Ti GAROU

A "Cadillac" Holland Mystery

H. Max Hiller

H. Max Hiller (signature)

INDIES UNITED PUBLISHING HOUSE, LLC

ISBN: 978-1-64456-127-0
Library of Congress Control Number: 2020935534

INDIES UNITED PUBLISHING HOUSE, LLC
P.O. BOX 3071
QUINCY, IL 62305-3071
www.indiesuited.net

For Karen and Carla. There would be no pages after this were it not for their encouragement and help in taking an idea and making it into a story.

1

I WAKE FROM ANOTHER NIGHTMARE and the familiar surroundings remind me that I am still safe from this memory in both time and distance. My breath and heart rate begin to return to normal and I step out of my bed to get a beer. I smile at the framed banner hanging in my living room as I make my way to the kitchen. It was the campaign banner for a minor candidate in New Orleans's first mayoral election after Hurricane Katrina named Manny Chevrolet. His too-honest campaign slogan was "A Troubled Man for Troubled Times." I adopted it for my own mantra the first time I saw it.

My name is Cooter E. Holland, and I am a troubled cop for a troubled city. My father named me after his hometown in the bootheel of Missouri. Six successive generations of the Holland family have lived on a farm bordering the Mississippi River east of Cooter with a long tradition of the younger sons leaving home to find work elsewhere.

Ralph Holland, the youngest of five sons, was a member of the New Orleans Police Department for over thirty years. He worked his way up from a beat in the Lower Ninth Ward to become Chief of the Detective Division. He also published a series of popular crime novels by the time I graduated from the military prep school he packed me off to after retrieving me from the First District's holding cell after one too many underage drinking incidents in the French Quarter. I abandoned the family's expectations for my future by choosing a military career which meant being apart from the city of my birth for nearly half of my lifetime before returning to a hometown that was as battered as I was. My career as a shadow warrior ended when I was pulled from the brink of death in an ambush on a back street in Baghdad that I knowingly lead my team into.

One of those killed in the ambush was wearing a jacket with my cover name written in the lining. This led to my family being notified that I was missing and presumed dead after the body was identified. I actually *had* died on an operating table, twice in fact, and it was over two months later before my family was notified I was alive, albeit in a coma and in a hospital in Italy. Hurricane Katrina brought fresh tragedy to my parents and sister less than a month after they were left reeling from the premature report of my death. My father disappeared without a trace after volunteering to assist with the search and rescue operations following the collapse of the city's floodwalls.

I was still in the hospital in Naples when I promised my kid sister that I would return to New Orleans and look for our father. As it turned out, the law enforcement situation was in a very critical situation in New Orleans during the first year after the storm. Over a third of the New Orleans police force had either resigned or been fired and National Guard soldiers, State police officers, and volunteer cops from across the nation were temporarily deployed to help out. NOPD was in no position to train new officers so I was encouraged to apply to the State Highway Patrol. My politically connected "fixer" uncle brokered a deal with my father's former NOPD partner and the Commander of the State Police to use my overseas intelligence work as work experience so I could graduate from the State Police Academy at the rank of Detective. The LSP could then assign me indefinitely to the use of the New Orleans Police Department. Bill Avery replaced my father as the Chief of NOPD's Detectives, and he willed himself to overlook a worrisome psych profile that my PTSD posed.

The arrangement fell apart almost immediately. Chief Avery and I did not share the same priorities. His focus was on the present and mine was squarely in the past; finding an answer to my father's disappearance. I was stonewalled and sent down blind alleys by people I had reason to believe should have been as concerned about my father's virtual disappearance as I was. My fury caused so many scenes that Avery had no choice but to relegate me to work solo and to help NOPD clear its pre-storm backlog of arrest warrants and handle a few minor investigations that were taxing his department.

I had just spent the previous week camped out in an abandoned house to monitor a FEMA trailer in the Lower Ninth Ward. The neighborhood was home to Chief Avery's favorite sous chef, but it remained mostly uninhabited since Katrina's floodwaters had devastated it four years ago. I had called in the Fugitive Task Force earlier that morning when I verified the squatter was a drug dealer wanted on homicide charges. The stakeout reminded me of similar missions I had done as a sniper with the Army's Tier-One operators and while working as a contractor with intelligence agencies I cannot name. I have compartmentalized that period in my life and those memories and lessons are stowed in a part of me that nobody is ever meant to find.

One of the other members of that near-fatal intelligence mission followed me home to New Orleans and assumed a new identity. Chef Tony Venzo, as Antonio Venzo Hussein al-Majid now calls himself, made me a well-compensated silent partner in the Creole-Italian bistro called Strada Ammazarre he opened in the French Quarter. I helped Tony buy the building on Decatur Street near the Old Mint building at a steep discount and we set aside the third floor for spacious loft apartments with a view of the Mississippi River for each of us. The first floor of the building was laid out for the bistro's kitchen, bar, and large, high-ceilinged dining room. The second floor was divided into private dining rooms, and it was in the smallest of these that I found my mother after I showered and pulled on a pair of jeans and a T-shirt.

"Is the staff following your orders?" I gave her a peck on the cheek.

My mother was taller than me in her heels and was impeccably dressed in a pale champagne Chanel skirt and jacket with a matching silk blouse. Her flawless makeup and improbable mane of lustrous blonde hair made her look much younger than sixty-eight years of age. A cosmetic surgeon had smoothed out what Estee Lauder could no longer conceal.

"Why wouldn't they?" She turned around to face me and looked at my clothes and then at my face, her frown growing by the minute. "Tell me that you are not wearing those clothes or that beard to your father's birthday party."

I was not about to defend appearing before her in jeans and a Jazz Fest T-shirt. Nor was I going to suggest that my father was unlikely to attend his party, mention that this annual party for a man she was divorcing at the time of his unexplained disappearance was a topic of discussion among her guests, or that some of them find any celebrations on September 11th to be in poor taste.

"Of course not, Mother. I just came by to say hello."

I made a strategic withdrawal and returned to my apartment to shower again and shave the week's growth of facial hair I had sprouted on the stakeout. I reached deep into the back of my closet for the white Armani dinner jacket and black slacks I wear only for this party each year. I then headed to the main floor in search of Tony so we could review the party's menu and proper plate presentations one last time.

I also checked the reservation book with Marie, our hostess, and said hello to a couple of the early diners I recognized. The bar area was filling up with locals who came to enjoy the tapas Chef Tony sets out each Friday to entice them to the Quarter rather than start their weekend in the revitalized strip of chic bars and cafes in the Warehouse District or further Uptown. The rain that began the night before finally thinned to a drizzle and the breeze coming through the open French doors carried the faint stench of decay from the gutters filled with water that had rinsed the rooftops and exteriors of the centuries-old buildings of the Quarter.

Chef Tony was standing at the bar with Chief Avery. The career lawman is a towering figure with the gait and bulk of the former LSU linebacker he actually is. His voice still has a very deep timbre and a distinctly local accent, but the silver in his closely cropped hair betrays the way this job has aged him. Avery was barely thirty years old when he started trailing behind my father as a rookie detective.

"I hear you found my bail jumper this morning," my boss said and patted my back.

"He was crashing in his uncle's place." I shrugged as though any detective would have thought to stake out a minor relative's house given as a home address when the suspect was arrested for a misdemeanor ten years ago.

"Well, good work," he complimented me and then turned his attention to the frosty mug of beer in his hand and leaned slightly towards Tony. "So, what's on the menu tonight?"

"Don't worry, whatever it is will taste good covered in hot sauce."

Avery thought about this for a moment before bursting into laughter. I couldn't help laughing as well, and Tony grinned because one of his jokes finally made sense. Our laughter was cut short by the sound of police cruisers and an ambulance racing past the double doors opening into the bistro from Decatur Street. Most of the regulars merely waited for the noise to stop and resumed their conversations, having long ago lost their sensitivity to, and curiosity about, the noise from sirens of any sort. Avery's cell phone buzzed about the same time the ambulance passed. He glanced at the text message and broke into a wide grin before he made a short text in response. I had seldom seen him this happy and I raised an eyebrow in query.

"Yes, indeed. I have to go. Someone just killed Biggie Charles Lynley at the Hard Rock Café."

"I'll go with you. Tony, don't tell my mother or sister where we went."

I poured our beers into plastic cups before following Avery out the door and heading towards Canal Street. My mother would not appreciate our being late to the party or regaling the table with gory stories from the crime scene. We walked slowly, so as not to spill our beers. Neither of us saw any reason to hurry to see the city's most famous dead guy. He wasn't going anywhere.

2

THE SIDEWALKS WERE PACKED with the usual late afternoon foot traffic of tuxedo-wearing wait staff on their way to work and gutter punks in filthy rags and expensive boots. There were also tourists in town for the Saints game against the Detroit Lions on Sunday. Avery and I were prepared for 2009 to be another in a long line of Saints' seasons that start well but end up in a shambles. Last year's fourth-place finish in the division did not inspire much hope for this year.

We walked past the bank of television reporters using the murder scene as a backdrop as they recounted the life of the deceased for the audience of their live-on-location newscast. The victim, 'Biggie' Charles Lynley, was a product of both the Calliope Projects and a failing criminal justice system. He was dealing drugs by the time he finished high school and was solidly in control of the heroin trade between St. Charles Avenue and the river by the time he was twenty-two. His undoing was the cold-blooded execution of two undercover DEA agents, but his murder trial was so poorly prosecuted that the DEA agents were being cast as the bad guys by the time the judge accepted a plea bargain to end the travesty. Biggie Charles was sentenced to fifteen years in Angola State Prison and paroled after serving only seven of them over the strenuous objections of everyone who could make one. He returned to New Orleans to build a rap music empire with money from an unknown source, which only added to his mystique. He spent a small fortune, but his label never posed any competition for other local labels because his acts lacked the level of talent at studios such as Cash Money Records.

BC Studios was better known for generating substantial

income as an after-hours club. They catered to local bad-boy athletes, twenty-something liberal college coeds, and thirty-something young white-collar wannabe bad boys who wanted to pal around with what they thought were gang members who had managed to pull themselves off the path of destruction. Biggie Charles Lynley's background ran the smarter celebrities off, yet Biggie continued to show up at places and events he should have been barred from and in photographs with people who should have known better than to stand so close to him. Avery's detectives mentioned Lynley from time to time in connection with an unsolved murder or some sort of drug or weapon sale on which they couldn't make a prosecutable case. The guy was more of a boogeyman than a crime lord. Maybe better yet, he had become a catch basin for any major crimes NOPD couldn't solve but needed to pin on somebody.

Avery led me to the knot of NOPD detectives dressed in sports coats who were milling about while their supervisors, all dressed in suits, were trying to decide how much effort to put into the case. A single New Orleans homicide detective might be assigned more active cases at one time than the entire police department of some communities will see in a year. Their active cases are often an intertwined mess of back-and-forth retaliation for some incident none of the participants can even remember. A detective's failure to make prosecutable cases on most of these homicides will have nothing to do with their personal ability to figure out who killed who, or even why. The arrest rate for the nearly two hundred homicides the previous year was under sixty percent and consequences were not something the city's gang members seemed very worried about. It was becoming an accepted fact that most homicides in post-Katrina New Orleans involved turf battles over drug dealing or other minority-on-minority crimes, both of which tended to be settled on the street and not in the courts even before Katrina.

"Big Chief and Cadillac have arrived. We can all go home," the beleaguered head of the Homicide detectives laughingly greeted us. Avery had been known as Big Chief for as long as he had carried a badge. NOPD's fleet of squad cars was sacrificed to the absolute necessity of patrolling neighborhoods still flooded with brackish water following Katrina. Sewell Cadillac's inventory was appropriated and pressed into service when the shortage reached a critical point. Avery assigned me one of these sedans when he decided I was no longer going to partner with his men. It gave NOPD's patrolmen and detectives an easy derogatory nickname for me. I was still patrolling in a Cadillac, but now I bought my own. This only served to justify the nickname.

"Back off, fellas. This is well in hand," one of the other detectives said. He held up a hand in a not entirely insincere effort to keep us at bay and whistled as he looked the two of us up and down. Avery was in his best Brooks Brothers suit and I was way over-dressed for this scene. "Did you two just come from a James Bond convention?"

"The hell you have this under control. You don't even have coffee yet," I countered.

"Whataya got?" Avery asked bluntly. It is one of those things he gets to do as Chief of Detectives. A large part of the respect and deference he gets has to do with his habit of reaching over and thumping anyone he feels is not in line with the program.

"Charles Lynley's new pit bull got hungry with just the two of them in the vehicle."

"How do you even know what kind of dog it is?" I asked. The afternoon's rain probably washed away anything of investigative value from the parking lot, but I thought there was little to have been lost by the look of things. The crime scene seemed neatly contained within the interior of the Land Rover. Its side windows were tinted to start with but were now further darkened by what appeared to be gallons of blood. The front windshield was nearly obscured by fresh splashes of arterial spray.

"Biggie's fiancée gave him a pit bull for a birthday present. She and the bodyguard had left the two of them alone for about twenty minutes and came back to this."

The Homicide Chief spoke up in an effort to regain control of the scene. "Who is going to shoot the dog? You can't see the thing so someone will have to open the door so someone else can shoot it."

"You can't do that!" We turned towards the unexpected objection. I had not noticed my sister's arrival at the scene. I wondered if Tony sent her or if she had noticed us as her cab passed the scene. "You can't just shoot the dog."

"Damn it, Tulip, the dog just killed a guy. What's the problem?" Avery didn't need to explain himself to her.

My kid sister is thirty-two years old but looks considerably younger. She has been saddled with a name, Tulip Holland, our parents found even more amusing than my own. I was over-dressed for the occasion, but Tulip was absolutely distracting. She had her auburn hair in a tight chignon and the salon-applied make-up accented the dark brown of her eyes. Her floral-print dress was short and featured a display of her cleavage that was distracting the detectives from the topic at hand.

"Dogs don't attack their owners without some sort of provocation," Tulip persisted. "And a trained pit bull would certainly be unlikely to attack its owner."

"It's also the only witness to the crime." I wasn't trying to make a joke. I turned to one of the uniformed officers who had been first on the scene. "Did they say it was acting funny?"

"No," he conceded and handed Avery his notes. He gave my sister and me a particularly nasty look as he left.

I looked at the Land Rover and then to where Biggie's dinner companions were huddled together. They looked a lot more nervous than sad about the way the evening was going. Perhaps someone told them they were going to have to take the dog home with them.

I walked over and introduced myself as Detective Holland, figuring that they could believe I was an NOPD detective if they wanted. I was not at the scene in any official capacity at the moment. The burly Black male identified himself as Bumper Jackson, Biggie's bodyguard, and the woman as Tyshika Barnes. She claimed to be Biggie's fiancé, to which the bodyguard nodded his head.

"How long has Biggie owned the dog?" I asked the bodyguard. He was probably in his mid-thirties and carried a lot of muscle on his nearly seven-foot frame, which he used quite effectively to block my access to the fiancée. I couldn't help noticing that Tyshika was not crying. She just seemed especially angry.

"Since today. It was supposed to be a surprise birthday

present from Tyshika. She picked it up on the Northshore a couple of hours ago."

"Well, I guess the surprise worked."

The fiancée did not react if she heard me at all. Bumper did flinch and started to say something, but he hesitated. This might have been because of his confusion over my possible rank because of the way I was dressed. My clothes certainly cost more than those of anyone else he had spoken with that evening.

"So are you guys going to shoot the dog or what? Because I will if need be." The bodyguard's heavy revolver was in a shoulder holster which was exposed now that he had draped his jacket over Tyshika's shoulders.

"We were just discussing that. Can you tell me if the dog was at all aggressive towards either of you?"

"It's a trained attack dog, man. It's aggressive towards everyone."

"A trained dog should have protected your boss from an attack instead of attacking him." I avoided commenting on Bumper's own dereliction of duty.

"Look, her cousin works at the kennel and trains guard dogs for a living. He wouldn't give us a dog he thought would do this. This animal is just nuts. Shoot it."

I assured the pair that NOPD had the situation in hand and walked back to where the detectives were beginning to trickle away. The arrival of DEA and FBI brass and their own agents suggested that there might be a jurisdictional turf battle over who handled any investigation.

"How are they going to get the dog out?" I asked Avery as I returned to the group, which now included SAC Michael Conroy of the local FBI office. I could not remember ever seeing him at a murder scene before. Tulip was still at Avery's side as well. She continued voicing her objections to any discussion of killing the dog.

The SWAT commander had been reached by phone and summarily refused to shoot any dog in front of a bank of TV cameras that desperately needed something interesting to happen. The K-9 unit also distanced itself.

"There has to be a better idea than shooting the dog!" my sister shouted in frustration. The Federal agents and patrolmen around us did not share her view and universally favored putting the dog down over opening the door and turning the beast loose upon the crowd.

"I can't think of one good reason to stop them," Chief Avery responded just as loudly and then led us both aside. "I do agree that the dog may prove more useful alive than dead if someone wanted it to kill Lynley. But, unless one of you has an idea, I'd say that removing it from the vehicle alive seems impossible."

The three of us stood there, studying the vehicle and the problem inside, while everyone else continued to kick around ideas on how to shoot the dog. Something had to be done before the vehicle could be processed as a crime scene. This would be a dead-end case for the detective that drew it and nobody would object if this was closed as a dog attack right now. The assembled representatives of the city, state, and Federal authorities all agreed that justice, long delayed, seemed to have finally come to Biggie Charles Lynley.

"I'll tell you what. If your sister has convinced you that this is anything more than a dog mauling, you can pursue it. You just have to go arrest the suspect."

I could tell Avery was barely able to hide his glee at coming up with a means of passing any blame and bad publicity for what happened next to the State Patrol instead of his own department. Even Tulip agreed that there were but two likely scenarios here. The first was for the dog to be shot while still in the vehicle. That would make using the dog to prove Biggie's death was anything but a dog mauling impossible. The second possibility was the dog might attack anyone trying to remove it from the SUV. That someone would now be me.

"I have never done a murder investigation and you know it." I didn't want to actually refuse the assignment.

"I'll watch over your shoulder. What are the odds this is ever going to wind up in court anyway?" There was no reason to believe the district attorney's office would want to do anything but pin a medal on anyone I might prove killed someone as loathsome as Biggie Charles Lynley. Tulip told me to hurry up as the three of us were already late to dinner.

"Fine, I'll take the case, but we'll both probably regret this." Tulip gave me a peck on the cheek and hugged Avery. He reluctantly agreed to open the Land Rover's rear driver's side door so I could capture my suspect.

I was now cornered into being the guy who got to arrest a murderous pit bull on live television. The thought of acting like I was going to do so and then shooting it in self-defense came to mind. This was not really an option because my sister was going to tell people about tonight and cast me as either her hero or as a dog killer. I stripped off the white dinner jacket and silk tie I was wearing and handed them to Tulip, telling her to bury me in them if this turned out poorly. I then borrowed a ballistic vest from one of the patrolmen and a set of heavy coveralls and jacket, as well as a helmet with a face shield, boots, and leather gloves, from a bemused fireman. What I really wanted was one of the training suits from the canine unit, but all they offered me one was one of their long-handled animal control snares so this hasty improvisation was going to have to work. I was going to have to rely on how fast the fire department was with a fire hose because I did not have a hand free to hold a pistol. My only hope would be if they could knock the dog off me before I was added to the beast's dinner menu.

I would like to describe the way I bravely wrestled the murderous animal into submission and awed the crowd, but I can't. Avery opened the rear driver's side door and pressed himself against the front wheel well with his pistol in hand. The crowd took a collective breath as the door opened, and shared a massive laugh in relief when nothing happened. I looked through the open door and found the dog was now calmly licking its victim's face, which was frozen in an expression of unimaginable terror. The dog had a metal choke collar on, with the heavy leather leash still attached. All I could think to do when I saw the grisly sight was to whistle for the dog to come to me.

The dog gave me a quizzical look and then simply walked across the bloodied interior and jumped down to sit at my feet. I could tell the breed only by the square shape of the head. The dog's fur was matted with blood. He shook himself, spraying gore all over everything within a ten-foot radius. I exchanged wry grins with Avery. I thanked him for his assistance before turning to the crowd and taking a deep bow to their greatly amused, and quietly relieved, applause. I then marched the four-legged murder suspect to the fire truck. One of the firemen offered me a hose to wash the dog.

Avery handed my borrowed costume back to its owners while I held the dog steady for the Crime Lab technician to photograph it and take swabs of the matted blood on its fur. The first question in the investigation came to mind as the technician washed the blood from the dog's fur with a slow stream of water. The coat of short hairs had been dyed a very deep indigo blue, so dark I could not make out the dog's actual fur color. The technician took more photos and wrote down my email address to send me copies of the pictures.

"Here's your dog, Tulip. Want to hold his leash?" She did not.

"I'll call Animal Control in Algiers and see if they can keep him until he can be evaluated," Tulip offered. We were going to have to make up a plan as we went along. "I do some pro bono work for one of the pit bull foster groups and they may be able to help."

"Let me know if you need anything else," Avery said and walked off to smooth the feathers he was going to ruffle when he announced his personal State Police detective was going to be investigating the dog's attack as a homicide.

Everybody believed this was a dog attack an hour ago, and nobody wanted to deal with the dog just ten minutes ago. Now that this had become The Blue Dog Murder Case everyone was going to want a piece of it. The news photographers and tourists were busy capturing the Land Rover's exposed interior for posterity, but the death tableau was never going to be broadcast or see the morning paper.

"So, tell me what kind of evaluation is necessary for a pit bull that ripped a three hundred pound Black man apart like something from a horror movie," Avery wondered as he came back to where I held the dog while the crime lab techs took more photos and blood swabs from its fur. "Crazy is crazy and knowing why it's crazy isn't going to matter, right?"

"Not unless I'm crazy," I tried to joke. "Maybe they can rule out whether or not anything biological triggered the attack. If it wasn't sick or deranged then something else had to make it attack."

"Even if someone found a way to remotely make the dog attack, what are you going to do with a healthy and sane dog that kills people?" Avery barely caught himself before he started to pet the quiet canine sitting between us.

"I guess we'd have to find it a new home," Tulip smiled at Avery. "Say, don't *you* have a birthday coming up?"

3

CHIEF AVERY RELUCTANTLY AGREED to stand guard over the pit bull while I went to get my car. The way the dog was grinning made him nervous. The openly relieved Chief of the Homicide squad remained at Avery's side to offer his detectives' advocacy for writing the death off as an animal attack rather than waste time on an investigation by an inexperienced State trooper. Avery thumped the captain for mocking my appointment to the murder investigation the captain had just declared was unnecessary. Tulip continued to let Avery know that she remained unapologetic for raising her objections.

I was back within a matter of minutes and took the leash from Avery. He walked with me to my Cadillac CTS-V sports wagon. I had just purchased the vehicle but was going to have to risk the dog shaking off more blood since my other car was a convertible with only two seats. I did not want to sit quite that close to any murder suspect.

"I have informed our Homicide squad, the FBI, and the DEA that you are looking into this for me and not just to pacify your sister. Homicide and the Feds are ready to close the case, so getting any sort of cooperation might be tricky. What do you think should be done first?" Avery and I watched the dog passively step into the kennel I borrowed from a K-9 officer. The officer helped me lift the kennel into the car once we had the oddly passive dog secured.

"We should make sure they process Biggie's vehicle as though it really is a murder scene. That car is probably going to give me the only clues I'll get." I realized Avery was quizzing me like a rookie patrolman. "I'm sure a lot of people wanted Biggie Charles dead. I need to expand the list of suspects beyond the dog, which I doubt had much of a motive. It may just be a good judge of character."

We both looked at the dog and I sensed Avery was ready to agree that the dog did not act alone. Humanizing the canine suspect for a second, I thought the next step in an assassination would be for whoever wanted the dog to kill its master to now be the loudest voice pushing for its death. My shortlist of obvious suspects consisted of the fiancée, the bodyguard, and the cousin that trained the dog. The bodyguard had already offered to shoot the dog. I was most likely looking at a combination of at least two of these people, but I was not interviewing any of them this evening. My immediate task was to quarantine the dog at the LA/SPCA facility across the river in Algiers as quickly as possible. My mother might forgive me for missing most of my dad's birthday party if I at least made it there in time for the cake cutting.

The LA/SPCA opened a new animal control center on the West Bank following Hurricane Katrina. The bright modern structure replaced their previous facility located beside the Industrial Canal in the Upper Ninth Ward. That cinder block animal warehouse filled with flood water and would have drowned every animal there had they not been evacuated in the last hectic hours before the storm hit.

"I'm bringing a dog in for quarantine, Steve," I told the after-hours receiving clerk when he answered the buzzer on the rear door. I read his name on the badge over the left breast pocket of his polyester khaki shirt. Steve was a young man of about twenty with a crew cut and a diamond earring in his left earlobe. The look on his face when he peered into the dog kennel changed to the face of someone wishing this had happened on a different shift.

"Is this the one the cops just called about?" Killer dogs traditionally arrived in the company of uniformed police officers, not shaggy-haired detectives wearing Armani and driving a Cadillac. That I had a badge and gun under my jacket was not going to assuage this young man's qualms.

"Yes," I said as I let the dog out of its transport kennel and took hold of its leash. The dog didn't pull on the leash. In fact, it laid down. It rode sitting up in the cage for the entire fifteen-minute drive, seemingly very interested in its surroundings, but uninterested in me personally. "The dog is evidence in a homicide and it's definitely the cause of death. We need to have a toxicology screen run to see if maybe drugs caused the dog to attack. It's a trained attack dog, so something triggered the incident. Make a note that I am to be the only detective with access to it."

"Let's get him cleaned up a bit more and we'll draw some blood. You won't get the lab results for a day or so."

Steve led the way through the neutrally painted hallways to a room set aside for quarantined animals. Steve was so practiced in his actions that I knew he had handled a lot of animals before this. He allowed the dog to sniff his hand before he reached over to replace the dog's metal collar with a nylon one and a metal lead. Steve made a disparaging remark about metal choke collars as he handed me the collar and heavy leather lead.

I rinsed the collar's tags in a hand sink so I could read them. There was little harm in doing this as the cleaning removed very little of the blood on the collar itself. There was an engraved metal tag with the name TAZ, the dog's veterinary tags and city license, and a yellow tag for its microchip.

Steve wanted to give the dog a proper bath to remove the blue hair dye from its coat, but I needed to be sure that the forensic team had what they needed before I let him muck about with the evidence. Steve approximated the dog's age to be three, making it nearly fully grown.

Three years is a lot of time to trace in a dog's life. The dog may have been trained and sold, and perhaps then returned and sold again. There could prove to be so many gaps in its record that I would never establish an accurate history. The possibility that Taz had a secret attack trigger nobody knew about was going to make handling the dog risky. I followed Steve and the dog to a room with a couple of other cages, both housing dogs that had also recently attacked humans. All of these dogs faced a certain death sentence unless their time in quarantine showed some reason beyond their own control for their attacks. I braced for the dog to respond viciously to the needle prick when Steve reached inside its kennel to draw the blood necessary for the drug screen I had requested, but it barely flinched.

I considered a variety of murder scenarios while I drove

back across the river. I also wondered why his fiancé hadn't just bought him a puppy. The fiancée might have killed Biggie over some real or imagined insult, but that would have meant kissing off her only means of support. There is a long tradition of bodyguards turning on their masters, but there is usually some sort of profit in doing so that eluded me in this case. I could not imagine what the guy who trained the dog might have had against Biggie, and I wouldn't think selling killer dogs would help the kennel's reputation. There was the tantalizing lead that two of the suspects were related, but this could just prove to be a coincidence. I found myself as lost on the matter of likely suspects as I was on a plausible motive. Biggie being gunned down in a drive-by shooting would have made more sense and offered a more traditional route to finding his killer. Someone being imaginative and original about this murder only promised to make my first murder investigation all the more complicated.

I RETURNED TO THE BISTRO much more concerned about my mother's disapproval than I was about why dogs kill their owners. This evening's dinner party was a cornerstone of my family's way of handling my father's disappearance. Mother refused to listen to even the suggestion that we might never know what occurred. Her steadfast opinion was that something explainable was simply delaying his return, and had done so for the past four years. The presence of his entire family and the empty chair at the head of the table were used to underscore her position on this matter to her children and guests.

The guest list this evening included Chief Avery and select Chiefs of other New Orleans police and fire districts who had been my father's peers and friends, three or four Federal officials and a couple of judges my father had known socially, my mother's favorite city councilman, my father's literary agent, a few businessmen who contribute heavily to the charities with which my mother occupies her days, and anyone else she needed to fill out the table. Mother used the introduction of new people as an excuse to exclude from her social circle anyone with whom she had grown bored, or who had made the mistake of letting it be known that they thought my father was dead and not simply missing for so long. My mother's view is that if Ralph Holland is dead to them then that offender is dead to our family. Mother bases her conviction that my father is still alive primarily on email exchanges she has with an online psychic who keeps telling her that his soul "has not crossed over."

I found my business partner standing at the bar when I dashed through the door and headed for the staircase to the second-floor banquet room. I took this as a very bad sign.

The chef should have been in the kitchen overseeing the four-course meal my mother expected me to pick up the tab for. Perhaps I had already missed the dinner.

"Am I too late?" I asked Tony so I would know what reception to expect upstairs.

"Your mother delayed service for an hour. They just cleared the salad course."

"Have a drink," Ryan Kennedy suggested and took a sip of his own. Ryan is one of our best regulars. He comes from a socially prominent East Coast family which followed the time-honored practice of packing its homosexual son off to the South on a generous allowance. He still speaks with a faintly East Coast-Brahman accent and was once the Quarter's most sought after caterer. He is retired now, but unable to enjoy himself because of the increasingly debilitating ailments which plague him. His hand shook slightly from the early onset of Parkinson's and the glass of Marquis de Perlade champagne was likely to exacerbate his diabetes. "I have things to discuss with you."

I motioned for the bartender, Jason, to pour a snifter of bourbon for me and braced myself with a drink before I listened to whatever absurdity Ryan had in mind. "What's tonight's subject?"

"I think I need a male nurse," Ryan declared and settled his gaze on our only male bartender. Tony and I prefer to staff the bar with female bartenders, but Jason was a former star pitcher of Tulane's baseball team and brought his own following when we hired him. "I don't see why you will not loan me that young man's services."

"In the first place, I get the impression it is you who intends to do the servicing. And we can't have our only male bartender beating up one of our valued regulars to defend his honor." It's a token argument we have to keep repeating.

"You are so provincial, my dear boy," Ryan smirked and sprang a different approach upon us. "Do you think Chief Avery might have some sort of prison trustee program I could call upon? Someone's former prison bitch could do as a male nurse, wouldn't you think?"

"I'll tell him of your interest," I lied with a smile and set my empty glass on the bar before stepping away to head upstairs.

I had hoped to slip into the private dining room and make it to my seat with minimal notice, but that was just wishful thinking. My mother set my place to the right of my father's empty chair at the far end of the table. This meant I had to pass her and walk the length of the table before I could even reach my seat. My sister was seated to the left of my father's seat and her subdued expression let me know to expect a full dose of our mother's anger for having made anything a higher priority than tonight's dinner party.

"Sorry to be late," I whispered in my mother's ear. I could see the tension in her jaw. She barely turned towards me before she spoke.

"Oh, so you're done playing with your doggie?"

"For now." It was all I dared say in response. My mother was undoubtedly aware of where I was and what I was doing with the pit bull. Chief Avery would not have been allowed to take his own seat in the middle of the table until he explained why it was necessary for my mother to alter her plans at the last moment to accommodate her absent children and himself.

My mother pulled the three of us aside once the other guests departed after dinner to remind us that her entire purpose in having Tulip bring me back to New Orleans, using Uncle Felix's connections to get my commission with the Louisiana State Patrol, and having Chief Avery be the one to supervise the son of his former mentor was strictly so I would have the resources necessary to investigate the disappearance of my father. She remains unlikely to forgive me for being reported missing but presumed dead, in a foreign country no less, until my father is found and given the good news that the last report he heard before his own disappearance and presumed death was neither complete nor accurate. My mother was an emotional disaster when Tulip begged me to come home.

I had consciously allowed searching for my father to ease out of my daily routine and was now waiting on someone to step forward with more information or a fresh memory they could share with me before I would take up the case again. There was no way Avery, Tulip, or I would ever confess to being in the majority which believed my father died and his body was lost in the floodwaters. The area he was patrolling would have washed his corpse out to Lake Ponchartrain or into the Mississippi River, and from either of those on into the Gulf of Mexico. There was no activity on his debit or credit cards after he vanished and his driver's license was not renewed when it expired two years ago. Not a single report of people turning up in hospitals or police stations with amnesia anywhere in the country fit his description, but I continue monitoring those reports out of habit.

5

I AM A PASSENGER in a convoy of three armored vehicles moving on a washboard of a side street in Baghdad's Mansour district under the light of a full moon. I ride in the middle seat of a lightly armored Chevy Suburban, listening to the Rolling Stones' song Far Away Eyes on a set of earbuds instead of the constant bursts of rage and indignation from the handcuffed Iraqi colonel next to me. He is getting absolutely no sympathy from anyone in this convoy, and can only hope for some from the Iraqi authorities we hand him over to with clear evidence of his role in years' worth of attacks on American and Coalition forces.

My world abruptly turns blindingly white, then goes nearly totally black, and finally changes to crimson red as RPG explosions rip apart the vehicle and shred the man seated in front of me, and the jacket I loaned him. I check the prisoner and find he has a piece of the seat frame lodged in his chest. He might live or he might die, but I feel like I am suffocating so I roll backwards over the seat to kick open the rear cargo door and escape the vehicle. I instinctively move to find a position from which to defend myself with either the carbine in my hand or the pistol on my hip. I have a brief, useless worry that the last thing I will hear is the sound of Mick Jagger's voice. The sound of gunfire draws closer and the vehicle is rocked by the impact of small arms rounds. I am barely free of the Suburban and in a drainage ditch before a startlingly young boy, maybe fourteen years of age, takes aim at my head and fires at point blank range. Three rounds strike my upper left shoulder before his gun either jams or he runs out of bullets. He begins pounding on my head until I free my pistol and fire blindly in his general direction. The battering stops and I am relieved when a deep and painless darkness overtakes me.

I bolt upright and find that what has saved me from dying this time is the thunder of yet another Louisiana rainstorm. I am wide awake in my bed and safe now from the nightmare, if not from the anger and feeling of futility it brings. I am tired of these nightmares, and frustrated beyond reason with mentally replaying hundreds of such incidents I can never alter. My every waking hour since I left the hospital has been filled with making certain I am never ambushed again.

The clock on my nightstand says it's after ten o'clock in the morning. Tulip and I left the bistro after the dinner party and argued about Biggie's pit bull as we drank our way through a string of Frenchman Street nightclubs before dining on beignets at Café du Monde as the sun came up. I would have been as happy as anyone at the scene to shoot the dog and close the case had my sister not been there. Tulip's argument as an attorney was that the dog deserved no less of a fair hearing than any human murder suspect. I pointed out that nobody would adopt Taz even if I could prove it had been induced to attack Biggie Charles, so it would still wind up euthanized.

I showered and pulled on a pair of khaki slacks, a clean polo shirt with the State Patrol emblem over the left breast and my steel-toed Merrell chukka-style boots. I hung my badge over my belt and chambered a round of ten-millimeter ammunition into the Glock 20 pistol I clipped to my belt before I headed downstairs for a light brunch. I wanted to review the costs of last night's dinner with Chef Tony, and to discuss any problems he saw with my assignment to what could prove to be a high profile investigation before I began what promised to be a long day of people swearing the dog's behavior came as a total surprise.

"I saw you on TV last night," Hannah, our daytime bartender, laughed as I sat at the end of the long, zinc-covered bar. She brought me a Bloody Morgan, which is a Bloody Mary made with spiced rum, and the day's *Times-Picayune*. "I asked my boyfriend to tape the late news."

"Great. We can show it at the Christmas party."

I contend that some people gravitate to the French Quarter because it is easier than joining the Foreign Legion. Hannah was not this bartender's birth name. She came from New Jersey to attend Tulane University with the goal of being a high school history teacher. She almost immediately abandoned this idea in favor of becoming a Quarter Rat. She took the name of a favorite movie character, dyed her blonde hair a coppery red and adopted a wardrobe that includes leather thigh boots with absurdly high heels. She is so short that she needs the boots to reach over the bar.

I booted up my iPad tablet computer and checked my email. There was a message from the pit bull rescue group Tulip represents. They wanted to assure me they were available for anything I might need. They drew the line short of offering Taz a foster home, but did provide a list of websites they felt had some helpful information.

I browsed through a few of them while I waited for my breakfast. What I found is that pit bulls are a dog breed with an unfortunate reputation. A summary of the articles would have you believe they either are a naturally aggressive animal with a particular hatred, or even an appetite, for young children or they were gregarious family-friendly dogs that also happen to be fiercely loyal to their owners. It was suggested that their occasional attacks were due to inadvertently mixed signals between the dogs and their victims; such as toddlers getting into their food bowls or strangers entering their territory. The truth hides in the middle.

I suppose if all I knew of airplanes was what I read in newspapers I would assume they are a ridiculously unsafe means of getting anywhere, because the news never tells us when they take off or arrive on time. We only hear about airplanes when one falls out of the sky and kills hundreds of people. You never see an article about any aircraft landing safely except space shuttles and Air Force One, and you almost never see articles about pit bulls saving lives. But they do this, a lot.

I noted that there was a consensus that pit-bulls actually make very poor guard dogs because of their friendly nature. I also noted, with no small amusement, their success in being trained as drug and explosives sniffers for police and military forces. The irony of a criminal like Biggie Charles dying in the jaws of a dog better suited to finding his drugs than protecting his life was something to savor over a cocktail with Avery when this was all behind us.

"Christ, boss man, what the hell is that?" Gina asked as she stared at the evidence bag holding the dog collar. I had not looked at the bag since sealing it the night before, but now I noticed that the smeared blood inside the bag gave it an appearance eerily similar to the car windows of the Land Rover.

"It's the collar from the dog that killed Charles Lynley last night."

I threw the Sports section of the Times-Picayune over the collar before anyone else saw it. Gina muttered something I was probably just as well off not hearing and retreated to the waitress station to finish her side work before the lunch rush started. Gina is the den mother of the bistro. She is in her late fifties and will happily be a waitress for the rest of her life. She is already getting a little stooped in her stance from leaning over guests and carrying armloads of plates at a time, but she never stops grinning with pleasure at meeting new people. Having her wait on you is like visiting your crazy aunt's house.

Gina's quirk is that she spends her time off stalking a former Saints quarterback living between her apartment in the Lower Garden District and the streetcar line to the Quarter. Her last Christmas card included a picture of her standing in front of Archie Manning's house while Olivia, his wife, unloaded groceries in the background. This behavior in any other city would be cause for a restraining order, but here she is tolerated as long as she keeps her distance.

I finished my eggs Benedict and gathered up the dog collar in its evidence bag. I could have carried the collar loose considering the odds against it ever being presented at a trial, but treating it as viable evidence was both good practice and a reminder that this was an actual police investigation. I would need to remember to drop the bag off at the evidence room and e-mail a complete report of my interviews to Avery later in the day.

"You have a phone call," Hannah waved the bar phone at

me as I started towards the kitchen to confer with Chef Tony.

"Who is it?"

There was a pause while she spoke with the person on the other end of the line. I have tried for some time to get the bartenders and servers to do this before they bother Tony or me with phone calls. They have permission to be as rude as they wish with unsolicited sales calls.

"She says her name is Miss Ann, and that she is Charles Lynley's grandmother," Hannah said and slapped her hand over the receiver. I am not sure what she thought I might blurt out. I leaned over the bar and motioned for her to hand me the phone.

"This is Detective Holland."

"You the one looking after my grandson's murder?"

"I am the detective who is trying to establish whether it even was a murder." No need to get her hopes up.

"I want you to come talk with me. Just you. I got no reason to trust no police, but you be the only one goin' to worry about my Charlie. I know somebody killed him because he were afraid of dogs and wouldn't ever want one around him."

The woman gave me an address in the St. Thomas Projects and I agreed to see her in an hour. She gave me half that long to get there after saying her lunch would be coming in a little while. I hung up and told Tony I would have to get with him later.

"Book 'em, Danno." Tony joked as I headed out the door. It was a reminder of how much of my friend's English, as well as his understanding of what I now do for a living, has been learned from watching late night re-runs.

I OPTED FOR THE JOY of driving my XLR roadster instead of the station wagon for my day's running around. I had some fear of it being taken for a joyride while I was visiting with Lynley's grandmother. I counted on the local thieves making a connection between the vanity plate reading COP CAR and myself and backing off. I am fairly well known in most of the bad parts of town.

Miss Ann Lynley was living on the top floor of one of the buildings which replaced the St. Thomas Projects' brick-over-concrete warehouses of the poor. The apartments these buildings replaced had been notorious, as much for the gangs using them as a base of operations as they were for the number of generations raised in apartments meant for short-term housing. The local housing authority and HUD took advantage of the evacuation of New Orleans to knock the old buildings down while they reconsidered the entire concept of low-income housing.

The replacement they came up with was being touted as "mixed-housing." These are neighborhoods of townhomes and smaller apartment buildings that mix the income levels of the tenants. Apparently, their goal was to provide role models for lower-income families, as though it is a lack of good examples that causes poverty. The displacement of the former tenants also had the unintentional consequence of dispersing the concentration of criminal gangs that had been like a cancerous growth thriving within the body of the projects and spreading them through the lymphatic system of the city at large. New Orleans quickly went from having a few good neighborhoods to only having a few safe blocks.

I parked at the Wal-Mart on Tchoupitoulas Street and walked across the street to the address I was given by

Biggie's grandmother. I hoped the parking lot cameras were working. I took the time to put the coupe's top up as a safety precaution and set the alarm. There was tenant parking beneath Miss Ann's building that I could have used, but it lacked security cameras. Building the units above a parking garage was one example of the renovation lessons learned from the flooding that followed Hurricane Katrina.

Two thoughts came to me as I was driving here from the Quarter: This elderly woman was likely to be the lone voice speaking on Biggie's behalf and that I might take what she told me at face value. The bodyguard and fiancée were my prime suspects, while any musicians under contract to the studio had a business relationship with the deceased. I also knew Miss Ann would likely want me to think of him as misunderstood or a victim of his surroundings, or however she learned to live with having such a monster as a relative. She might have some insights and background on her grandson's associates and business dealings that could be useful but, to be honest, I was coming here mostly because she had asked me to do so and I considered paying my respects to Biggie's family to be something of a duty.

"Get in here, you," the slight woman that answered the door snapped at me and grabbed my arm. "I don't need to be seen talking to the likes of you."

"You were the one who asked me to come see you, Ms. Ann."

The apartment was immaculate and smelled faintly of bleach beneath the odor of the boxed lunch someone from Meals on Wheels must have delivered just before I arrived. I looked through the sliding glass door to the balcony and realized she had one of the city's best views of the river. Walmart's parking lot and the massive metal roofed brick warehouses along the river were beneath her line of sight unless she was on the balcony.

Biggie's grandmother was probably in her seventies or early eighties. Black women grow old in a fashion that makes it impossible to accurately judge such things past a certain age, and I have learned not to ask or speculate. She was barely five feet tall and walked with a metal cane.

Ms. Ann waved me to the well-worn sofa and stepped into the kitchen for plastic glasses she filled with sweet tea from a plastic pitcher. She handed me a full glass and then set the pitcher on the wobbly TV dinner tray between the sofa and a wing-backed chair she settled into before muting the game show on the television set in the corner. There were family pictures on the wall behind my hostess, but I was unable to make out any resembling Charles as a child.

"You mentioned that your grandson was afraid of dogs." This was the thing that caught my ear earlier.

"Yes, indeed. Charlie was born in the Calliope but his momma sent him to live with his grandpa and me in Bogue Chitto until he got to be about ten. He started acting up in school, but that weren't why we sent him back. My husband had himself a coon dog that Charlie liked to pester. Charlie started whipping it with a stick one day and that dog bit him so bad we had to take him to get stitches. The sheriff made us put the hound down and his grandpa beat that boy with that same stick until he couldn't scream no more."

"Wow."

"After that, Charlie wouldn't go nowhere near no dog, least not till he got outta Angola." We settled into a silence that only ended when I spoke again.

"Ms. Ann, did your grandson have any brothers or sisters, maybe any cousins, who might tell me anything else that might be useful?"

She shook her head and took a sip of her sweet tea. I felt bad asking her to dredge up any bad memories.

"Charlie had an older brother, but he got blowed up in Vietnam. His aunties and uncles is all gone now, too. My Franklin died on an oil rig the same year as the World's Fair; then I moved here to take care of Charlie's momma when she got cancer. He was still up in Angola when she died. After she passed it was just Charlie and me."

"And when was the last time you spoke with Charlie?"

"Must be three or four years, but he sends me a card at Christmas and my birthday."

"Why is that? Did you two not get along?"

"Ask that girlfriend of his. I ain't spoke to him since she moved in with him. Now I guess I won't never get to again."

I had nothing much to say about that family history. It sounded tragic, but it was no more so than a dozen others I could have listened to in this building alone. The city's death toll includes a long list of young Black men who died from either the kinds of street-justice retribution that used to be settled with fists instead of guns or from the kinds of work their lack of education relegates them to do.

I had a front-row seat to the civil war and the grudge killings in Baghdad in the aftermath of Saddam Hussein's totalitarian regime, but it had nothing on what was happening in my hometown as the police department struggled to find its post-storm footing. Under-strength police districts were still working out of temporary trailers half a decade after Katrina. The criminal turf battles settled years earlier returned because of haphazard repatriation and the leveling of the projects' disruption of the pre-storm gang turfs.

As the saying goes, "People gotta eat" and the city's gangs are made up of young men who feel justified to take up a gun because it is the only way they believe they can be empowered. Statistics show gang members are dedicated fathers, even if they are lousy husbands and boyfriends, but make especially poor role models. NOPD lost nearly a third of its force in the first year after the storm, which forced it to focus its increasingly limited resources on keeping the most-occupied neighborhoods and tourist districts safe from the crime wave stymying recovery in the remainder of the city. That wave was now a flood that covered more of the city than Katrina inundated.

"Could you tell me why anyone would have dyed a dog blue as a present for Biggie?" This was not something I was going to figure out on my own.

"Blue? Someone colored a dog blue and give it to Charlie?" Her voice rose as she repeated what I'd just said.

"Probably the darkest blue they could find."

She was silent for a long moment but stared at me as though she were debating on what to say next.

"You know about the rou-garou?"

"It's the werewolf story the Cajuns tell their kids. There's a painter who made a fortune putting blue dogs in his paintings. Think there might be some connection?"

"Hell, yes! Charlie's granddad used to tell him that old hound was going to come back and get him if he didn't behave. That hound turned into his own rou-garou we used to tease him with. It was why he stayed afraid of dogs until he got outta Angola. He saw one of them paintings you was talking about at some gallery on Royal Street and he started collecting them pictures to show he ain't ever gonna be afraid of nothing no more. He didn't want anyone to think he was afraid of anyone or anything after he left Angola."

"So who would know this about him and maybe use it against him?"

"Anybody what knows Charlie knows about it." Finding my suspect promised to be a very time-consuming process of elimination. Her answer less helpful than knowing the background story. I finally had a reasonable answer for why someone dyed the pit bull blue, but Lynley told a lot of people his motive for collecting the Rodrique paintings. Every one of them just became a suspect. I might as well include the painter. He wasn't going to be very happy to find his artwork was tied to the likes of Biggie Charles Lynley.

"Well thank you for your time," I sighed and stood up. She remained seated but reached out and clutched my elbow.

"You really gonna try to find who killed him or you just gonna poke around and call it an accident?"

"It's my job to figure this out, Ms. Ann, whatever I may have thought of your grandson's past. My job isn't about working only for the good people in this city. If someone was responsible, I'll find them and then we'll both have to let the courts have their turn. You don't think he might have poked the dog that killed him with a stick, do you?"

"I'll do more'n poke you if try to make a joke about this," she snarled. I had not really meant to make the question sound like a joke. "You call me when you find who done this to him."

"I sure will."

I heard the door chain slide in place behind me. She may have simply wanted to put a face to the name of the man who was charged with finding the killer of one of the city's most notorious villains, or maybe she just wanted to see if I would make time for her. I did not think she considered her grandson's violent death to be unexpected, but neither of us liked the timing or the method.

I headed to my Cadillac coupe. It looked undisturbed.

There were two Black youths in baggy jeans and crisp white T-shirts watching it from the nearby cart rack. They may have been engaged in some sort of legitimate activity, but they were trying too hard to make it look as though they belonged here. Neither of them had a store bag in their cart and both of their heads swiveled to follow my approach.

The part of my brain that instinctively translates my tactical training and experiences overseas into survival skills in New Orleans kicked in and I began watching the pair much more closely, and to scan for additional threats. I had been ambushed once too often and swore I never would be taken by surprise again. An intern shrink at the VA diagnosed me as being hyper-aware, but he also thought my new line of work could benefit from this form of PTSD. He's right, because I never make the mistake of believing that being a cop in New Orleans makes me any safer than I was when battling insurrectionists in Afghanistan or Iraq.

The oldest of the two youths was probably in his mid-twenties and older than the other boy by only a few years. They were both about six foot tall, the same as me. The older one carried less muscle and weight than me, but the younger one had the brawn of a defensive lineman. The older boy was keeping his hands where I could see them while the youth kept patting his front pants pocket. He was unconsciously telegraphing where he carried his weapon.

"Why you bugging that old woman?" the older youth finally called out to me.

"What old woman?"

"Ms. Ann. Biggie's grandma," the younger one now spoke up.

"She asked me to come see her." No harm in either of them knowing that much.

"Well, you don't need to come back." The younger one was pressing his luck with me. I stopped in my tracks and faced them from about fifteen feet away. I could clear my holster and drop them both by the time either of them had time to point their own weapons, but I didn't want to start my day, or end theirs, that way if it could be avoided.

"You do know I'm a cop, right?" I went so far as to point to the badge hanging over my belt. I unsnapped the holster to the handgun on my right hip in the same move.

"Yeah. You've busted a bunch of my friends on bullshit warrants," the older one snarled. "You're the detective the other cops call Cadillac."

"What's your beef in this anyway?" I didn't really care.

"I made a CD with Biggie. He was supposed to release it next week," the older kid explained.

"Well good luck with that," I said and opened my car door. They did not move until after I backed out of the parking space. I watched them in my rearview mirror as they began walking across the parking lot, away from Ms. Ann's building.

MY SECOND INTERVIEW OF THE DAY was with the veterinarian whose vaccination tags were attached to the metal choke collar. The collar also held a yellow tag for the sub-dermal microchip this vet implanted in the pit bull's shoulder.

The veterinarian's practice was in a building anchoring a pricey strip of shops on Metairie Road, the sort of stores favored by old-money widows in the habit of paying too much and the newly rich for whom spending an outrageous sum of money let them feel elitist. That may have been why someone like Biggie Charles chose this vet. Biggie might have figured that having his dog treated by the veterinarian of people who made their fortunes legally would somehow rub legitimacy off on himself as well.

My first impression of the owner of the practice was that he was one of those men over the age of sixty who have chosen liposuction over actual exercise, hair plugs over a receding hairline, and who spend hours in a tanning bed to maintain the nice glow on their plastic surgery. The second impression was that of a very successful man with a thriving business. I was counting on his balancing the protection of that reputation against any sort of privacy issues he might harbor towards a dead felon's business dealings with him.

"Good morning, I'm Doctor John, but not the famous one." He laughed at his own practiced joke for the locals before leading me into a vacant treatment room. "How may I help you, Detective?"

"I need some information on a dog you treated recently," I said and placed the evidence bag with the collar on the examination table. He looked at it, frowned, and looked up at me.

"This is the about the pit bull from last night. Right?"

"Yep. What can you tell me about the dog?"

"Not much you don't already know. It is a mature, pure-bred American Bull Terrier weighing about seventy pounds. The animal is healthy and a good example of the breed, which is why the kennel used it for breeding. Tyshika told me she paid to have it trained as a guard dog, but all I can say to that is that the dog was well behaved and responded well to orders. It just needed some flea and heartworm medicine, and I also inserted its microchip."

"What I have really been wondering was why Biggie chose you in the first place. Why do you suppose he picked yours out of all the practices in the city?"

His hesitation betrayed the lie even before he spoke.

"It wasn't Mister Charles who chose me. It was his fiancé, and I really have no idea why she did. I would guess she saw our ad in the Yellow Pages."

"Does she strike you as a Yellow Pages sort of person?" I figured he would come closer to the truth on his next try.

"I know the owner of the kennel."

"Is there any reason to hide that?"

"Jerome Washington was suspected of being involved in dogfights a few years ago." I waited for him to explain the rest of whatever he was trying not to say. "It could never be proved, and I never asked him about it. He moved his kennels to the Northshore after Hurricane Katrina and I understand that he is doing quite well there."

"How would any suspicion of his involvement in dogfighting splash back on you?"

"I was Jerome's veterinarian when he started out as a dog breeder. I had a smaller practice then and he was a steady customer. None of the dogs he brought me ever showed any injuries consistent with dog fighting. I did, though, sell him medical supplies so he could treat his own animals. Whether these supplies were used to treat the injuries he did not bring me is not something I could say one way or the other."

"And certainly would not speculate on now, right?"

"No, I would not."

"Did Tyshika bring the dog in alone?"

"It was Tyshika and some huge guy she said was her

boyfriend's bodyguard. She told me the dog was going to be a surprise present. I guess it really was a surprise."

"Yeah, that's what I said."

We shared an inappropriate laugh at what we both had blurted out before he herded me to the office manager and told her to give me whatever I asked for. All I needed was a copy of the medical records for the dog, which fit on two pieces of paper I folded and tucked into the messenger-style bag I always carry with me.

MY FINAL INTERVIEWS of the weekend were at the kennel that trained and sold the pit bull to Tyshika. I hoped to be able to build a working profile of Taz based on speaking with those who had been around the dog the most. There was no reason to change the methods I used to sort out situations between humans just because my prime suspect had two extra legs.

The drive from the city took nearly an hour, partly from the usual Saturday traffic jam at the Lakeside Mall on Veterans Highway and partly from the never-ending road improvements meant to relieve that congestion. The second half hour was spent driving through spotty rain on the elevated roadway spanning Lake Pontchartrain.

Alpha Dog Kennels moved from Downman Road, in the heart of the mostly Black part of town known as New Orleans East, to the very center of post-Katrina white flight following Hurricane Katrina. The business was now on the outskirts of Mandeville. The town's population had exploded following the storm as people with both no trust in rebuilt floodwalls and large insurance settlements came looking for a fresh start on higher ground. It would seem that Jerome Washington saw the graffiti on the wall and took the opportunity to go from being a suspected dog fighter to become the Northshore's largest purveyor of premium canine protection.

I did not know what I'd find. I had never been to a real kennel, only to the pound, as my parents never allowed my sister or me to have a dog. My father always said that if we really wanted to protect our house then we should get a goose because nobody ever sneaks up on a goose. I do not think my father ever considered the possibility of having a dog merely as a companion, but he was most likely right in the belief that neither of his children would ever properly care for a pet. I was surprised, then, to find that the kennel looked like the campus of a prosperous junior college. There was a German shepherd carved from a cypress log and a large sign bearing the name Alpha Dog Kennel at the turnoff from the highway. The small parking lot held more family cars and mini-vans than tricked out SUVs and sedans with absurd rims and gaudy paint jobs, but both types of vehicles were present and the only parking space I could find was well away from the front door.

An attractive young blonde in her mid-twenties, whose uniform and teeth were both white enough to set off her summer tan, asked me to sign in and assured me someone would be right with me. I did so before I passed her my business card with practiced discreetness and asked to speak with Jerome Washington. The trick to being discreet is to be sure nobody is nearby when you announce you're a cop and to smile really big before you make them think you are about to drag their boss off in shiny handcuffs in front of a roomful of paying customers.

"Mister Jerry, code one at the main lobby," she paged.

I figured that anyone as used to police officers as this man probably was would have some sort of warning in place, even after he went legitimate. I wondered if there was a signal in his being paged as 'Mister Jerry' instead of 'Mister Washington.'

I moved a few feet away from the counter and watched the driveway in case her page had been the Abandon Ship cue. I also noticed that the receptionist was watching the double French doors leading through the back of the building out of the corner of her left eye.

The kennel owner came into the building through those doors barely a moment later, smiling broadly and offering me a firm handshake that held little sweat. He must have been remarkably young when he first started Alpha Dog because he looked to me to be barely in his thirties. He was shaved bald, with a very close-trimmed goatee and medium chocolate colored skin over a muscular but average sized frame. We were almost eye to eye in height, and he moved very confidently into what could be a very nasty meeting. He surprised me by showing absolutely nothing but a genuine interest in answering my questions. His voice was calm and there was not the least sign of concern in his eyes.

"Jerry Washington," he said. It occurred to me that using 'Jerry' as a name probably worked better with his clients on this side of the lake than 'Jerome.'"

"Detective Holland." I showed him my badge. "I'm here about Taz."

"Yesterday's dog attack?" He seemed relieved that this was why I was there. The efficient girl at the desk handed him a manila folder he pointed to beside her arm and he quickly passed it to me. "These are copies of our records on the pit bull. We knew the dog as Roux, because of its dark fur, and I must confess that we were all quite surprised."

"That Biggie changed the dog's name or that it killed him?"

"I knew he changed the name to Taz. He said he loved the Tasmanian devil character from the old Bugs Bunny cartoons." Jerry gave a bemused shrug. "What surprised us was that it attacked him so viciously. I was most surprised that it actually killed him."

Jerry was deliberately steering me outside, away from any client's earshot. I trailed along in order to get a better feel for the operation. The rear of the main building opened onto a well-manicured courtyard. A fountain was set at the end of the courtyard, which was backed by the pine trees meant to obscure the view of the buildings housing the kennels. A dozen dogs and their owners were on the paver-stone patio we crossed to reach the fountain.

"The secret to dog training is to train the owner," Jerry said when he noticed my interest in the group. "The animal just wants to please its owner. The owner needs to decide what he expects of the animal, and then convey that desire on a consistent basis. People ruin the training every time they make exceptions. If you tell your dog to stay off the sofa then never invite it to join you on the sofa. Do you think Lassie understood what an exception was?"

"No, but Lassie loved Timmy and never ripped anyone's throat out that I can recall. You said the attack was a surprise. What surprised you about a guard dog attacking?"

"Other than attacking and killing its owner?"

"Well, how long had he owned the dog? I recall it was a birthday present."

"Everyone is required to take at least a basic course, such as these people are taking with their animal, before we complete a sale. It would be irresponsible to turn a trained defensive animal loose with anyone not trained to handle such a creature."

"So Biggie trained with this dog?"

"They were acquainted." Jerry was suddenly hedging. "The truth is they had only done four of the twenty hours we require. I got a message from his office asking if we could gift wrap the dog so it could be given to him as a surprise birthday present. I don't remember who left the message. Mr. Lynley was supposed to leave the dog in its kennel and bring it back today when he took part in their weekly training class. It would not have stayed with them until the training was complete. All the same, Mr. Lynley knew how to behave around the dog."

"And how should Biggie have acted? Did he forget something?"

"He should have made no sudden aggressive moves, especially towards the dog. No teasing the dog. No acting less than the alpha. If he excited the animal and then acted afraid of it, something like this might be the result."

"Like poking it with a stick. What do you suppose the odds of that kind of scenario happening would be?"

"I would not have thought this would happen. I really have no idea why the dog would have attacked without provocation, or why Charles was unable to control it."

"Some of that might have to do with the nature of his injuries." Jerry gave me a confused look. "It looks like one of the first bites may have been to Biggie's crotch. I would think that if he went to grab what was left of his manhood then his throat would be an easy target. Do you actually train these dogs to go for a man's crotch?"

The kennel owner gave a soft laugh, leaving me unsure if it was a laugh at the image or the question.

"No. That's something dogs fighting one another might do, but with humans that move actually makes the dog vulnerable. It puts its head in an easy position to be struck."

Jerry brought his hands straight down to demonstrate.

That act may have been harder in a seated position, but so would the attack on the fat man's genitals.

"Did he ever mention he had been bitten by a dog when he was a kid?"

"No, and I would have discouraged his getting a pit bull had I known. I would have suggested he get himself a Setter or something a lot mellower than something like a terrier."

"And how is it that you had Biggie Charles as a customer?" I knew the answer to this question but thought it would be interesting to see what he said.

"My trainer's sister is his fiancée. Was, I mean."

"How did you feel about that?"

"Feel about what?"

"Your trainer knowing a guy like Biggie Charles."

"I would have much less business if I was choosy about my customers. I didn't care one way or the other as long it didn't impact our business."

"And did it ever affect your business?"

"Not until last night. Don't get me wrong. I was no pal of Charles Lynley, and I know what he did to go to Angola, but he was making a good name for himself, the same as me, and I had to give him props for that," the kennel owner's response made me rethink how I questioned him.

Jerry had quietly deflected all of my insinuations. Both of these men had pulled their names out of the mud and overcame improbable odds to build apparently successful legal businesses. Biggie, whatever else he may have been, had a reputation as the go-to guy on the Gulf Coast to jump-start your career in hip-hop music, and Jerry obviously came a long way from selling puppies off the back of a truck in the poorest part of a poor community.

"I guess my only other question, for now, is why Biggie Charles would want a three-year old dog instead of a younger one. Wouldn't a younger dog be easier to train or bond with?"

"Well it wasn't really a guard dog," Jerry confided. "I mean, we planned to train the dog in the basics of defending its master but it would not have been a dog I could have sold as a true protection animal. The truth is, it was part of a litter from two of our blue ribbon show dogs and I was using it for show and stud until Charles' fiancé saw the dog a few weeks ago and made me a very generous offer. We planned to train it to act like a big mean dog for Charles because he didn't really want a dog that might actually attack someone by accident. The people he hangs with are always acting like idiots around him and a real protection animal would have been biting everyone in the damn room."

The two of us shared a laugh at the truth of this observation. The idea of someone waving a gun near Biggie to tell a story or make a point only to lose the use of their arm to a confused pit bull was within the reasonable expectations of a well-trained attack dog's behavior.

"So, the fiancé's cousin trained the dog?" The idea that these two had conspired to use the dog to kill Biggie was too obvious to ignore, and yet was so obvious it was unlikely.

"Right. His name's Cisco," Jerry said, then thought for a second before adding details he probably thought would discourage my making his employee a suspect. "He is one of my best trainers. Cisco's been with me from the start, so he knows what he's doing. He's about through with the morning class. I'll have him speak to you before you leave."

We had walked only as far as the fountain in the middle of the wide courtyard in the course of the interview. I noticed that the kennel owner began glancing at his wristwatch in the past few minutes and made no offer of a tour of the facilities. This may have been because I'd used up what time he was prepared to take from a busy day to answer my questions. It may have been a lot of things, but the one I held onto was that Jerry Washington answered my questions so thoroughly because he did not want to give me any reason to come back with any fresh questions.

"Thanks for your time." We shook hands in parting and his handshake remained dry and firm. "You really seem to have made something for yourself here."

"I'll be honest. When I heard the page, I figured you were some guy bringing a lawsuit from Cisco's cousin. It will be just like her to sue me for the dog attack."

"You're kidding."

"You haven't met Tyshika, have you? Let's just say she knows how to find a buck if there's one to be found."

"Duly noted." Jerry left me with that thought and went to speak with his trainer.

Cisco was about a head shorter than me, but he made up for it with a narrow-brimmed hat that reminded me of the style favored by the late coach Bear Bryant. He wore oversized eyeglasses. Their lack of magnification left me wondering if they were just for show. He had a good handshake, though his was much moister than Jerry's. I considered this for a moment and understood that the owner had only sold a dog, while this young man had been responsible for training it not to kill its owner. A task he failed spectacularly I might add.

"Cisco Barnes," he introduced himself. "I guess you have some questions about Roux. Oh, I mean Taz."

"Just one, really. What went wrong?"

"Honestly, I have no idea. The two of them seemed to bond as well as any dog and their owner in my experience. I have been at this for years and this attack is absolutely unprecedented in our history. I only wish that I could have done some sort of evaluation before you shot Taz."

"Do you really think it would help if you were able to work with the dog again?" This elicited a very reflexive blink from Cisco.

"Why do you ask that? Didn't they shoot the dog?"

"No. It's now part of an active murder investigation."

"Murder?"

"Of course," I noticed his sudden anxiety. "You, and your boss, just confirmed this is unusual. I think you just said it was unprecedented. I'm supposed to figure out why the dog attacked and if someone trained it to do so."

"I'm open to helping any way I can. Just give me a call."

I smiled and nodded at the offer, but there was no way I was going to let this man anywhere near the dog ever again.

"Whose idea was it to dye the dog blue for the day?"

"Beats me. There was a note in my message box that said to do so and to have him gift and ready to go in a gift wrapped cage at four yesterday afternoon. I figure Tyshika or maybe Bumper thought it would be funny."

"Okay, thanks." Nobody seemed to know who ordered the dog's dye job, but someone thought up the idea because the dog was most certainly blue when we first met.

It was going to be nearly five o'clock by the time I made it back across the lake. I'd get there just in time for a light dinner before the kick-off of the LSU football game against Vanderbilt. The contest was likely to be about as evenly matched as the one between Biggie and Taz. I was going to enjoy it all the same and any meeting with Lynley's supposedly grieving fiancée, or that bruiser of a bodyguard, was just going to have to wait until the first of next week.

I noticed a dark colored Lincoln Navigator as it pulled out of the parking lot across from Alpha Dog and into position three cars behind me. I kept an eye on it as it followed me onto the entry road for the Causeway and into one of the other cash lanes to pay the toll. This put only a few car lengths between the two of us as we drove the twenty minutes across the bridge. It matched my movements as I intentionally changed speeds and lanes to confirm the vehicle was genuinely following me, but it never came closer than four car lengths. I would not have imagined that following a red Cadillac XLR convertible across a bridge would be as much work as the driver behind me was making it into. I gradually slowed down at one point until I could make out what I thought were at least two occupants. Both were Black and male, but neither of them looked like the boys in the Walmart parking lot.

I allowed my mind to split concentration between driving and deciding who else might have any personal stake, beyond the comfortably short list of suspects, in my investigation into Biggie's death. The hardest question was not why they were following me but rather how did they know where to find me this afternoon? I had not seen them until I left the kennel, and I doubted they started as far back as Biggie's grandmother's house. I was really slipping if I allowed a vehicle that conspicuous to follow me around all afternoon and had not noticed it until now.

The driver of the Navigator stayed with me all the way to the parking garage where Tony and I keep our vehicles on Chartres. I took a moment to visually inspect my auto for any sort of electronic tracking devices but came up empty. I debated mentioning the incident in my report to Chief Avery. I chose not to do so because I wanted to give him something more to worry about than that my PTSD was making me paranoid.

9

BIGGIE'S DEATH WAS FRONT PAGE NEWS in the *New Orleans Levee,* a satirical gazette whose publication date is based on accumulating enough things to be sarcastic about to fill an edition. The article featured a picture of a pit bull dressed as McGruff the Crime Dog, bragging about having 'taken a bite out of crime' by killing Biggie Charles.

Biggie also made the *Times-Picayune* again. This time it was on the Sunday obituary page. The obituary included a picture that made him seem far nobler than he had ever been and ran in a large box above the fold. I figured it was a paid obituary. The *Times-Picayune* was not going to miss writing about him so much that they would have created such a display for free. The lengthy obituary mentioned his having been born in the Calliope Projects and graduating from George Washington Carver High School. The obituary made no mention about the time he spent with his grandparents in Bogue Chitto. It also brushed past all of his crimes and the years in Angola. Whoever wrote this wanted him to be remembered as a successful music producer and promoter who worked tirelessly with young local musicians to give them a viable alternative to a life of crime themselves. There was also no mention made of his locally famous quote about being smarter than a slave owner because he owned careers and not just people. His grandmother was listed as a surviving heir but not Tyshika. The omission of the fiancée indicated to me that she was definitely not the one to have posted Biggie's obituary, nor had she made the funeral arrangements at the newly renovated Rhodes Funeral Home on Washington Avenue. A brass band was scheduled to lead the second line to his final resting place in one of the cemeteries near City Park. The funeral was set for Thursday afternoon so there was plenty of time to decide whether or not I should attend the funeral. I didn't need to stake it out to observe the grieving suspects, but I did consider going just to hear the band.

I joined our bar full of regulars and tourists to watch the Saints crush the Detroit Lions later that afternoon. The Saints won but also displayed a distressingly familiar degree of sloppy play, including three turnovers. They came away with a winning score which was half of what they should have racked up.

I spent the rest of Sunday evening preparing my report for Avery and watching the surveillance tapes from the parking lot between the former Jax brewery building and the Hard Rock Café where Biggie died. Nobody approached the vehicle between the time Bumper and Tyshika exited the vehicle and when Bumper returned to have what looked like a fairly heated conversation with Biggie. The next time the bodyguard checked on his boss it was time to call the police.

10

I WAITED UNTIL LATE Monday morning to drive the two dozen blocks to the studio of BC Productions. I had a porter bring my Cadillac CTS-V station wagon from around the corner in case my stalkers were waiting for me to leave the garage in the coupe I drove on Saturday.

BC Productions was at the corner of Iberville and Broad Street, within sight of the parish courthouse and jail. The neighborhood surrounding the building was still struggling to get back on its feet from the flooding four years earlier. Multiple generations grew up in the mostly shotgun-styled houses their grand-parents built during the rare period of economic prosperity the city had during both world wars. The reason the neighborhood was still a ghost-town was that their impoverished grandchildren had to spend all the money they should have invested in flood insurance to buy things like food and clothing.

BC Studios' company logo looked like it had been spray painted with garish colors in graffiti-style across the front of the building. The former grocery building provided a large loading dock and plenty of room for its offices, a digital recording studio, and the facilities for producing and shipping the CDs and DJ vinyl, plus the live sound stage with a large dance floor and a multi-level VIP section which allegedly actually paid the bills. Biggie was repeatedly cited for operating the studio as an unlicensed after-hours nightclub. Biggie's attorneys successfully beat the charges each time because nobody ever had to pay a cover charge for admission and the liquor that flowed was supposedly free. Apparently his guests bought a ton of memorabilia. Biggie was also smart enough to never be armed or on drugs when the place was raided.

The business offices occupied the front quarter of the cavernous space inside the building and took advantage of the only windows. I saw nobody in the office area behind the two women at the reception desk. A large glass panel bearing the BC Productions logo separated the reception area from the actual offices and, while I had the impression that I had access to the area, heavy double wooden doors at either end of the desk barred actual entry. The glass turned out to be the same protective laminated glass used in banks. I had to appreciate the illusion of transparency. Anyone coming in to conduct business would feel that they could see what was going on in the office, but anyone coming in with mayhem in their heart could stand there all day but never get any further. The glass barricade did not run to the ceiling, and it offered no protection against the sound of Tyshika Franklin ranting.

"I said get him on the phone!" She was screaming at the switchboard operator from what had probably been Biggie's domain on the far side of the office space.

"I am trying," the beleaguered Black girl tried to explain through the safety of the intercom system. "But his office says he ain't in at the moment."

"Just find the asshole."

Tyshika came out of the office with the phone still in her hand. She was barely past thirty years of age, having been a minor when she first hooked up with Biggie, and the fullness of her angry voice was in direct contrast to her slight but attractive frame. She was wearing a tight white blouse and a blue skirt that would have made it indecent to sit down were it an inch shorter. I wondered if her idea of appropriate office attire had come from a rap music video. She jabbed the long nails on her free hand at me.

"You! I wanna talk to you!"

"More than I do her," I whispered to the second receptionist. She grinned so only I could see and then buzzed me into the vacant office space. "What can I do for you, Miss Franklin?"

"Have you killed that dog yet?"

"No, it's still considered to be a material witness."

"You know that thing killed my Charlie. What more witness can it be? Why is my Biggie dead and that dog still be walking around?"

"Well, I need to determine if the dog was working alone or if it was part of a larger conspiracy." I wanted to see her reaction to this idea. She did not disappoint my taste for theater. Tyshika screamed and threw the phone at my head.

"Are you kidding me? How can a dog be part of some conspiracy? You think the dog was sitting at some damn table making plans with somebody to kill my man? Dog talks, does it?"

"In a way, yes." I returned her flying phone. "I found out it wasn't really trained to kill at all. It knew Biggie well enough to have attacked him long before now if it really hated him. So, now I need to find out who might have trained it to do the deed."

"Good luck with that." She laughed shrilly and turned to head back to Biggie's office. I sensed I could forget getting her cooperation for the moment, but followed her to make the effort.

"The kennel owner says he's afraid you're going to sue him." I just tossed this out as a means of keeping the conversation flowing. It had absolutely no bearing on my investigation.

"Damn right I am. I'm gonna sue Alpha Dog Kennels for two million dollars. You want to talk about pain and suffering? That jury will give me whatever I want when I show them the pictures of what that bitch dog did to my Charlie."

I paused for a moment before picking at her argument. "Well, two things to consider then. First, it's not a female so it is not a bitch. Second, I take it you didn't see Biggie's obituary in yesterday's paper."

She had, by now, figured out this was not a social visit, and that I certainly was not going to offer any sort of condolences for her loss. She was burning through what little sympathy I had been able to muster for her as it was.

"What about Biggie's obituary?"

"It's just curious that you weren't listed as a survivor, or mentioned at all for that matter. Did you write it and forget to mention yourself?"

"The funeral home said he had one written and they had it on file." She could not consider the full implications of what I was saying and maintain her anger at the same time. Many of the things I found curious or amusing about the obituary were explained by Biggie's having written it himself. He made quite an effort to control how he would be remembered for the permanent record.

"Am I interrupting?"

I looked over to see attorney Daniel Logan standing in the doorway. Logan stands just over six foot tall, is baby-faced, but borders on obesity. The attorney is in his early fifties with slicked-back hair he keeps dyed black. He has a penchant for seersucker suits and bow ties. The suits are not inexpensive, but he buys them off the rack and never pays for a proper fitting. His Brooklyn accent also marks him as a modern-day carpetbagger in New Orleans. The real story of why he had shifted his practice from New York to New Orleans is a favorite topic of speculation among those who have regular dealings with him.

Logan has made himself a reputation and a very lucrative career out of representing criminals with enough cash in hand to hire him. His two special skills are making certain he only defends clients with the assets to pay his hefty fees and convincing the courts not to seize those funds so his clients don't drain the meager coffers of the Public Defenders' Office. His attorney fees usually clean the accounts just as thoroughly as a court order might have done.

"I've been trying to reach you all day." Tyshika rediscovered her store of anger and turned up the volume once again. "Are you trying to avoid me?"

"Obviously not, Tyshika." Logan flashed his most reptilian smile. "Here I am."

Logan greeted me by my nick-name and plopped into the chair next to mine, leaving the two of us facing the exceedingly angry woman. I could see Tyshika was now having a difficult time deciding which of us posed the greater threat and where she should focus her attention. It was likely that the attorney and I were going take turns making her angrier. I let him go first.

"Tyshika." He used a very calm and patronizing voice. Perhaps he had found some success with this approach in the past. "What are you doing here?"

"Somebody's got to run this place, right? I figure Charlie would want me to." The volume in her voice came down as she spoke. It softened in direct proportion to her increasing realization of the position in which her late fiancée had actually left her. The attorney and I were about to finish what the obituary omission began.

"Well, yes," Logan agreed, speaking slowly. "But it will not be you. Mr. Lynley designated Bumper as the one to step in for the time being, until the estate is settled."

"You mean to tell me," her voice started skywards immediately. "That the one person he trusted to keep him alive, and *didn't*, that's who's gonna to run his company?"

"It's an unfortunate way to describe the situation, but yes," the attorney said with a faint shrug and a smug grin. I was now utterly forgotten by both of them and just strapped myself in for the rest of the ride. "Per his instructions, his designated manager is to run things until his son can assume control."

I feared her head might actually explode. Her eyes bulged and her entire body shook until her hair was flying about and a sound probably only heard by animals came out of her open mouth. Then she found her voice and shrieked. "Are you freakin' kidding me?"

I was no less dumbstruck than she was. This was the first I had ever heard of there being a Little Charles Lynley running around somewhere.

"I'll give you a moment," the lawyer said and stood up. He saw my hopelessly confused look and motioned for me to follow him into the empty office area. Logan hastily explained the situation while Tyshika prepared herself for her next attack. I kept her in my sight in case she had a handgun within reach.

"You can imagine the difficulty for someone such as Charles to find legitimate work upon his release from prison. Tyshika took him in and supported him. They had a son that they both realized stood almost no chance of a life that did not involve eventually following in his father's footsteps. I arranged an adoption for the boy and, to the best of my knowledge, there has been no contact between the biological and adoptive parents since. The boy should be seven years old now. He surely has no idea who, or what, his father was. I am absolutely surprised that this is something Biggie decided to do."

I was dizzied by the thousands of possible follow-up questions to this increasingly bizarre situation. "Why would Biggie give his son up for adoption and then leave him the family business anyway?"

"I admit it does seem strange." I could see the dollar signs in Logan's eyes as he estimated the legal cost of straightening this mess out. Best of all, at least for him, was that this was a mess he had also been paid to help create.

"How do I contest the will? I deserve something for putting up with that bastard for this long. He is not going to use me, make me give up my child, and then just leave me out in the street like a piece of trash. He's the trash!" Tyshika finally screeched as she thrust her head out of the office into the empty workspace where the lawyer and I had taken refuge. She did not physically leave the office, perhaps thinking that her continued presence there might give her some sort of squatter's rights.

"Well, you could hire a lawyer of your own and drag the whole thing out for as long as I allow. But you would need money for a large retainer, which is money you do not have to the best of my knowledge. My suggestion is to let me meet with the boy's mother and look at some sort of mediation. I cannot imagine that she will want her son involved here and, as he is a minor, she may want to appoint an administrator. Why don't you go home and work on your resume for that position and I'll be in touch?"

Tyshika knew Logan well enough to know when she was cornered and getting close to the end of what little patience the attorney had for scorned widows and mistresses. The women who get involved with the Biggie Charles Lynleys of the world must surely know the kind of men they are investing their lives in, and yet so few ever think to protect themselves financially against the near certainty of a bad ending. Tyshika gathered her things and left the office quietly. Her hair was still a mess but she held her chin up high as she marched past the openly smirking receptionists. You had to be blind not to notice that the two girls on the desk had waited a long time for this day. There would be an office celebration somewhere later that night.

"So, what is your interest here, Cadillac?" Logan asked once we were alone.

"I'm investigating Biggie's death on NOPD's dime. There's a theory that the dog didn't work alone."

"No canine Oswald, then?"

"It doesn't seem likely. Someone had to train that dog to attack him the way it did," I explained my working theory without giving up any secrets. I had none to hide anyway.

"Well, I guess I owe you for being here to protect me from the grieving fiancé if things got really ugly."

"We've known one another long enough that it would have been a tough call on who to shoot." This was hardly the worst dead lawyer joke he'd heard.

"You may as well follow me to see the boy's mother. You're going to have to know about this eventually and one of these women may yet decide to kill the messenger." He started to lead the way out of the now deserted office area then stopped and turned to face me. "Do you know what really surprised me? I am surprised that someone like Biggie Charles even had a will. I handled all of his legal work but he never expressed an interest in making one. The one I have was something drawn up by the attorney that defended him in his murder trial. That was before he even had a kid."

"Why are you so surprised about Biggie having a will?"

"For someone in Biggie's line of work, having a will meant accepting that he might not outlive his enemies. It would, though, mean being sure of what happened after he died."

"Like screwing with Tyshika?"

"Absolutely. Tyshika turned tricks to support Biggie after his release from Angola, but she also encouraged him to take back his turf and go back to the same things that had landed him in prison. He knew every cop in New Orleans was waiting for him to do so. She lived damn well off of him while he built this record label. In his mind, she has already been repaid a hundred times over."

"I doubt she's going to like that explanation. What are you going to do for her?"

"Not a goddamn thing." The lawyer looked at me as though I was questioning his dedication to his client's wishes. "I guess I could help her sue the dog kennel."

I let that comment pass. "Have you been knowing Biggie Charles very long?"

"I knew his father first, so I guess for most of his adult life. Biggie was one of those kids from a bad neighborhood who had the brains and determination to have done anything he wanted. He could have been one of the few success stories, but he was lazy and drugs are the only career path for ambitious young men who lack the character to stay on the higher path."

"But you didn't represent Biggie at his murder trial?"

"Noooo!" Logan held up both hands. "Someone else has that black spot on their resume. The prosecutor was caught trying to suppress an audio tape of the agents saying they should shoot Biggie and say he drew first. Personally, I think that the agents were daydreaming, but I can't say one way or the other how the jury would have voted. It didn't matter because catching the prosecutor was enough to force the DA to give Biggie a very good plea deal. It proved to be enough prison time that Biggie understood the price he'd pay if he went back to his old ways when he got out."

"Rumor is that he did go back to the life."

"Rumor has it that the Saints will go to the Super Bowl this year, too. I am sure Biggie knew a lot of the dealers and shooters out there, because they frequented his club. This place was raided every few months but they never found drugs or guns on Biggie or any of his people. He insisted on running a clean operation. He really was dedicated to building something with the record label and was making a positive impact in the community."

"So, where did he get his start-up money? As I vaguely remember it, he didn't start out small. It was like he sprang to the top of the heap overnight."

"I don't have an answer for that," Logan said much more cautiously than he had been so far in this discussion.

"I don't think he is still covered by any confidentiality clauses."

Logan said nothing and started out of the office. He was willing to share only what he felt was necessary to make me think better of his dead client. Logan and I said a polite goodbye to the secretaries and I trailed behind him as we stepped into the bright mid-day sun.

"I will follow you. Where are we headed?"

"Oh, we aren't going very far." He had a good laugh at my expense when he caught sight of the station wagon I was driving. "I know they call you Cadillac, but I didn't know you were a soccer mom in your spare time."

I didn't take the bait and waited as Logan put his briefcase in the trunk of his Mercedes convertible. He was parked well away from the entryway. He may have anticipated Tyshika taking her keys to the car's paint job on her way out.

I followed him as he pulled onto Broad, then almost immediately turned right on Orleans and led me back into the Quarter. I kept an eye on my rear view mirror for any sign of the Lincoln Navigator or any other vehicle following us. Logan proved to be right about our not traveling very far. I could have parked in my own garage a few blocks away had I known our final destination.

The attorney pulled into a parking lot behind the former Jax Brewery across from Jackson Square, and waved for me to park next to him. The spaces were marked as reserved, but with my license plates and police placard on the dashboard, I was unlikely to be towed. I parked next to a newly purchased Volvo XC-90 with a temporary plate sticker still on the rear windshield. The new owner, according to the sticker, was named Amanda Rhodes.

11

AMANDA RHODES WAS ONE OF the Hollywood and New York celebrities and artists to have bought property in New Orleans in lieu of staying in hotels while they are in town either working or on vacation. Access to her penthouse apartment was by way of a private elevator with its own marble-floored lobby at ground level. Logan led me through the lobby and punched in an eight-digit access code to open the elevator doors and waved me inside.

The wood-lined elevator doors opened onto a sun-washed living space with floor to ceiling windows overlooking the Mississippi River and French Quarter. I was impressed with the way the living room's decorating blended antique and modern pieces so well. The furnishings were chosen to create unobstructed and stunning views in all directions through the walls made up of laminated plate glass panels. I could see St Louis Cathedral, the Crescent City Connection Bridge, the office towers of the CBD and a panoramic view across the Mississippi River to Algiers from where we were standing. I could even hear the calliope on the excursion boat Natchez docked close by.

I tried to remember what I could of Amanda Rhodes. I knew she was one of the rare former child stars who could still find work as an adult in a difficult industry. She was approaching her forties now and a display case held the awards she won over the years. My favorite movies were the ones she had done just for the money at the middle of her career. Those were the ones when she still did nude scenes. She stopped sharing her body with the paying public after she married a prominent entertainment lawyer. I couldn't recall his name, but I'd never meet him because he died in a carjacking a couple of years back.

We were met at the elevator by a petite black-haired young woman with dark features and a caramel tan in a string bikini top and floral print wraparound. Logan greeted her as Miss Georgia, leaving me to decide whether she was Amanda's personal assistant or a beauty pageant contestant. She was not unattractive; but her face showed a hint of hardness around its child-like qualities. She had lovely brown eyes and her dark brown hair was cut close to her shoulders. She was in her mid-thirties and looked physically fit, but I guess chasing after a seven-year old would do that for any person. Her smile was friendly, yet she was not being especially helpful; her stance and position blocked our path beyond the elevator.

"You didn't mention bringing anyone with you." Georgia glared at the two of us. Her opinion of the attorney was obvious. It almost made me wish I had come alone.

"This was a last minute opportunity, Miss Georgia. This is a State Police Detective named Cadillac Holland. He is the detective investigating Charles Lynley's death. It would only be a matter of time before he came knocking, so I think we can all agree this is the best way to meet your boss."

"He doesn't look like any cop I ever saw."

"Summer uniforms." Granted, a polo shirt and denim jeans are not what one expects a police detective to be wearing when he shows up at a famous Hollywood actress' door on business. Georgia slowly turned from appraising me to focus her facial expression of displeasure about my unannounced intrusion upon the attorney.

"Wait here and I will see if she will speak with you." It wasn't until she had turned away that I remembered I didn't need her permission to be there.

Logan waited until she was out of earshot before saying another word. "I've always thought that she and Amanda have a thing going. She was with Amanda before she moved here. Georgia hated Amanda's late husband so much I am surprised she wasn't the one who killed him. I warn you, she is even more protective of her boss than she is of the kid she nannies."

Georgia returned a few moments later and marched us across the dark bamboo floor to a large wooden deck that surrounded a lap pool and overlooked Jackson Square.

Despite being in full sunlight, the deck felt much cooler than the tourist-packed sidewalks below.

A tray of sandwich meats, sliced cheeses, and large croissants was laid out on a table shaded by a massive umbrella. The actress greeted us as her assistant poured sweet tea for each of us before excusing herself. Georgia reminded Amanda that this was the day she was taking someone named Parker to the zoo after school and needed to run an errand before picking them up from school. Amanda ignored us while they decided on where Georgia should bring their take-out dinner from on the way home.

Amanda Rhodes, in her own home and off the big screen, was a trim woman not much taller than her assistant and a head shorter than myself. Her lustrous sun-streaked blonde hair was cut just short of her trim shoulders. The arms and long legs exposed by her white bikini were well tanned and toned without being overly muscular. The bikini tantalized with a generous display of cleavage as well. Her ostrich-skin Tony Lama cowboy boots were an unexpected touch. I realized I was distracted because she had to repeat her question.

"I asked how you came up with a name like Cadillac."

"Oh, umm, it's a nickname. It was all we had to drive right after Katrina," I said without really answering her question. I took a seat on the wide padded bench across from where she sat in a high backed deck chair. Logan was busy making himself a roast beef sandwich.

"I think I have read all of your father's books. I remember reading that he had disappeared or something." She seemed interested and wasn't just making conversation.

"Or something," I deflected this subject as well. I needed to be the one asking questions.

"You don't have the accent of someone raised here. Are you sure you're who you say you are?"

"It was better to have a neutral accent in my last line of work. Besides that, I left here when I was about sixteen. I didn't move back until after the storm. I have been trying to get my old mojo back, though."

"I had to lose my accent for work as well. I grew up in a small town over in Alabama." She said the last words in a sultry Southern drawl that would have done Miss Scarlett proud.

"There, the introductions are done," Logan mumbled around a mouthful of sandwich. "I brought the detective along so we could get this over with in one sitting. I didn't think you would mind, Amanda. This way he has no reason to come back and bother you further."

"Ignore the man. You're welcome any time."

"Tell him about the adoption," Logan instructed her and went back to eating.

Amanda took a sip of her tea and then leaned towards me just a bit before speaking. "John and I were, of course, aware of the history of our son's parents. It was a large part of why we chose this particular child to adopt. Parker was more certain than most to wind up wasting his life and to get mixed up with drug dealing and guns. I mean, what other future could he have with parents like he had raising him? It was worse than being raised by wolves."

"There aren't wolves in Hollywood?" She sounded a lot more uncomfortable discussing this than she wanted me to know. I had never heard anything about the adoption until now, not that I was an avid reader of the tabloids.

"Mostly that's among the paparazzi. Well, we do have lawyers there as well. My husband was one, but I married him anyway. That has made it so much easier to get over losing the bastard."

"And it's why you decided to raise your son in New Orleans, I take it?" I tried to refocus the conversation but noted for myself that she was not a grieving widow. The idea that she had sought a place to raise her adopted child in a place that is largely free of photographers lurking in the shrubbery came to me a little slowly. She had done a good job of hiding the adoption so far, but the secret wouldn't have lasted a week on either coast.

"I see no reason to expose Parker to that world just yet. Mr. Logan was able to get the adoption handled quietly by a friendly judge in a parish somewhere up north. I'm glad we adopted Parker, but he's still too young to be put in that terrible spotlight the tabloids shine on our children. We can make a big announcement or something when Parker is old enough to understand things better."

"I would think that your son being the beneficiary of

Biggie Charles's will is going to be difficult to explain if the boy's biological mother contests the will in court, which she is likely to do."

"Mr. Logan has tried to explain this all to me, but I just keep bursting into tears. I don't deserve this. First I lose my husband, and now I have to fight Parker's mother over something I do not even want him near. I will not let my son get sucked back into that world at any age."

"You are not alone in this." Logan sounded like his meter was running.

"And now you're going to drag us into the murder investigation."

"Do you know who killed Biggie Charles?"

"No." She groaned more than denied. I realized just then that one of the condo's balconies overlooked the Hard Rock parking lot where Biggie had died.

"Then you aren't a suspect in my murder investigation. There is no reason to make this any more interesting by putting your name in the mix."

"Then why are you investigating it at all?" She was not yet convinced that I wasn't going to destroy her world.

"Because my sister didn't want me to shoot the dog."

"So, do you do everything your sister wants?" Amanda wasn't sure whether to laugh or to mock my reason.

"I also doubt the dog came up with the idea of killing Biggie Charles on its own unless it's a really good judge of character."

Amanda relaxed enough to lean back. Leaning towards me displayed her cleavage and her exposed right leg was proving to be another effective distraction.

"Anyway, back on the subject," Logan again interrupted. "What would you like to see happen?"

"Well, I really do not want anything to do with any of Biggie's estate." Amanda smiled when she caught me looking at her thigh. "Can't you just give it to someone else?"

"Only your son, or you on behalf of your son, could do that, but we will have to go through probate either way."

"Well, how long before you have to start that process?" I wondered aloud.

Logan looked at me with that look all lawyers develop as a means of telling a third party to mind their own business.

"I can hold off a couple of weeks without drawing too much notice. There really is nobody else getting much out of this than the boy."

"What about Biggie's personal holdings?" I persisted. Logan brought me to the meeting and I was going to use the opportunity no matter how much he now regretted doing so. "Who gets those?"

"Charles didn't have much in his own name, and just about all of that is going towards paying the burial and probate costs." It was obvious the attorney had already done the math on those financial assets and expenses.

"Can't I just sign a quit-claim or something? You could sell the company and donate the money to charity."

"It could be a lot of money." I was certain that Logan knew the exact value of Biggie's estate by now.

"I have enough money that I don't need his," Amanda snorted. She certainly did seem to have enough money to raise a child in this crystal palace.

"I will look into all of this for you," Logan assured Amanda and stood up.

I started to get up as well, but Amanda placed a hand on my arm and motioned for me to stay. She told Logan to see himself out and then stood to refresh my glass of tea. This allowed her to sit down next to me on the bench, and then to move close enough to rub flesh.

"So, if Cadillac is just what people call you, what is your real name?"

"Cooter."

"I'm sure there's an interesting story behind a name like that."

"It's really not that interesting. I mean, compared to your own story of becoming a famous movie star and all." The disappointed look she gave me made me elaborate a bit.

"It's an inside joke of my father's. He was born and raised in the boot-heel of Missouri. I wound up named after his hometown. Being Detective Cooter doesn't make it very easy to get taken seriously so I use the nickname an NOPD officer gave me most of the time."

"Yeah, about that." She set her tea on the table and placed one hand on my knee. I did not move her hand or my knee. "What sort of detective are you, anyway?"

"I actually work for the State Patrol, but I was assigned to New Orleans from the day I left the academy. My unofficial title here is Reserve Investigator. I was injured in Iraq and was still in the hospital when I first learned my father disappeared. I came back to New Orleans to look for him as soon as I could travel. My dad retired from NOPD and his old partner has his job as Chief of Detectives. My uncle used his connections in Baton Rouge to get me into the State Police academy under a deal that assigned me to New Orleans once I graduated. The Chief of Detectives agreed to allow me to use NOPD's resources to look for my father so long as I helped him put his department back together. It didn't work quite as planned and a friend and I opened a bistro down by the French Market a couple of years ago. Now I split my time between the bistro and handling anything NOPD doesn't have the man-hours to justify bothering with. Biggie's death is the first homicide investigation I have handled, but it's in that same category."

"I remember reading about your dad's disappearance. So you never did find anything out about what happened?"

"All I know for sure is that he was rounding up known felons who stayed behind. The idea was to evacuate them for their own protection. I think the real purpose was to get the hard cases out of here so the people left behind needed less protection."

"How do you think he disappeared?" Amanda asked.

"What I have been able to piece together is that he was on a night patrol and got separated. He likely drowned and his body floated into the lake as the floodwaters began to fall. I was only able to track down a couple of the NOPD cops he patrolled with. Both of them have left town and were particularly unhelpful when I called them."

"Why do you suppose that was?" Her hand was still on my knee.

"Maybe because I said that they should have searched harder at the time."

"Now here you're trying to understand why a dog would murder its owner." Amanda leaned back as she laughed and took her hand from my knee.

"Funny little world we live in. Everyone else is ready to close the case."

"Then why are you even bothering?" Her hand was back, but now on my thigh.

"I want to know who came up with the idea." It was the absolute truth. I couldn't think of many people more deserving of a death like Biggie's. I also believed the dog was a pawn and should not suffer disproportionately for its part in the murder. I placed my hand over hers and looked her in the eye. "So, you don't have to seduce me to get me to keep what I have learned about your son a secret. I promise."

"Oh, I've already figured that out. There are plenty of other reasons to seduce you." Amanda stood up and took off her skirt. "Why don't you join me in the pool?"

"Sorry. I didn't bring my suit."

There was, admittedly, a part of me hoping that what came next was skinny dipping with my shapely hostess. What happened instead was that she gave me directions to a small closet just outside of the half bath off the living room where she kept an assortment of swimsuits. I selected a set of baggy surfer-style trunks and returned to the deck wearing the shorts and my shirt. I set my shoes and folded jeans atop my messenger bag, with my pistol tucked inside, beneath the table. The bag is my mobile office. It holds a tablet computer with mobile internet, spare batteries for it and my telephone, a digital pocket camera and small voice recorder as well as extra clips for my sidearm and a first aid kit meant to treat a gunshot wound.

"Much better," Amanda said and motioned for me to join her in the pool. She had set two rafts adrift in the rather limited space of the pool. I hesitated before taking my shirt off, but did and jumped into the waist deep water and climbed aboard the empty raft. She paddled to my raft and we sat facing one another with our waists roughly side by side and our legs stretched out on the rafts. She had the more even suntan by far.

Amanda looked at my exposed body for a very long moment without saying a word. I knew what she was studying but waited for her to make the first comment. It had taken me a long time to be comfortable looking at myself in a mirror after I was ambushed.

The scars, but mostly my struggles with their emotional counterparts, had cost me a few promising romances since my return. I nearly convinced myself that the only women who could look at the mess I had made of my body required money to do so. The Quarter has more than a few very attractive women willing to make that transaction, but I was tired of being the one who felt empty in those exchanges.

"That is a very impressive collection of scars." Amanda reached out a hand and touched the long vertical scar on my left knee. "Someone did some high-quality work on your face, but I'm sure you were handsome anyway. What happened here?"

"Bad landing," I said as her fingernail traced along the scarred knee and a bit higher. I saw this was not enough of an answer to satisfy her curiosity. She showed not the slightest bit of repulsion at what she was touching or seeing. "I was fast roping from a helicopter on a night time mission in Afghanistan. I shattered my kneecap when the helicopter hit a downdraft and I hit the ground a lot too hard."

"So you were some hotshot Special Forces guy."

"Only if you think that's something sexy," I joked rather than answered. I had, in fact, been a Delta Force operator.

"Well, it's sexier than falling down the stairs, right?" Her thin fingers traced the silver dollar sized puckers of purplish flesh around my left chest and shoulder. "And here? That doesn't look like anything you did falling down stairs."

"AK-47 rounds. All but one went straight through." I leaned forward to show her the two larger scars on my back. This was not a trip down memory lane I wanted to make. I tried to joke that being hit at point-blank range meant the bullets flew through me so fast they didn't have time to kill me. The one that didn't go through nearly did kill me. I flat-lined twice on the operating table.

"What were you doing?" I could tell she was tilting back and forth between being absolutely fascinated and utterly appalled at what she was looking at.

"Zigging when I should have been zagging," I continued to distance myself from discussing the incident. My resume from the Middle East isn't something I talk about with strangers, even pretty ones.

Amanda spent another ten minutes searching out my lesser scars and getting my minimal responses to each new discovery. I tried to brush them all off as being old war wounds I got from fighting old wars. This was actually a way my grandfather used to describe his own war wounds. The truth is that being lucky to be alive just means we weren't lucky at all when we were wounded.

Amanda's hand traced across my cheek and torso before it settled again on the scar on my knee. I rested my own hand on her soft tanned thigh, only in part to keep us from drifting apart. We floated together for another hour or so listening to the street musicians in the square below while drifting inches apart beneath the cloudless Louisiana sky. We barely spoke another ten words before I had to leave.

I could not find the words to express what I felt in those silent moments we shared. There had never been a moment since the day I didn't die in the ambush that I thought I might ever feel quite so glad to be alive. Amanda's smile seemed to say she understood.

12

IT TOOK A SUPREME EFFORT to accept that floating in a movie actress' swimming pool was not going to provide the clues I would need to answer what happened to Biggie Charles. Neither of us was quite ready to part ways so soon. Amanda offered a tour of her condo after she changed into a halter-topped wisp of a sundress and shimmied across the glossy dark wood floors barefoot.

There were three balconies on the main floor, each with its own impressive view. The one off Georgia's room looked down on the spot where Biggie Charles died less than a hundred yards away. There were four bedrooms on the second floor, each with its own full bath, and an office at the opposite end of the floor. The most stunning room proved to be the master suite, which occupied the entire top floor of the three thousand square foot home. Amanda and I lingered outside of her spacious sun-lit bedroom, facing one another across the distance of the open double doorway. I sensed she would not have resisted any sort of sexual advance. I was sure she knew I would have allowed her to make the first move. I hesitated because it would have shown incredibly bad judgment to leap into bed with anyone remotely connected to the case.

This was not my real concern, though. I just wanted to be invited back to experience intimacy with someone who seemed comfortable with the damaged goods I considered myself to be. Amanda pointed out that all of the bedroom windows were tinted, which no doubt disappointed any police helicopters patrolling the afternoon skies, as she closed the distance between us.

"You are going to come back, right?"

"If that's what you would like."

She leaned in and really studied my face. My hairline had been restored with hair plugs and my rebuilt smile of implanted teeth was straighter than it had ever been. The metallic plates holding my skull in place were hidden by the tanned flesh over my restructured facial muscles.

"I'm glad they decided to make you so handsome."

"Thank my sister. She gave the plastic surgeon a picture of someone better looking than I ever was."

"I don't know that I have ever met anyone with this much expensive plastic work that wasn't an actor," she commented offhandedly. "The difference is that you are actually a real person under all that work."

"Well, at least they did a good enough job to get your attention."

"Being able to be discreet is what got my attention. I don't want you telling the tabloids about any time we spend together."

"Then I guess I should leave this afternoon out of my report."

"Only if you ever want to visit me on any unofficial basis." Amanda touched my lips with one long index finger for a lingering moment. It certainly seemed like a good trade to me. It was also the right time to make my exit.

I invited her to dinner, but she suggested a late dinner the next evening. She wanted to have her son tucked into bed before she left the house. I left her place unsure if I was more surprised by the existence of Amanda's son or the possibility of an entirely unexpected romance.

I walked through the French Market to my place above the bistro to collect the slim files I had been given by the dog's veterinarian and its breeder. I needed to give them to the dog handler hired to advise me. I was not so distracted by my thoughts that I was unaware of the kid watching me as I passed the steps to the Moonwalk across from the mule carriages lined up outside of Jackson Square. He fell into step behind me as I passed Café du Monde. My immediate thought was that he was one of the pair I encountered at Wal-Mart, but he was built leaner than either of them. He would have done better a better job of being inconspicuous by staying on his side of the street.

My stalker tried to hide his face with a ball cap and

sunglasses, but he was staring a hole in my back. I monitored his reflection in the shop windows along the way. He repeatedly gave himself away by bumping against tourists because he focused on me rather than upon his surroundings. I probably could have lost him easily, but I was trying to learn what I could from him by his appearance and actions. I kept an eye out for the Navigator.

I shoved the paperwork into my bag and headed back to Amanda's to pick up the station wagon. I noticed I'd picked my shadow up again as I passed the gift shop to the Margaritaville bar and grill. He was either working alone or his partners were better at tailing me than he was.

I stared up at the Brewery building before I tossed my bag on the passenger seat of the Cadillac. I realized that it would likely be very hard to ever pass the building again without thinking of this afternoon, no matter how things turned out. It was a vastly better way to remember the old brewery than as the parking lot where Biggie Charles died. My shadow melted into the crowd surrounding Jackson Square by the time I backed out of the parking space and went to meet the dog sitter Tulip had lined up.

13

THERE HAD BEEN JUST ONE CALL call from the animal shelter regarding the dog since I dropped it off. It came Sunday afternoon to inform me that I needed to find my suspect another home. The dog was attracting too much media interest and distracting the staff from their regular duties. The shelter was not afraid it would attack anyone else. I privately thought it doing so would give me a fresh clue to follow. It would have been easier to blame things on either the dog or some fault in its training were the dog inclined to randomly attack, or had one of the shelter's handlers inadvertently stumbled upon its attack command or trigger.

I had relayed news of the dog's imminent eviction to Tulip after the Saints game was over on Sunday and told her to find the dog either a new shelter or a dog sitter. I thought she was joking when she called back two hours later and told me she could not find a foster home among her pit bull loving friends, but had talked our mother into letting me board Taz and a volunteer dog trainer in her boathouse.

My surprise at my mother opening the door to the family's first dog was severely offset by the fact she only agreed to let it live in the space Tony and I kept for those times we needed to get out of the city. The dog could only destroy things which belonged to me personally, and to do so to its heart content unless this handler did his job.

The former dog trainer Tulip lined up was named Roger Kline. He worked part-time at the SPCA facility and was one of the foster owners that volunteered for the pit bull rescue charity Tulip represented. Roger had not hesitated to agree to work with Taz, and she claimed he shared our belief that Taz's attack was not solely the dog's idea. He had been waiting for my call and agreed to meet me at the dog pound in Algiers because he was working at the facility that day as it was. He was already familiarizing himself with the pit bull when I arrived.

Roger Kline looked and dressed like a former roadie for some touring rock band when he wasn't wearing his work uniform. His personal wardrobe seemed to consist of weathered denim jeans and vintage concert tour T-shirts. He was gaunt, bearded, and thin in that way men who do yoga become. His beard was nearly as gray as the ponytail in his hair.

"So, how's Taz?"

"Well, he's definitely a pit bull." Roger grinned and shook my hand. I must have looked confused about what he was trying to tell me, so he elaborated. "I took him out for a walk through the holding pens and he was way too interested in the other dogs. We passed close to a beagle mix and he made an attempt to attack it, which is not unusual for any pit bull. Then I let him get near one of the German shepherd bitches. He lunged at the shepherd. Taz is all about being the alpha dog anywhere he goes."

"Does any of that tell us anything else about Taz?" This was becoming a lot like conversations I find myself in with people that have a deep understanding of the complexities of beer or wine. I know something they are telling me is significant, but not what or why.

"It's pretty strange. Tulip said you told her this was a show dog but show dogs are better behaved around other dogs. This fella wants to completely dominate them."

I moved next to the kennel and looked at Taz as though it were the first time I had really seen the dog. He had been properly cleaned and the brown two-tone coat made him look almost as though he had a leopard in his lineage. Roger explained that it was called a merle coat, and was fairly rare among pit bulls.

"I can't thank you enough for agreeing to watch Taz." I was very sincere about this as I had no idea what I might have done if he had not agreed to do so.

"The pay has a lot to do with it." Tulip unilaterally told him I was offering two hundred dollars a day, which I could probably bill to NOPD, but she added a generous amount of trade at the bistro to sweeten the deal. "Are we ready to load him up?"

"I had an idea on the way over here." I paused before pursuing the thought. I did not want Roger thinking the dog was fine and I was the one out of my mind. "I want to wrap the kennel before we load it. The dog traveled that way from where it was picked up and I want to see how it responds to the isolation."

"That makes sense. I'll bet he just lies down and takes a nap."

"Why do you say that?"

"Well, he won't have any visual stimulation and he'll have a hard time smelling anything besides the paper we wrap him in. He'll feel trapped and that usually makes them withdraw."

All we had to work with was adhesive tape and a copy of the day's newspaper, but we wound up with a double thickness of paper that approximated the wrapping paper Taz was concealed beneath before he made his murderous lunge upon Biggie. Roger's prediction of the dog becoming withdrawn proved correct as we wheeled the dog through the hallways to the loading dock. The two of us had no difficulty loading the kenneled dog, which made no sound during the entire drive to my mother's house.

I apologized to Roger that I would be taking a circuitous route to our destination. I was driving the Cadillac wagon and would have easily outrun anyone following me with its powerful motor and suspension if need be, even the Lincoln Navigator. I was less concerned about concealing where I had taken the dog than I was with protecting my mother from anyone who might be intent on harming Taz. She was already unhappy about the situation, and having an attack on her home was the very last thing I needed to have further upset her. Roger was driving a decades-old Dodge pickup truck, but he managed to stay right behind me.

My father purchased the property my mother now called home with the advance from his first big publishing deal. I refer to its current style as "Ill-Considered Post-Katrina." It's a two-story masonry structure covered in white stucco, with lots of glass, built on a slab foundation in an area that took a twenty-foot hurricane storm surge. The renovation expenses after Hurricane Katrina were higher than the original construction cost. All the same, it had been a very restful place to recuperate after I left the hospital. It has great views of historic Fort Pike, a heavy brick structure built after the War of 1812, and the Rigolets waterway connecting Lake Catherine to Lake Borne and the Gulf of Mexico beyond. My father used to tell me we could ride his fishing boat from our dock to where he grew up in Missouri, all we had to do was cross Lake Ponchartrain to the Industrial Canal and head up the Mississippi River. I think we might have enjoyed the time together.

I feel my mother was manipulated into moving here rather than rebuilding our home in Lakeview, which was fifty yards from the massive floodwall breach that destroyed the neighborhood. I initially thought she was being sentimental or had some lingering fear about the new levees, but it turned out that she had moved here on the advice of her online psychic. The psychic told her she would be "close to the answer" to my father's disappearance. Neither of us understood what this last part meant, but her neighbors were all either retired police officers or active duty ones with weekend camps so I felt she was safe living in such an isolated area.

My father's fishing boat was washed away by the storm surge and my mother, who was never a fan of deep sea fishing, quietly pocketed the insurance payout without ever replacing it. The boathouse became bachelor quarters for Tony and myself when we arrived. It was where I finished my recuperation and where Tony lived for over a year after he emigrated here on an EB-5 visa. The boathouse is thirty yards from the main house. Most of the furnishings I decorated the second-floor living area with were chosen as much for their comfort as for my lack of attachment to them when the next hurricane washes them away. I gave Roger the two-minute tour and showed him the groceries our mother's housekeeper stocked the place with earlier in the day. I warned him to expect a visit from the "lady of the manor" at some point. Roger shrugged and tossed his duffle on the bed in the front bedroom while I pulled cold beers from the refrigerator.

"Here are the files Taz's veterinarian and dog breeder

gave me Saturday." I handed Roger the files I had been dragging around with me. He just nodded and tossed them on the kitchen table.

"I'll look through them and let you know if there's anything interesting." I don't think either of us expected to find the answer to the pit bull's actions in either set of files.

"Are you up to a little experiment?"

"Sure, what do you have in mind?"

"I was thinking about having Taz attack one of us." Roger turned so he could see if I was serious. "I am willing to bet that he won't."

"That's not a particularly safe bet, you know."

We went back downstairs and pulled the still wrapped kennel from my station wagon and set it on the ground. Roger set about removing the heavy newspaper wrapping while I watched the dog's reaction to its new surroundings. Taz blinked in the bright light but still made nary a sound. He remained curled in the center of the cage, watching us with interest but no intent.

"If he does attack me, he's going for you next. Neither of us is trained as his alpha, so we are both fair game if he goes for the neck." Roger warned me.

"Ah, but I brought a gun. Did you?" I was glad to have found someone as reckless with this idea as I was so I didn't have to order him to help with this stunt.

Roger snapped the lead onto Taz and gently pulled him from the kennel. The dog gave a long, open-mouthed stretch and then sat down to wait for whatever came next. We both extended open hands towards his nose, one at a time, and neither of us were worthy of more than passing interest. He did, though, lick Roger's hand.

"The hand that feeds him no doubt," I tried to joke. I paced off a distance two steps longer than the combined length of my extended arm and the heavy leash holding the pit bull.

"Okay, let's try this then." My arms were at my sides and my pistol was gripped in my right hand, cocked and ready if necessary.

"Taz. Stand." Roger gave each direction in an even tone. The dog stood up, letting us know that it was open to following commands given by someone it had not been trained to obey. Roger and I exchanged nods and he proceeded. "Taz. Attack."

There is a certain relief when a stupid idea fails miserably and nobody is hurt. Roger tried a couple of other commands and even tried repeating the orders in French, Dutch, Spanish, and German. He explained that some trainers taught the owners to give commands in languages that the average person attacking them would not think to use. Taz never once took up the slack in the leash and we both thought it odd that a defensive animal would refuse to follow even basic commands. We assumed he was trained to obey only Biggie. The problem with that theory was that the dog and its victim were only barely acquainted, at least according to Jerry Washington.

Roger moved closer and took an empty swing at my face, but Taz still gave no real reaction. Roger finally resorted to making an open-handed slap towards Taz himself, and the dog would have taken any level of smacking we chose to give it because there was absolutely no indication that there would have been any sort of defense or retaliation on the dog's part. It seemed to accept that any human was its personal alpha.

"What we seem to have here is the Manchurian Candidate of dogs."

"I don't suppose the dead guy wore any sort of cologne?" Roger seemed full of suggestions. "Maybe this attack was a sensory response. Something had to set him off."

"Maybe so. I'll ask the coroner. I doubt that it made it into his report, but that may well be what they used to get the dog to single Biggie out."

"Well, that and the fact he was alone in the car, right?"

I glanced at my Breitling watch as I walked back to my Cadillac. It was almost five o'clock. I could drive back into the city or I could go over to the main house and have the conversation in which my mother would link what she had already told Tulip was my "obsession with the dog case" with the lack of progress on resolving my father's disappearance. It took only a second to choose to retreat rather than fight and I headed back to town as fast as I could get out of the driveway.

14

I DECIDED TO STOP by the NOPD crime lab because I'd heard nothing from them regarding the forensic evidence collected the night of Biggie's death. The department's laboratory and evidence rooms were utterly destroyed and all of their contents compromised by the flood waters that covered eighty percent of New Orleans after Katrina. Even so, their new facility was built on the lakefront near the University of New Orleans. The important parts of the operation were placed well above the likely crest of future storm waters, which was easy to determine now that that depth had been determined.

I made pretty good time driving against the rush hour traffic and was able to drop off the dog collar at the evidence locker and still catch my two favorite forensic technicians, a pair of females in their late twenties named Christen and Julie, before the end of their shift. Christen was from somewhere near Eunice. She had the caramel coloring and thick black hair of a Creole, and an accent that only a fellow Cajun could completely understand. Julie was a recent Florida transplant, a blonde with a figure she maintained through kickboxing. The two were wise beyond their years when it came to processing evidence. They grew up watching all of the forensics-based television shows they could find and held themselves to the standards of their imaginary TV peers.

"What do you have for me, ladies?" I asked them as I entered the office.

"It looks like the deceased may have bled out," Christen said when she handed me the autopsy report. "We just got the vehicle so it will be a while before we have anything you don't already know."

Biggie Charles's ruined SUV would certainly give them a lot of blood evidence to work with. I barely glanced at its interior when Biggie Charles was still sitting in a pool of his own blood and shredded flesh.

The two techs and I took the elevator to their garage and I made a more critical assessment of the crime scene in the Land Rover. Biggie's arterial spray was dried onto one of the tinted side windows and the windshield. The early spray patterns were strong enough to have sprayed across the headliner and still reach the front windows. A pool of blood coated the cargo area and the back seat and floorboards looked like buckets from a slaughterhouse were poured on them. One wide spot in the gore marked where Biggie was seated. It indicated how little Biggie had been able to struggle after he began bleeding. The door to the gift-wrapped kennel was wide open, with a large piece of silver wrapping paper still attached.

"What became of the dog, by the way?" Julie wondered.

"Taz, that's the dog's name, is doing great. He's with a handler at my mom's house." Both girls stopped what they were doing and looked at me.

"The dog is still alive?" Julie's eyes went wide. "At your mom's house? *Your* mom's?"

"Why didn't they shoot it on the spot?" Christen wondered.

"I took it into custody as a material witness." They laughed at this explanation, so I felt compelled to explain further. "The theory is that the dog was trained to kill its victim. I need to find its trigger to figure out who used it as the patsy in Biggie's murder. It may be the work of one person, but it almost has to be two or three people. I'll tell you something funny, though. We have not been able to get the dog to attack anyone else since I took it from this vehicle."

"Maybe it's just faking it, so it can plead insanity," Julie said and laughed. "Or maybe it hated rap music."

"So, the dog is a material witness, a piece of evidence, and a murderer?" Christen asked for confirmation of my theory and then just shook her head.

"Yep. So, what does the car tell you right now?"

"We think the dog went for the neck first, but was

pushed away and settled for the victim's manhood. There were bite marks on Biggie's arms and hands so he held it off for a while. See that big splotch of blood across the windshield? The dog almost had to have been in front of him when it attacked to get that blood pattern."

I helped Julie remove the kennel from the rear of the vehicle. This time I paid particular attention to the pit bull's heavy travel kennel. There was a layer of blood soaked wrapping paper over the entire kennel. Biggie would not have seen the dog, or its level of agitation until he opened its door. Opening the door would have occupied one hand, and he would not have been in a position to defend himself as the dog charged out of the kennel and over the back seat. The momentum of this lunge, coupled with Biggie's almost certain surprise, gave the dog at least five seconds before Biggie was able to try to defend himself. The fight was probably over in less than half that time. The dog didn't need to get in front of Biggie to bite his throat if the fat man was turned around in his seat.

Julie was the one who first noticed the amount of paper still attached to the kennel's door. Nearly half the gift wrap from the front of the kennel was ripped apart in opening the door. The three of us all agreed that we would have torn just enough of a hole to see the dog if it began sounding agitated, and removed no more than what was necessary to open the door. This looked more like the door had been forced open from the inside.

"Well look here," Julie said and took a couple of photographs of the door to the kennel. The latch meant to hold the kennel door closed was pulled back. The wrapping paper still covered that portion of the cage so it was all but certain Biggie had not pulled the catch open to free the dog. The only thing that seems to have been holding the door closed at all was the light pressure of the wrapping paper against the cage.

Biggie would not have had time to unbuckle his seat belt and turn to face the kennel as the carrier's door came flying open. The only question I had now was what made the dog come flying out of the cage in such a murderous rage? Biggie would have been a sitting duck no matter where he was when that dog came over the seat in a dark blue flash. The color of the dog might have distracted Biggie for a few valuable seconds. The bites to Biggie's left hand and forearm meant he realized the pit bull's intentions and fought back as it attacked him. Biggie may have tried to shove the dog down and away, so perhaps the initial attack was at crotch level. The shock and pain of such an injury would have been enough to take the fight out of Biggie, or any man, and left him defenseless against the fatal neck wound.

"Did you find a handgun?" It occurred to me that I would have tried to shoot any dog attacking me if I were armed. I had no doubt that Biggie Charles, convicted felon or not, kept a gun close by at all times.

"There was an automatic in the glove box." Julie held up an evidence bag with the handgun and its full magazine inside and the loose round from the chamber. "We haven't printed it yet."

"That would have been a long reach. I wonder why it wasn't in the center console."

"I put mine in the console when I am driving," Christen weighed in.

"What else did you find?"

"Just this." Christen held up another evidence bag, containing a single recordable CD. "It was in the CD player, and the player was on during the attack."

"It might be interesting to hear the soundtrack to this mess." I doubted it was a collection of classical music. "Can I get a copy?"

"Sure." Christen headed off to make a duplicate of the CD for me. Julie and I continued poking around in the vehicle. There were no drugs or liquor in the glove box or the center console; in fact, the center console was empty. I have never seen an empty center console.

"Oh, this is good." Julie stepped back from the open rear hatch and took a photograph of something sticking out of the pooled blood and then pulled it out of the vehicle. We studied the item under the bright overhead lights of the crime lab's garage.

It was a ridiculously large sized birthday card, but it was in scale to the kennel. The card was still in the envelope so Julie carefully removed the card and then took a photograph before opening the card so we could read the inscription:

Hope you get everything you deserve.
Tyshika

"That's going to come back to haunt her, huh?" Julie almost laughed. It was a most unfortunate choice of words for anyone to have written, assuming Tyshika wasn't actually involved in Biggie's murder.

Christen returned with the CD copy, and a form for me to fill out. I tucked the CD into my messenger bag while Julie showed her partner the greeting card.

"How soon can I get a copy of your report?"

"The preliminary one will be available in the morning, the final one by the weekend. I can email them to you if you want," Julie offered.

"Do you still have my e-mail address?"

"Sure thing, if it's still cooter h at Yahoo."

"That's it." The girls did their usual snicker.

"You do know what cooter means, don't you?" Christen asked, using her very deepest coon-ass accent. While everyone knows the word for its sexual slang, I knew she was from a part of the state where the word is just another name for a turtle. My sister also compares me to a turtle when I draw into my own hard shell whenever she asks one of her occasional questions about my previous career.

"It means 'wise old man' ladies. Get your minds out of the gutter."

15

I GAVE TYSHIKA ANOTHER DAY to adjust to her new situation before interviewing her. I knew she would have made a dozen self-incriminating statements if I followed her from the office and questioned her. I would have been happy to wrap the case up in three days and was still fully prepared to see Tyshika convicted of the murder, but I was having a harder and harder time convincing myself of her involvement. Family, friends and especially lovers are invariably the prime suspects as they usually have the best opportunity and often the most to gain by the death. Tyshika turned out to have everything to lose. Whether she knew that or not at the time of Biggie's death remained a question.

I spotted the Navigator as it pulled away from the curb nearly a block away as I left the parking garage. I drove out of the Quarter on Orleans Avenue and turned onto Basin Street and then Claiborne Boulevard to get to westbound I-10. My tail remained a full block behind me until I entered the highway. They chose to try to hide in my passenger side blind spot as we headed west during the short drive to Biggie's condo in Marina Towers.

Marina Towers was constructed with storm surge in mind and survived Katrina intact. It was built just barely inside the high floodwalls adjoining an area known as The West End. This area had been a casino and brothel haven ruled by the sheriff in Jefferson Parish not too many years before my father joined NOPD. It was a place with family-friendly nightclubs and restaurants during my youth. The home where my sister and I grew up was about six blocks away from Marina Towers, but it fared far worse. The storm's winds forced storm surge from Lake Ponchartrain against the Seventeenth Street Canal's poorly built poured concrete floodwalls until they toppled and washed away everything but our memories.

My knock on the door surprised Tyshika, as the doorman should have announced my arrival. I'd flashed my badge and marched right past him. Tyshika was surprised to see me, but she didn't act in the least bit concerned that I was there to arrest her. The look on her face was so sad that being arrested might have improved her day.

"Moving day?" There was a stack of open cardboard boxes in the living room waiting to be filled.

"I thought so, but Mister Logan says I can stay until the will gets settled," she moped and flopped onto the oversized white leather sofa. She was a subdued version of the wildcat I had seen at the office. "If you want a beer or cold drink you can help yourself."

"I'm good." I sat in one of the low chairs opposite the sofa. There was one overstuffed chair between the two of us, which sat higher than the rest of the seating in the room and must have been Biggie's throne. "What all did Logan tell you?"

"He says the car Biggie gave me and this place are in the company's name. Biggie didn't have my name on nothing."

"So, what are your plans?"

Tyshika was especially unprepared for transforming from Biggie's arm candy to self-sufficiency. Being a kept woman is a transportable skill, but right now Tyshika was a hungry remora without a shark.

"I got none." She fidgeted with her hands in her lap for a long time as the conversation faded into silence. "Mister Logan says he would help me sue the kennel."

I had to refrain from smiling at Jerry Washington's apparent clairvoyance.

I broke the silence which kept returning to the room. "Okay, I have to ask you something for the record, Tyshika." She looked at me, already formulating an answer. "Did you kill Biggie?"

"Hell, no. I would right now if he walked through that door, but I had nothing to do with this."

"This?"

"You know, him getting killed and all."

"Do you still think the dog did it all by itself?" I

remembered how adamant she and the bodyguard had been on Friday about wanting the police to kill the pit bull. She looked at me for a long moment. I assumed she was replaying the whole day through in her mind.

"No. Biggie was afraid of dogs but he and Taz was good together."

"Was it your idea to dye the dog blue? Did you think it would be like giving him a real live blue dog?" I had noticed a number of paintings in the condo had a blue dog in them.

"I didn't know the dog was blue." The way she said it seemed honest. "I guess somebody might have thought that up, but it weren't me."

"Who do you think could have wanted Biggie dead bad enough to go to this much work?" Tyshika was reacting viscerally enough just then to make a pretty good snap judgment of the players she knew.

"Beats me. There's plenty of people that be glad Biggie's dead, but most of them would have just capped his ass."

"This does seem both personal and impersonal. Someone wanted him to suffer, but not at their own hands."

"I hope he still suffering. Bastard."

"You mind if I look around a bit?"

She shrugged and waved her arms by way of permission. I wasn't sure what I expected to find. Honestly, I only wanted to see how someone like Biggie chose to live when he felt successful. The man came from next to nothing, so it was interesting to look at what he considered to be the stuff of success. I remembered gawking at the opulence and bad taste of Saddam Hussein's palaces when Baghdad was secured. The two men may have shared a decorator.

The first thing I noticed was that every wall seemed to have an original painting or signed lithograph of George Rodrique's blue dog. There was a lithograph of an Absolut ad from years ago hanging over the bar. The art collection was worth more than the combined value of everything else here. The lithographs were commemorative or fund-raising pieces done in the last few years or, put another way, since Biggie had the money to buy them.

Every room also had a plasma screen television; the smallest was a twenty-two inch one over the vanity in the guest bathroom. Two rooms were knocked together to create an adult playroom, with a large pool table and a projection television and enough theater-style seating for a dozen people. The master bedroom had a king sized bed and way too many mirrored surfaces. It also had a great view of the lake from its balcony. Everything was either painted white or upholstered in white, so only the wall and ceiling textures and the floor colors changed from one room to the next. What color there was in each room came from the artwork on the walls. It had a faintly dizzying effect as I made my way from room to room.

I checked out the master bathroom and envied the oversized steam shower and twin vanities. I opened the drawer to one of the nightstands by the king sized bed and was not in the least surprised to find an unmarked bottle of Cialis and enough lube and condoms to last a lifetime, which it turns out they had. I picked up a nearly empty bottle of cologne in a cut glass bottle from among the half dozen identical bottles on a shelf in his walk-in closet. I smelled it and was not impressed enough to buy a bottle. There was also the fear that wearing it would attract women like Tyshika. I did, though, keep hold of the cologne bottle as I walked back into the living room. Tyshika had not moved an inch. She was still trying to absorb all of this expensive view of the lake so she could carry it with her to her new life.

"Do you mind if I take this with me?" She looked at the bottle and then at me.

"Why? You gonna wear it?" She was able to laugh at the idea.

"I just want to try something with it." I didn't elaborate. If the dog responded to the cologne then it was not meant to attack anyone other than the guy wearing this scent. That would mean whoever trained it had to know this particular cologne was the victim's favorite. All of this was making me understand just how brutal of a death someone wanted Biggie to suffer, the absolute realization by Biggie at some point that he was doomed and what a painful process of being chewed open and allowed to bleed to death had been. The dog attack was as cruel and efficient of a means of killing someone as I could imagine that didn't involve using a chainsaw.

"Knock yourself out. Anything else?"

"What can you tell me about your son being adopted by Amanda Rhodes?" It had been intended as a fairly routine question but Tyshika's head snapped towards me in shock.

"Who told you about that?"

"You were present when Logan said Biggie left the business to his son. I just followed up on where his son is now. So, what can you tell me?"

"Biggie and me agreed to keep it a secret when we signed the papers. Mister Logan and Mister Rhodes had it all worked out. They had a judge in Monroe handle it and Miss Amanda used her real name, not her made up one, so nobody knew it was her."

"Why did you let them adopt your child?"

"Biggie and me was having a hard time making it after he got out of prison and a kid was more than we could handle just then. I didn't want to do it, but I met with Miss Amanda and knew my boy would be brought up with more chances and stuff if they had him. Besides that, it weren't like Biggie was giving me any choice."

I imagine Biggie didn't offer her much in the way of a discussion once he made his mind up to let a rich white couple adopt his son. Her story didn't explain how they had crossed paths and what Biggie's real motive was.

"How did you meet the Rhodes couple?" I did not want to let her know I'd already spoken with her son's adoptive mother.

"Biggie was looking for someone who could help get him into the record business. I guess Mister Rhodes was a big-time music lawyer and offered to help him. Next thing I knew Biggie said we was letting them adopt our son and everything was going to be better from now on. I met Miss Amanda at that dog park on Melpomene with Parker and she was so nice to him and me and she told me all the things she wanted to do for him."

"And did things improve after the adoption?"

"Biggie was able to buy his studio a few months later so I guess it all worked out."

"How do you feel about it all now?"

"How do you think I feel? My man's dead because of some dog I bought him and a rich white woman's got my son. I got nothing anymore," she nearly hissed, but then lost steam and started to cry. I found some tissues in the bedroom and set the box on the coffee table beside her. I waited silently while she composed herself. I had not meant to peel the scab off any wounds, but I needed to try to figure out the connection between Biggie and Amanda as best I could.

"Have you had any contact with their family since the adoption?"

"None. Have you seen my boy yet?" She sounded oddly hopeful that I might have. I gave a slight shake of my head and told her no. I tried to imply I might never do so, even though it was just a matter of time before I did spend time with him if Amanda and I actually started dating. Tyshika was in no condition for that sort of news. I thanked her and started for the door, but she gave me another strange look and I stopped with my hand on the door handle.

"You didn't ask me about Biggie's guns," Tyshika said, with a faintly reproachful tone. I had the feeling that she had been saving this knowledge as some sort of bargaining chip and nobody was offering her a chance to cash it.

"Okay, you have my attention. What about Biggie's guns?" I had an image of handguns and a maybe a rifle or two in his closet, something I fully expected someone like Biggie to have in his possession.

"They're stored in a locker out by the Huey P," she told me. "He makes everyone he signs a contract with give him all their guns. He told them they had to give up being bangers for real if they was going to work for him."

"How many guns are we talking about?" I still couldn't imagine it was very many.

"Biggie could have started a war," she assured me. "It's a big locker and it was full the last time I saw it. That was over a year ago."

That would be a lot of guns. My mandate with Chief Avery, however, was to avoid letting any of my investigations balloon out of control. Taking a murder that nobody cared about and turning it into the seizure of a massive arms cache, which would draw not only media attention but the involvement of Federal authorities, was exactly what I was not supposed to do.

"I'll tell you what, Tyshika," I said and wrote down a

telephone number on the back of one of my State Patrol business cards. "Call my boss at this number and tell him what you just told me. There may be a reward you can collect, and I know you could use the money."

"You ain't going to look at them?"

Tyshika was obviously quite perplexed at my apparent ambivalence to what she clearly thought was important information about her dead fiancé. She may have thought telling me about the guns was something she could trade for a favor in the future, or it may have simply been her way of thanking me for being nice to her when nobody else seemed to be interested in her feelings.

"That's somebody else's circus and monkeys," I half-grinned at her and headed out the door.

16

BIGGIE'S BODYGUARD WAS LAST on my list of interviews. I called to confirm he would be at the recording studio. He was probably still trying to get a grip on his new duties. I pulled out of the condo's garage and headed to the studio by way of the lakefront. I had to accept that the Navigator was going to be following in my wake for the time being. I didn't think the occupants meant me any immediate harm, but I decided to test their driving skills and let them know mine.

The route I chose, taking Robert E. Lee Boulevard to Elysian Fields and then along Broad Street to BC Studios was all area I patrolled after the floodwalls were patched and people were able to rebuild. The route passed through the prosperous neighborhoods near the lake as well as the poorer parts of Mid-City. The floodwaters had been a great equalizer in what they damaged, but the rebuilding was a glaring example of the city's long history of privilege and denial. FEMA and the insurance companies shamed themselves badly in Katrina's aftermath by categorizing almost the entirety of the city's damage as flood damage the insurers didn't have to cover. Flood insurance was required on mortgaged properties; such as those at the lakefront, but many of the city's poorest citizens inherited houses with no mortgages and didn't have the money to spend on insurance against something they never thought would happen. The front-running mayoral candidate in the up-coming election was pledging to demolish any unrepaired homes. It would finish the city's racial transformation that the storm began.

Tony was the only person who truly appreciated how the utter devastation of my hometown made my transition from Iraq to New Orleans easier. He also felt that we had traded one place full of jittery military checkpoints, dangerous neighborhoods, murders in the dead of night and no apparent plan for dealing with any of it for yet another city dotted with barely habitable neighborhoods, military patrols, a crippling murder rate, and a massive rebuilding effort hamstrung by conflicting local interests and Federal bureaucracy. The cities also shared a similarity in the violence being perpetrated by angry young men who felt a gun was the best way to express their sense of disaffection. The continuing failure of the local and United States governments to create a coordinated recovery created nearly identical feelings of distrust and betrayal among the weary residents of both Baghdad and New Orleans. The recovery was proving to be more devastating than the destruction itself. The PTSD I fully expected to suffer when I was released from the hospital initially manifested itself as a depression and anger which was little different than the average Katrina survivor's. Voicing these sentiments raised the first of many red flags at the State Police during my psychological evaluation to join their ranks.

I was buzzed through the lobby at BC Studios and found Bumper Jackson in the office of the man whose life he had been sworn to protect. The desks out front were occupied once again and the place looked like something close to business as usual.

"Bumper?" I asked as I poked my head into the office. I recognized Bumper from the crime scene, but also from the occasional photograph I had seen of Biggie in the paper and local magazine articles. Bumper was always just out of focus and a step or two in the background or off to the side. His shaved head made him look all the more like a human bullet. His mouth was framed with a neatly trimmed mustache and goatee. He would have made a human shield between Biggie and anyone approaching, and he looked capable of twisting the limbs clean off of anyone Biggie wanted him to hurt.

"You're that cop." He barely glanced up from his desk.

"Which cop is that?"

"The one I talked to by Hard Rock. I hear you want to prove that Biggie was murdered."

"That's not entirely correct. I'll settle for knowing what

happened." I extended my right hand. "Detective Holland."

Bumper stood up, ignored the hand, and motioned for me to follow him. He led the way to the VIP lounge located beyond the offices and the sound booths of the recording studio. Bumper opened the door of a three-door stainless beer cooler behind the bar and offered me a bottle of Heineken. We moved to the sofas and sat across the room from each other, both with our feet on the glass coffee table between us. I guessed the beer was his way of testing my adherence to the State Patrol's work rules.

"What was the chronology on the day Biggie died?"

"Chronology, huh? You're testing my vocabulary?"

"Just trying not to insult your obvious intelligence." Part of my mind was still working on his name. It was familiar to me from somewhere unrelated to what he was doing now. I took a large swig from the bottle of cold beer.

"Biggie and I were in the studio from about seven that morning until we left for Hard Rock. Tyshika stormed in at two o'clock and wanted us to leave for the kennel. Biggie was pissed and told her to just bring the damn dog from the kennel by herself. She got back around five o'clock."

"So whose idea was getting a dog in the first place?" I decided to not challenge his memory by mentioning that the veterinarian placed him at Tyshika's side the day Biggie died. It didn't take much to understand why he wanted me to believe she acted entirely on her own that day.

"Biggie was always looking for more street cred and I agreed that it might make some of the bangers respect him more if he had a pit bull." Bumper shrugged but didn't really answer the question. He tried to distract me by changing the subject. "He made Tyshika ride in the back seat with the dog while we drove to the Quarter."

"The kennel said someone called from here and asked him to dye the dog blue. Was that you?"

"I haven't got a clue on that. Ask Tyshika." I saw no reason to let him know I had interviewed the woman he seemed ready to implicate whenever possible.

"Whose idea was it to gift wrap the kennel?"

"I think I remember hearing Tyshika asking her cousin to have it ready that way. I don't know why. It wasn't any surprise what was in the box."

"Oh, yeah, it was." Bumper didn't initially see my point, but then he grimaced.

"What I don't get was why Biggie was being presented with a dog the kennel owner said he shouldn't even take out of the cage."

I phrased the statement to intentionally let Bumper know he was not my first interview. I wanted to shake some of his smugness by making him wonder what I already knew. He was doing a fairly good job of deflecting my questions and pointing me towards people other than himself about his boss' murder.

"Tyshika didn't have any money for a birthday present so she asked her cousin if she could just borrow the dog Biggie bought so they could act like it was something she got him." The derision in his voice was not necessary to make it clear what he thought of Tyshika.

"What did you get him for his birthday?"

He started to say something but caught himself. He chose to change the subject again.

"Anyway, we had reservations at Hard Rock for dinner. I parked in the lot beside the restaurant and went with Tyshika to be sure that everything was set."

"Why did you leave him alone in the car? Is that any way to be a bodyguard?"

"Biggie didn't need a bodyguard any more than he needed that dog to protect him. Biggie just needed to look like he needed a bunch of protection so people would take him seriously. He couldn't be the bad ass hip-hop producer if people thought he was just another fat man in a suit. It's why he kept hanging out with the gangster boys," Bumper finally told me something I didn't know. "I don't remember one time anyone threatened him that we took seriously."

"Well, you'll always remember to check the dog next time," I suggested. He held his tongue again, but he was clearly growing tired of being subtly criticized for his job performance.

"Right," he said and paused for me to focus on his story. "We got out and Biggie moved to the back seat."

"I noticed that when I watched the security camera footage." This made his nostrils flare. "Why did he do that?"

"He never wanted anyone walking by the car to think he

didn't have a driver if I wasn't there. He wanted people to know that this was his big fancy car."

"I also saw you came back to the car for a couple of minutes. You opened his car door and then slammed it pretty quick. What was that all about?"

"I went out to tell him it was going to be a while on the table and he got mad about me leaving Tyshika alone in the restaurant. He's the one that closed the door so quick."

I made a mental note to review the footage one more time. Bumper was caught off guard by the mention of there being video footage of the incident. He was also too quick to respond to everything I asked. I couldn't decide if they were honest or practiced answers.

"Is there anything you would like to tell me about Biggie's operation that would be better for me to learn from you than to find on my own?"

"Such as?" Bumper asked cautiously and then grinned. "Oh, I get it. You want me to tell you if Biggie was breaking any laws and want me to believe I will be the one left holding the bag if you find anything now that he's dead."

"Well those are your words," I shrugged. "But, yes, that's what I am not telling you. I have already found one interesting lead. I was just wondering if you might cough up the same one."

"I am not coughing, sneezing, or farting until I have spoken with an attorney."

"Fair enough. Tyshika gets the first deal," I sighed, but he didn't take the bait. "I don't suppose you'd be willing to say whose gun was in the Range Rover's glove box?"

"Biggie's. He put it in the glove box that morning because he had a stack of CDs in his hand when I picked him up, and he shoved all of those in the console. They are still sitting on his filing cabinet, right where he put them when we got here that morning."

This explained the empty console but not why the gun wasn't returned to the console when it was empty again. Biggie may have left it in the glove box because the pistol would have been handier for him as a passenger than in the console. Bumper's answer let me know that he would not volunteer anything about Biggie's illegal activities unless doing so placed the blame squarely on someone besides himself.

"You're aware it was against the law for a convicted felon to have a firearm."

"I do," he said tersely. "I also know Biggie didn't give a damn, and it wasn't my job to tell him what to do."

"Did he keep it chambered?"

"Not much use if it isn't. Nobody gives you time to load when the shooting starts, right?"

"Not in my experience, no. Talking about loaded guns, how was the relationship between Tyshika and Biggie?"

"Relationship? No. There was no relationship as far as Biggie was concerned. He felt he owed her some for having been there for him when he got out of Angola, but he did not love that woman and he sure did not intend to ever marry her."

"Why not?"

"Two reasons. First off, having her around meant other girls were only too happy to sleep with him to get one over on her. Biggie could have any woman he wanted around here, but he could also use Tyshika as the reason he couldn't take anything too far. Second, and this is the real reason, he never forgave her for not fighting him about putting their kid up for adoption. He thought it meant she didn't really love their son. Biggie wanted her to have to depend on him so she'd really feel the knife when he cut her off in the will."

"She certainly seems to be feeling it. So you knew what was in the will?"

"Umm, yeah." Bumper realized he had said more than he meant to say. "He told me some things, but I never read it for real."

"What did he leave you?"

"He left me a condo and my choice of his cars." I could have asked if he had learned this from Biggie or Logan, but the answer wouldn't have made much difference.

"Would that be enough reason to wish him dead?"

"Man, I was making close to two hundred large a year watching his ass. I got so much money socked away I won't know he's gone for some time to come. I really liked Biggie, and I sure liked my job, so why would I screw any of that up?"

"Others have for less. You sure you haven't been

measuring his office for new drapes all this time?"

"Oh, hell no." He laughed and went to the fridge and offered me a fresh beer. I had only taken the one drink from mine and left it sitting on the table beside me. "I was getting so much gravy I didn't need to eat the potatoes. You know how much work I gotta do now?"

"And how do you feel about Tyshika?" I tried to get back on track with the handful of questions I had when I came in the door.

"She's a street girl." He said this and then looked at me directly to make sure that I knew he wasn't calling her a prostitute. "She saw that their son had no future. She was working two straight jobs and was still on welfare. She was afraid Biggie was going to get back into his old ways and knew the kid would either grow up with a dad back in prison or dead in the ground and that her boy would probably follow his daddy down that same path. I think she did the right thing, but I sure wasn't going to tell Biggie how I felt."

This was likely a total lie or just more of his obvious campaign to make Tyshika a better suspect than himself. It did sound plausible, but I doubt there had been such a personal conversation with Biggie that the fat man would have ever told his bodyguard any of this.

"Maybe you could tell her now. She might like to hear someone say something nice for a change. I noticed you have a bit of a limp. Is that something new or old?"

"Old. I played for Oklahoma but I blew my knee out in a game late my junior year. I had to sit out my senior year. It doesn't bother me much and Biggie didn't hire me for my ability to run from things. He just wanted someone to look mean, just like that dog that killed him."

"Did you get the knee fixed?"

"Nah. I was never going pro so I laid up most of the summer with it, but I never got back to where the coaches wanted me to be so I lost my scholarship. Now I just wear a knee brace." He showed me a standard compression brace. It was not what I would have expected for a career-ending injury. Now I knew where I had heard the name Bumper Jackson before. He had been a great player.

"I know the pain. I had to leave a dream job when I blew mine out and now I'm just a borrowed cop for NOPD. It's like prepping for the big game and then falling just before you get there." I sounded pretty sad, but I was lying. I love my new job. "How did you handle not being able to play?"

"Not well. It was how I got into this line of work in the first place. I went on a bender and wound up doing so much damage to a guy's bar that I had to work as a bouncer until I paid off all the damages. I was working at a strip club in Hollywood when Biggie came in and hired me to cover him."

"Lucky you, huh?" Bumper just shrugged at this comment.

"Don't you own that Italian joint by the French Market?" Bumper changed subjects again after we had lapsed into a rather awkward lull.

"Yeah." I must have looked surprised at this.

"What?"

"I was wondering how you knew about it. It's not like I advertise the fact."

"I could say I saw you there, but the truth is I did a little checking up on you."

"Find anything interesting?"

"No. Not much. Your sister is a big attorney and your dad's missing, but that's about it other than you being a State Trooper assigned here since you left their academy. You supposedly spend less time working for NOPD than you do at your cafe."

"But I do enjoy being a detective more than being a bar owner."

Bumper had tipped his hand with his disclosures. I now knew he had a source of information that could access my records with the State Patrol, which meant he either had a crooked cop on his payroll or was perhaps a cop himself. I couldn't decide if this was his way of telling me to back off or just his way of trying to intimidate me.

"Any more questions?" Bumper stood up to leave.

"Just two. First off, did you kill Biggie or do you know who did?"

"I still blame the dog, just like everyone but you. What's the other one?"

"What can you tell me about a storage locker full of guns out in Harahan?" I had no idea what there was for him to know because I still had no idea what was actually in the locker Tyshika was supposed to call Avery about. I was sort of hoping Bumper could jump me ahead of the actual search warrant.

"Not a damn thing."

He turned around and walked away, showing just a bit more of a limp on his lame side than when we walked through the office. He left me alone to consider how much of what I had just seen and heard was to be believed, and so far what I'd seen told me not to believe much of what this man said.

It's a bit funny that people who know almost nothing give up everything they do know just to make you think they have something valuable to trade. It's the ones who tell you the least who tend to know the most. I expected Bumper's version of things to be easy to check out, but I still wanted to see if I could get anyone else to verify his stories. I made a big mental note that Bumper wasn't denying any knowledge of Biggie's storage locker full of guns. He was only refusing to discuss it.

17

AVERY'S REACTION to my suspicion that Bumper might be an undercover cop, or that he had an informant in Avery's own department, was to allow my investigation into Biggie's murder to grind to a halt. I initially used the excuse of conducting follow-up interviews to spend time with Amanda, but she had been the one to suggest we drop the charade and our time together became devoted to my introducing her to the city as locals know it. We were seldom able to find time alone until Parker was asleep, but the New Orleans I wanted to show her did not really exist until well after dark. We did take her son and Georgia to a football game at Avery's and my alma mater. It was not my intention to have them witness Amanda's home state team, Alabama, crush LSU.

Avery expressed little interest in the investigation when he came by the bistro to have breakfast or for Happy Hour. We both knew the questions about Biggie's death would eventually need to be resolved, if for no better reason than that Avery's budget could carry Roger for only so long. I also needed to rescue the dog sitter from having to deal with my mother on a daily basis. I will admit another part of this inertia was my private concern that I would lose Amanda once the case was closed, as though it was the only reason she remained involved with me. Amanda mocked me the only time I shared this thought. All the same, I knew I was not misreading the expression on Georgia's face when I came for Amanda after Parker was asleep. The nanny made me feel like a teenager running the gauntlet past a prom date's parents.

Two full weeks passed between my short interview with Bumper and when the dust began to fall from the case once again. It started with an unexpected call from Amanda. She woke me from a sound sleep well past nine o'clock in the morning. I was with her barely six hours earlier, after taking her to see Amanda Shaw play zydeco at Rock-N-Bowl on Carrollton and Marcia Ball's second set of honky-tonk piano at Tipitinas'. This was followed by a slow dance to a street musician's rendition of Rocket Man on Frenchman Street and a pre-dawn breakfast of bacon and eggs at the colorful, but less than romantic, Clover Grill on Bourbon Street.

"I need you."

"I need you, too." It's always easier to be the second to make such a declaration.

"I need to talk to you." Amanda wasn't confessing her affections and what I mistook for moans were actually the sounds of Amanda sobbing.

"Then I'm on my way."

I managed to hang up on her as I hastily pulled on the jeans I'd worn the night before. I pulled a clean shirt from the closet and socks from my dresser. I tracked down my shoes under the end of the bed. I grabbed my messenger bag and tossed in the keys, wallet, and pistol from atop my dresser and headed downstairs. It occurred to me that it would be faster walking the short distance than driving.

Amanda greeted me in the lobby. She had obviously been crying, but the look on her face was one of unmistakable outrage. She was stamping about the lobby's polished marble floors barefoot in a floral print blouse and shorts. She fell silent as we ascended to her place and she motioned for me to follow her when we stepped off the elevator. The sound of the elevator doors hissing as they closed behind us magnified the stark tension in the house. I matched Amanda's brisk pace up the stairs towards her office, allowing myself a long look at her tanned legs and happier thoughts of my recent visits to the top floor.

The office was large, as were all the rooms in this place, with a hand-woven rug, a heavy antique mahogany desk, and comfortable upholstered seating for anyone sitting across from her. The room looked out on the Mississippi River and the Algiers ferry dodging towboats and freighters as it made its way to Canal Street from the Westbank. Amanda's distraught appearance dispelled any comfort I might have felt in being the person she called to calm her down. She gave a deep sigh and collapsed into the high backed leather chair behind her desk.

"Here." She moved a thin folder across the desk as she explained that the paperwork inside had arrived by courier barely an hour earlier. She dropped her head on the desk, resting her forehead on her crossed arms as I read the sheaf of legal documents now in my hand.

The paperwork came directly from Dan Logan's office and informed Amanda that Tyshika was asking a court to revoke Amanda's adoption of her son. Tyshika was going to claim Biggie Charles sold the child to the couple against her expressed wishes.

"She's lying." This was a decision I had more hopes was true than I had any evidence to support my conclusion with after I read through the paperwork twice. I looked for a shredder to make my point. "Any court gets a look at Tyshika and you'll automatically win. Let me make some calls."

My first call was to my sister at her law office. She listened as I read the paperwork to her and brightened Amanda's day with hysterical laughter so loud it could be heard through the phone. Tulip immediately agreed to represent Amanda in court if need be, and then explained exactly what she found to be so funny.

I was still grinning when I dialed Logan's office. Logan answered the phone himself. He was probably watching the caller ID on his phone in anticipation of Amanda calling in response to the paperwork. His vision would have included her holding a checkbook and pen in hand.

"Logan Associates," he said cheerfully.

"Exactly who associates with you? We need to talk about the papers your lackey delivered to Amanda Rhodes this morning."

"Oh, my." I could hear his voice tighten just a bit. "I did not expect you to be the one who called."

"Are you seriously looking for disbarment?"

"Don't threaten me, detective." Logan was now acting as defiantly as he could, and he had the capacity to muster a lot of disagreeable characteristics on cue.

"You handled the original adoption, right? That means

you would have known all of the sordid details of what you are now threatening to expose. You are either violating attorney-client privilege to admit that you were party to an illegal adoption, or you are part of a cheap extortion attempt based on a lie. Which one are you going to let take you down?"

There was a very long pause as he weighed his options for moving ahead with his thinly veiled threat. "Well, I suppose something can be worked out, right?"

"The next sound I want to hear is your paper shredder. Got it? If you want to contact Miss Rhodes in the future you will need to contact her new attorney, Tulip Holland. Do you need the number?"

"No. I will review the case notes and please tell Amanda I am sorry to have bothered her with this prematurely."

"Thank you for not asking if it is true," Amanda said after I hung up the phone.

"Well it's not, is it?"

I ruined the moment. Amanda pulled her knees under her chin like an emotionally conflicted child and looked at me for a very long time before saying anything.

"It's complicated." This is never a good response to questions of a legal nature. I stood up and moved to sit on the edge of her desk and looked her in the eye.

"Complicated, huh?" Her expression still bordered on one of terror. I used my thumbs to rub some of the ruined mascara from her cheeks and then leaned forward to kiss her moist forehead. Her facial expression softened a little more and she was able to force a smile. "Complicated means lunch on me. Let's get out of here and you can tell me all about it, okay?"

"I'm not going anywhere looking like this." She took my hand and stood up. I gave her a long hug and then moved aside so she could step past.

"Why not? Nobody would ever recognize you." I tried to joke, but she was already out the door and on the way to her room. I debated following her but lost the argument with myself and remained in the office. I looked at the paperwork again and considered the situation from every angle I could imagine.

It was obvious that Tyshika would drop the whole thing

and go away if money were paid. There was probably a clue hidden in Logan's choosing to have the papers delivered here rather than actually filed in court, but it eluded me. Even if Logan had no case, there would certainly be huge publicity once the celebrity news circus got wind of the filing. The tabloids would have a field day with the lawsuit since Amanda kept the adoption a secret for so long. I decided Logan knew Amanda's weakness was the fear of any publicity that might tarnish her public image. The one thing I couldn't ignore was that, if Tyshika's allegation were true in any way, Amanda's status changed from being a bystander to being a prime suspect in Biggie's death. Killing him may have seemed like a good way to end any sort of current or potential blackmail over this same thing.

I was still mulling this over when Amanda returned. Her hair was pulled into a ponytail and she wore just a touch of makeup to accent the smile she always wore in public. Amanda also did a wardrobe change to a peach-colored tank top, denim jeans, and Roman sandals. She was not about to let her appearance betray anything going wrong in her private life when she appeared in public. She leaned forward to give me a light kiss before tugging the papers out of my hand. She folded them into her purse and held out her other hand.

"Where are you taking me?"

I should have stopped her right there and explained how much the paperwork changed everything for her, and for us. I could not entirely excuse myself for a romantic entanglement with a suspect. I was counting on Amanda's explanation clearing things up and removing her from suspicion once again, but remaining a couple was going to take a great explanation from her and would undoubtedly require my willingness to ignore some very glaring facts.

"I know this romantic bistro just down the street."

I looked up and down the street as she locked the lobby door behind us. I was relieved, but also a little surprised, to not see my new shadow or the mysterious Navigator. I spotted him the night before while Amanda and I barhopped Frenchman Street and strolled through the Quarter's less traveled corners.

"Hello, and thank you for coming," Gina greeted us at

the bistro's hostess stand. I pointed to the largely deserted patio and she gave me a quick wink after setting our menus down on the glass-topped metal table. "Let me get Tony!"

"Friendly service. You must eat here often." Amanda joked. I started to say something but realized, too late, that Ryan had followed us from his seat at the bar.

"Thank you, thank you." Ryan took hold of Amanda's hand after imposing himself upon us. "I have no idea what we would have done if you had not come to our dear boy's rescue."

"I don't know what you mean. Really." Amanda was whispering in an effort to keep this from becoming a scene. She had no idea the sort of scenes this man was capable of creating. The few tourist diners nearby were already beginning to look our way. Locals would have made a point of acting as though they were ignoring us.

"The staff was beginning to think Cooter is a monk. I can't remember the last time he has been seen in public in the company of such an attractive woman." Ryan took a seat, uninvited, and grinned at me as I said silent prayers that he would leave before he could truly embarrass me. The prayers didn't work. "I just wanted to tell Cooter here about my latest doctor visit."

"Please don't," I begged with a forced grin. Amanda was laughing at my panicked look.

"I had to meet with a new doctor this morning. I'm dying, by the way." Ryan informed Amanda. He gave her no time to react to this self-diagnosis before he began what I knew was going to be an intentionally risqué story. I couldn't stop him now without shooting him.

"And how did that go?" I fulfilled my role in setting up the punch line.

"He had the gall to ask me if I am a homosexual." He enunciated each syllable of the last word in as exaggerated of an outraged gay man's rising tone of voice as he could muster and raised his eyebrows and hands in protest at the very idea any doctor would suggest such things about him.

"Why would he ask you that?" Amanda was now playing along. She saw how uncomfortable Ryan was making me but she also seemed to be enjoying his intrusion.

"I set that dear boy straight. I told him that I am no

homosexual, and that my boyfriend would tell him so!"

Amanda burst into a loud laugh, which I could not long resist sharing. My feigned intolerance of Ryan's antics is a form of envy for his capacity to simply be himself. My past dictates that I will forever have to hide many things I have done and some of the places I have been. Mine are not the sort of truths that will ever set me free from their telling.

Tony and Gina arrived too late to save us from Ryan, but they brought wine.

"Amanda this is Ryan, one of our slight irregulars." I now resigned myself to introducing him. "This is Tony, my business partner, and Gina is our waitress."

"Oh, my," Gina said and froze for a moment. "You're Amanda Rhodes!"

"Yes. I guess I am."

Amanda seemed relieved to put the morning aside as she was fawned over by my friends and the diners nearby on the patio. It took a few minutes to get the autographs and photos over with, but things finally calmed down and we were left in peace. Gina poured generously from a bottle of Pinot Grigio and set the remainder in an ice bucket before she left again, after whisking away our menus with the promise of a special meal from the chef. Amanda took a sip of her wine and then leaned forward to say something. "I envy your life. I really do. How did you meet your chef?"

"We met in Italy a few years ago. Tony arranged my medical care after I was seriously wounded in Iraq and then he emigrated here about a year after I came back to New Orleans. He made me a partner in this place because he thought I might need an option in case being a cop didn't work out." Most of this was a pack of lies, but they were the ones Tony and I agreed to tell until the day we died.

"I'm sure the long version is much more interesting," Amanda frowned and poured herself a little more wine. Her first glass was gone in three gulps.

"No, not really. We've really only known one another a few years."

"It might take you that long to solve Biggie's murder," she said over her wine glass.

"Things would go faster if the list of suspects stopped growing." I couldn't hide that I was trying to ease us into the complicated conversation we needed to have. She gave me a wary look and took another sip of her wine before bracing both hands on the table and taking a deep breath.

"Okay, here's what happened. My husband and I were unable to have a child of our own, so we decided to adopt. This was right after Hurricane Katrina and I had convinced John we should move here in order to be part of the city's recovery. I have made a number of movies in New Orleans and just wanted to try to give back some of what the city has given me over the years."

"But how did you wind up with Biggie's kid?" I saw that she would spin this out for as long as possible and had a feeling that there was a nasty ending to her story.

"John was an entertainment lawyer in Los Angeles, remember? He made a number of contacts locally and one of them was Dan Logan. Dan said he had a client who had fallen on hard times and was trying to get his life back on track, but he was afraid of falling back into his old ways and he had a two-year old son. Logan told us the boy's parents were very concerned about his future, maybe more than their own, so Logan made a suggestion to them and my husband that he had an idea that would make something good out of everyone's negative situation. My husband could help Biggie meet people in the music business and we would raise the young boy away from the world his parents were afraid he would be part of when he grew up."

"That sounds real noble." I lied. It sounded as insane as adopting a rabid animal found on the side of the road.

Gina interrupted us with a platter of shellfish to start the meal, most of it involving shrimp or crab meat. She told Amanda how much she liked Amanda's last movie and then left us alone once again.

"I would have told you about this sooner," Amanda sighed before she continued. It was a nice bit of acting. "I am really afraid that you will have to arrest somebody or make a big deal out of this now that you know."

"My boss told me to investigate the dog. Your problem with this sounds more civil than criminal. I don't want to break up a happy home if I can avoid it, and I can."

"Well, thank you." She smiled and took my hand.

"Feel free to speak to an attorney before answering this

one. Did any money change hands?" I had to ask.

"Speaking of attorneys, who is Tulip Holland?" I didn't want to pursue the matter much further so I let her get away with not immediately answering my question.

"My sister. She handles civil litigation when things start becoming uncivil. I'll call her later and set up a time for the two of you to meet."

"Lawyers seem to be how I got here. My husband and Logan worked out the adoption and had some attorneys in Monroe that Logan knows file everything through a court there. Looking back, there may have been some corners cut and that might be what Logan thinks he has on me."

"What sort of corners?"

"There were no home visits or interviews with any adoption agencies for one thing. And we used my birth name, even though I have had my name legally changed."

"Those are more than corners. There may well be some question of how legal this whole adoption is and Logan being involved only makes that more likely."

"I am willing to pay whatever it takes to straighten things out."

"The first dollar you pay Logan or Tyshika will open an artery in your bank account. They will just keep coming back for more and more."

"You're probably right." Amanda poured herself more wine. I poured myself a second glass and moved the bottle out of her reach. We sat for a long moment and worked our way through the appetizer. Gina returned with a bottle of red wine and plates of thinly-sliced smoked Muscovy duck breast drizzled with a demi-glace sauce laced with raspberry flavored Chambord liqueur and presented upon a stack of freshly fried Yukon Gold shoestring potatoes.

"One question remains. I have to wonder why the attorney who handled the adoption would threaten to file a lawsuit that he knows might lead to his own disbarment. Was there ever any money to Biggie?"

"Sort of." Amanda said nothing else for a moment and then accepted that she had to finish the story. "Right after the adoption my husband loaned Biggie Charles the money to set up his studio and did the contracts on the first couple of acts Biggie signed to his record label. But Biggie and John had already fallen out by the time my husband died."

"Do you know why?" I couldn't imagine every possible reason a weasel lawyer and a crooked client might argue.

"John took a piece of Biggie's business every time he gave Biggie money. He did that with all of his clients. His estate is still getting sorted out by a million accountants."

"And has any of the money Biggie borrowed been paid back?"

"I don't believe so. I know none has come back since John died anyway."

I might have accepted her version of things at face value if Amanda and her husband had used any other attorney, but what she was telling me indicated that Logan should have stopped Tyshika's suit instead of threatening to start a court case that would certainly leap to the tabloid headlines. I have no respect or affection for Dan Logan, but I never think of him as being a stupid or impulsive attorney. He had picked up a scent of something and was, at best, merely fishing and, at worst, knew something Amanda was still keeping from me.

"Alright." I didn't try to conceal my skepticism as I leaned back in my chair. "Just know that I cannot protect you from anything I am not aware of. I don't think you have given me the full story, but I hope that's because you don't know the full story yourself."

"Well," Amanda hedged. "I should also tell you about the money I started paying out after John died."

"Paid out for what?"

"Georgia came to me right after John died and said Biggie's bodyguard confronted her in front of Parker's school. She said Biggie was demanding that I keep paying him to stay quiet about the adoption. She said Bumper told her it was part of the arrangement between John and Biggie."

"I doubt that. Why didn't Biggie come to you himself?"

"Georgia said they said they didn't want me to be able to go to the police. I was to give her ten thousand dollars on the first of each month, in cash, and she would pass it to the bodyguard to give to Biggie. It wasn't that much money and I needed to keep him quiet. I still need to."

"But you stopped paying when Biggie died, right?"

"No," she said. This time she seemed even more nervous about telling me what was going on. "Georgia said that now the bodyguard was going to sell the story if I didn't keep paying him."

"So you've been paying the bodyguard ten grand a month to stay silent."

"Yes," she sighed. "And he will tell everyone about the adoption if you arrest him."

"Well I'm not going to run right out and do that," I took her hand to reassure her. I wanted to, but I wouldn't.

"So, does this make me a suspect?"

"The prettiest at the line-up, but you definitely had a motive to kill Biggie Charles." It was the best motive I had found yet, which brought me back to my ethical dilemma.

Gina brought our dessert; strawberries rolled in graham cracker crumbs, flash-fried, and placed on a bed of home-made vanilla bean ice cream drizzled with a glace made using dark Belgian chocolate. I wanted to change the subject so I began asking Amanda questions about her relationship with Georgia while we nibbled at our dessert.

Amanda's husband once beat her badly enough that she was forced to drop out of a movie when they were days away from the start of principal shooting. She took refuge in a celebrity rehab center. She preferred to be thought of as a substance abuser rather than as a woman too weak to leave an abusive husband. Amanda told me Georgia was in the same rehab program and she decided to take Georgia on as her personal assistant. Amanda claimed their time in rehab forged a symbiotic friendship that helped them both. I told her I have a pretty similar relationship with Tony.

Georgia proved her real worth when she began stepping between Amanda and John whenever his mood turned ugly. John Rhodes quickly learned the odds of his winning a fight with a street-wise woman who felt her meal ticket was threatened. The stint in rehab was six years in their past, and the strength of the women's bond was obvious. I did not come away from the conversation sharing Logan's lurid interpretation of their closeness.

I began to realize that Amanda was one of those women who needed a stronger person in her life. She'd traded the shadow of a domineering husband for the sheltering wing of her loyal assistant. I also understood that Georgia's open hostility towards me was her way of displaying both her protective nature and expressing how concerned she was that any romantic relationships Amanda developed might weaken her own position.

As much as I appreciated learning these very personal details and seeing signs of Amanda's increasing trust and affections, our relationship was now clouded by my sense that there were other forces at work between us than simply Amanda's biological or emotional desires. I had to add blackmail as a possible motive for the murder I still needed to resolve, and I could only hope that the clues and motives would somehow stop bringing me to Amanda's door.

"So, how was the meal?" Tony poured the last of the wine evenly between our glasses and perched on the arm of one of the other wrought-iron chairs, making it obvious that he was not planning to intrude for very long.

"Excellent. I'll tell you what, give me your card and I will recommend this place every chance I get." Amanda raised her latest glass of wine in a toast to the chef.

"You don't have to do that." Tony actually seemed embarrassed by her praise, but he wasn't about to stop her either. A celebrity endorsement was beyond his wildest dreams. It's the American equivalent of a Michelin star.

"I have to know. What does the name of your restaurant mean?' Amanda asked Tony. He whispered the answer in her ear and she burst into laughter. Somehow the phrase 'road kill' is more appetizing in Italian than it is in English. It alludes to my appearance when Tony rushed me to the nearest hospital from the scene of the nearly fatal ambush.

Amanda signed more autographs and posed for a selfie with Ginger before we could leave, but I could tell that my companion was still upset about her morning as we left the bistro. I wasn't likely to improve her mood by returning to the topic of her being a suspect, but I did so anyway.

"You are someone who obviously benefits from Biggie's death. I see no evidence that you were ever in a position to arrange or to do the killing. I doubt you are in cahoots with the bodyguard or Tyshika. I just don't see that. You may have had a motive, but you lacked the means or a way to put that dog in Biggie's car. It makes you a lousy suspect."

"That's something worth celebrating. If you can keep it a secret, we can go back to my place for a while. Georgia and Parker aren't due home for quite a while." Amanda kissed my cheek as she slid her hand into my hip pocket.

"Are you trying to seduce an officer of the law? And aren't you afraid I might make some sort of deal with one of the tabloids?"

"Oh, you aren't going to tell anyone you are having sex with a prime murder suspect, now are you?" Amanda was suddenly playing our little game just a bit cruelly.

"No. No, I am not."

Nor was I not going to join her if she really wanted me in her bed, ethics be damned. We had shared nearly every evening together since our first date, but that time was always spent in public where we could never really act like the romantic couple I hoped we were becoming. We enjoyed the rest of our afternoon together and I left her bedroom silently thanking Dan Logan for his part in bringing it about, but I was now also determined to finally solve the murder and clear Amanda so we could see where our romance would lead without any clouds hanging over us.

18

THE UBIQUITUOUS LINCOLN NAVIGATOR was parked next to a pile of construction debris a block away on Wilkerson Row. I spotted it as I leaned over Amanda's bedroom balcony. It took me another minute to find my young shadow. This time he was lurking on the steps leading to the Moonwalk, which put him on my side of the street. He blended in better than usual and was going to be able to fall into step behind me if I followed my usual route. It worried me that he believed I followed a pattern or routine. I needed to work on that, beginning immediately. My primary concern now became making sure these guys were far away from here before Georgia and Parker returned and piqued their interest.

"What are you looking at?" Amanda asked as she molded herself against my back. She was wearing nothing but a sheer dressing gown that stopped short of her knees. I could feel the warmth of her body against my own. It did not make leaving any easier.

"Do you recognize that Navigator? Paparazzi perhaps?"

"I have never seen it before. Why?"

"They have been following me off and on since I started looking into Biggie's murder. It's time to shake them off."

I turned around without losing contact with the touch of her body. I kissed her deeply as I began to back-pedal her into the safety of her bedroom at the same time.

"Are you in danger?" She sounded more excited than concerned at the prospect.

"I won't be soon."

"My hero. Just play nice, alright?"

"I'll call you when the coast is clear."

I can tolerate the occasional car chase, and it was sort of

fun to play along while the young man followed me through the Quarter. I felt no serious threat from either the nameless kid trailing me or his friend driving the Navigator, but I was annoyed with the lack of privacy. I also realized my visits to this address would inevitably draw the attention of whoever these young men worked for to Amanda and her family. I doubted if Chief Avery would soon forgive me if I managed to convert a dog mauling case into the stalking, kidnapping, or something worse, of a Hollywood celebrity.

My choices were to either call Chief Avery or to ask for help from Chef Tony. I felt more comfortable exploring the options with my chef than I did with creating a situation requiring paperwork and following NOPD's stringent use-of-force restrictions. Tony was already concerned that any media interest in the murder investigation might attract deeper scrutiny of our mutual history, so he readily agreed to what I had in mind when I called him.

I waited in the lobby for five minutes and then headed past Jackson Square and walked slowly towards the bistro. I paused at Café du Monde to listen to a rail-thin street punk playing one of the slide guitar tunes in his limited repertoire and gave him a buck to buy dog food for the mongrel tied up beside him. The local vagrants had discovered having a dog decreased the odds of their going to jail. Beat cops don't want the hassle of finding someplace to lodge the dog while they roust its owner.

I glanced back just in time to watch the Navigator pull out of the side street and pass through the traffic light behind me. It passed me and continued towards Esplanade Boulevard. I was beginning to wonder if I was about to be abducted or if the Navigator was simply going to turn around and come back the other direction on Decatur Street as it had the last few times I walked this route.

I resumed walking and then abruptly mixed things up for the youngster. I normally crossed the street at the statue of Joan of Arc. My tail would then fall back and we would both walk the short distance down Decatur to the bistro. The Navigator would then pick him up at the corner of Barracks Street.

Today I stayed on South Peters and entered the tourist-crowded French Market. I stopped at a produce stand just inside the entrance while I watched the youth following me talking into his cell phone. This was the first good look I had at the kid, and I was finally able to confirm he wasn't one of the punks I encountered in the Walmart parking lot when I spoke with Biggie's grandmother. He needed me to make my next move so he could get new orders. My intention was to isolate him so his friends weren't able to rescue him at the moment I sprang my own ambush.

I walked very slowly past the stalls of produce and tourist junk to give Tony time to move into position, and to be sure my shadow's focus narrowed to just watching me. I spotted Tony standing at the entry to one of the produce companies across the street from the market and set about trapping the boy in my wake.

Tony set a course that intersected mine in the cramped center aisle of the open air market. I hastily let Tony know which of the many faces around us belonged to the boy following me. I continued walking forward while Tony browsed until the youth passed him, at which point Tony began following my stalker.

I stood still for a moment and then headed towards the public restrooms. I stepped into a dingy toilet stall and waited with my pistol drawn. My shadow waited until he heard me bolt the door on the stall before he entered the restroom and took up a position near the sink.

I flushed the toilet, which was Tony's signal to make his own move. He stormed into the room as my tail acted like he was washing his hands while focusing his attention on my stall in the mirror. Tony jabbed a Taser into the young boy's diaphragm and the powerful electric shock drove the air from his lungs. I stepped out of the stall with my gun drawn just in time to watch Tony empty the youngster's pockets and pull a .45 caliber handgun from the waistband of the boy's baggy jeans and press the muzzle against the gasping youth's forehead.

"Would you mind telling me why you're following me?" I holstered my own pistol.

"You be tripping. I wasn't following you."

"Sure you are. You personally have been watching me for the last two days and you or your pals in the Lincoln Navigator have been on me since Biggie died."

"You got no right to hold me."

"We can discuss that topic at Central Lockup, or you can shut the hell up." I showed him my State Patrol badge.

"This guy ain't no cop." I had to admire the young man's willingness to antagonize a stranger holding a gun barrel against his sweaty hairline.

"That means he doesn't have to follow the rules I have to follow. So, you can either start talking or I can walk out of here and leave you with my friend since you insist I can't do anything to you."

The kid just sat and glared back and forth at the two of us. Tony and I tried our best to respect his show of bravado, but I finally had to grin. I busied myself with the wallet Tony pulled from the boy's pants along with the pistol.

"Your name is Arnold Dupry?" It took a moment before he grudgingly nodded an acknowledgment. Arnold was fifteen-years old, and should have been sitting in a high school classroom right then.

"Call me Shooter. That's what my friends call me."

"You need better friends, Arnold. What's with the pistol?"

"I'm gonna kill the guy what killed Biggie. I'm gonna shoot the guy when you catch him." He said this with a certainty and a vengeance beyond what I thought anyone so young was capable of harboring. Then I remembered the angry child who bashed in my skull.

"No, you're not." I wagged a finger at him. "What's your beef in this, anyway?"

"Biggie was good to me and my brother and didn't deserve to have that dog being put on him. Now that Bumper guy says he doesn't know if he wants to release the record my brother and cousin made and might want the money back that Biggie give to them. We wouldn't have no problems if Biggie still be around."

"That's how you bozos can afford a Navigator?"

The SUV probably represented the bulk of the money Biggie had advanced the boys against their imaginary future royalties. It actually represented the talons Biggie sank into them. The odds of the first record by any of Biggie's so-called artists making enough to cover a royalty advance were slim to none. He would milk them for a number of records before they came close to drawing even with what he would say they owed him. "Biggie's been like a dad to us. Our real dad stayed here when we went to Houston during Katrina and we ain't heard from him since. I think the cops shot him."

Tony pulled the pistol from Arnold's face and helped the teen to his feet before stepping away from him. The kid gave Tony a pretty hateful look but said nothing. Tony patted me on the shoulder and then pocketed the boy's cellphone before silently tucking the confiscated weapon under his chef jacket and leaving the restroom.

"Here is how we are going to leave this. You are free to go, but you need to stay far away from me. Being bushwhacked is the least of what you can expect next time. And try not to be such an angry young man, okay? It's not very becoming at your age."

"Yeah." Arnold snatched the wallet I handed him.

"Who told you I was looking into Biggie's death anyway?"

"Bumper told my brother to keep an eye on you."

"Tell Bumper I burned you. Are we clear on the matter of you boys following me?"

"Yes, sir."

Arnold finally found his manners and sullenly nodded agreement. I grabbed his shirt collar and marched Arnold out of the Market and towards Decatur Street. Tony was waiting for us at the corner of Barracks and Decatur.

The Navigator was parked down the block and I nudged Arnold into the street and told him to wave for his ride. He hesitated before he did so. Maybe he thought this was another trap. The vehicle approached very slowly and parked a few yards short of where we were standing.

"Make sure your brother knows this is over. If I arrest anybody for Biggie's murder you'll see it on the news like everyone else."

Arnold climbed into the back seat and a moment later the big SUV pulled past me at a parade pace. I assumed the Black man of about twenty-three or four behind the wheel was Arnold's brother. There were two passengers riding in the back seat, but I could not get a good look through the tinted windows. Tony wrote the license number down on his wrist with the Sharpie marker he keeps in the pocket of his chef jacket and we walked into the bistro for a drink.

"All clear," I reported to Amanda when I called her from the bar phone. I continued to watch the double French doors open onto Decatur Street in case the boys in the Navigator decided to try to try their hand at a drive-by shooting. I saw little reason to really believe I had seen the last of Arnold or the Navigator.

"What did you do?"

"I engaged the young man in direct dialogue and he and his friends understand that following me is not acceptable behavior."

"Did you hurt him?"

"I did not." This was semantically accurate, though not entirely honest.

19

ROGER HAD NOT CONTACTED ME since I'd left him at my mother's place with the pit bull and its medical and training records. I wanted to test the theory about Biggie's cologne being used in the dog's attack so I figured it was time to check in with him. I knew that finding what triggered the attack was going to be necessary before I could begin to understand how the dog was used to kill Biggie. I was going to have to know who killed Biggie to know why they did so. There seemed to be as many reasons to kill the man as there were people who knew him.

I called Roger at the boathouse the next morning, but there was no answer. I tried his cellphone and found he was at the animal control center, and that he already planned to see me at the bistro after his shift. Roger said he needed to show me some unexpected things he found in the veterinary and kennel files.

I was curious enough that I said I would drive over to see him. Roger was walking the long rows of kenneled animals when I found him. He alternated between making notes and taking a moment to pet each dog in his care. He greeted me and we shook hands before he set the clipboard atop one of the kennels.

"How are things going with my mother?" This was not just polite conversation. I was genuinely concerned that he might be tired of getting a daily earful from my mother.

"Oh, it's fine." He said this with a rather amused grin. "Your mother is a real piece of work, isn't she? I can see where Tulip learned some of her tricks."

"Is everything okay?"

"We're fine. She makes sure I pick up after Taz when we exercise in the yard, but she's begun walking with us. She also wanted me to be sure to remind you that Taz is why your folks didn't want you to get a dog when you were growing up. Apparently, she mentioned all of this to some psychic she met online and he supposedly told her that maybe she needed someone around who was good with animals. I don't think she read that the way I did."

"At least he said animal and not bitch," I sighed and we shared a laugh. The psychic's incessant messaging was wearing me out. "It's so typical that she'd use Taz to justify a decision made forty years ago. You said the files proved to be helpful."

"A lot, but I don't know if they solved your case or just made it harder to solve."

Roger took a digital camera from his pants pocket and pulled up a slideshow of pictures of the pit bull. "Look at Taz and tell me what you see."

I swiped my finger across the screen to advance and study the dozen or so pictures in the camera's memory. The animal looked the same as it had the last time I saw it.

"It's a mature male pit bull. It has a brown on brown coat of fur consistent with the length of hair of the breed. There are a few scars on its flanks. You yourself have already said it is healthy." I was looking for clues in each photograph. I hastily swiped past the two photos of the dog's genitalia, not even caring if they were clues to what Roger discovered. I was disappointed these responses did not crack Roger's poker face. I sensed he was testing me.

"What do you know about show dogs?"

"They tend to be temperamental and expensive."

"And there are very specific criteria for each breed." Roger was obviously trying to give me a clue of what to look for in the dozen or so photographs.

"Just tell me."

"Taz has what is called a 'merle' coat. Two-tone coats like this automatically disqualify the dog from being shown in competition. This dog cannot have been entered in any major dog show. The coat on the dog in both of the files you gave me is simply listed as brown."

"Okay." I still had no epiphany. It did occur to me that Jerry might have been lying about the pedigree of the dog he was selling to Biggie, but that was hardly a crime I would be inclined to pursue.

"You also told me the dog was used for stud, right? Why would you breed a dog with such an obviously disqualifying defect?"

"You probably wouldn't."

"You couldn't breed this one anyway." Roger thumbed through to one of the uncomfortably close-up photos of the dog's genitals. "The dog is not only neutered but has been for some time. Those scars are well healed."

"Alright, then we have a dog that could not have been used for show or stud as we were led to believe. What point is there to lie about something like that?" I had to admit defeat. I didn't really see how Roger could have the answer to this figured out.

"This dog is also larger and heavier than the one you gave me records for."

"Different dog, right?" It was obvious once I thought about it. Knowing the dogs were switched changed little.

"Bingo!"

"Why switch dogs?"

"My first thought is the dog Biggie actually bought would not have attacked him. But, whatever the reason, somebody absolutely switched the dogs."

I pulled the bottle of cologne from my messenger bag and handed it to Roger. "I took this from Biggie's bathroom. Do you suppose the dog could have been taught to kill anyone wearing this scent?"

"You can train a dog to use just about anything as a cue and something had to have set the dog off. I guess it could be cologne, but terriers usually hunt by sight, not scent."

Roger was showing no enthusiasm for my idea. The trouble we both had with the theory was that the dog would go for anyone wearing the scent, and the dog would have trouble differentiating between the Land Rover's occupants in the time the dog took to lock onto its target unless his killer or killers knew Biggie would be alone in the vehicle. Or maybe they didn't care how many people the dog killed.

"Hey, Roger, they're here." I glanced at the animal handler standing at the end of the aisle. The unmistakable sound of dozens of dogs barking made the announcement redundant. Roger apologized for the interruption and explained why he was really at the shelter in the first place.

"We're doing the intake on some dogs rounded up in a dogfight raid last night on the Northshore." I instinctively followed him towards the sound of the commotion.

The hallway was full of animal handlers, LA/SPCA animal protection officers, State Troopers, and very agitated canines in dozens of kennels. The dogs had been in the back of a truck since the middle of the night while waiting for someone to make a decision on their fate. Some were still ready to get back to the fight, but most were now just anxious and excited about these new surroundings and unfamiliar people. The people most experienced in handling a fighting dog were either in custody or hiking out of the woods where they hid to avoid arrest.

"Any arrests?" I asked one of the uniformed State Troopers I knew.

"Some of the spectators and a couple of guys new to the game, but most of the old timers were in the wind the minute we sprang the trap."

I looked at a couple of the pit bulls that were sitting still and not part of the barking chorus. I sized them up against the dog I had and the one I was supposed to have. These were all similar sized animals to the killer and all had scars from previous fights similar to those Roger found on Taz. Roger was inspecting the dog I was standing next to and rubbed it behind its ear. The dog turned towards him, not in the least bit aggressively, and managed to flip its ear atop its head, exposing the ear's inner skin and a small tattoo.

The tattoo was a simple blue design I recognized as the Greek symbol of Omega. Omega is the opposite of Alpha, so it should make a bad name for a fighting dog, or a fighting dog operation. Alpha Dog, it just so happened, was the name of a Northshore kennel I was now very familiar with. An inspection of the remaining dogs turned up seven more dogs with similar tattoos from the Greek alphabet; five more pit bulls, and two Rottweilers. Roger and I simultaneously thought the same thing and he pulled the camera from his pocket. He thumbed through the digital images to find the one which showed Taz's pulled up left ear. There was no tattoo, but there was a scar inside the ear where one may have once been.

"Looks like I may need to pay another visit to the kennel, huh?"

I was inwardly relieved that, for the first time in a while, there was a clue that did not immediately lead to Amanda.

"Like I said, this either just got easier or harder for you."

The case had definitely taken a turn. There was no longer any question that someone used the dog to murder Biggie Charles Lynley. His death was clearly a homicide, which would not please Avery. He would have to press for an arrest, but at least it wasn't likely to be Amanda Rhodes. Cisco was the last person to handle Biggie's pit bull. It made him the only suspect on my list I was certain could be indicted at this point, but I was also convinced that he did not decide to kill Biggie on his own.

I READ THE LATEST EDITION OF *Gambit,* the city's weekly arts and politics gazette, while I waited for Chief Avery to join me for lunch at the bistro. I read an article about Biggie and his supposed efforts to get young men involved with music instead of drugs. The reporter offered no theory on how Biggie financed his operation. At least there was no speculation about John or Amanda Rhodes, or any mention of Biggie's son. Bumper and Tyshika each received passing mention, but only the bodyguard was interviewed. The local television and radio stations barely mentioned Biggie's second line and funeral. I felt that I could work comfortably below the media's radar. *Offbeat,* the monthly music magazine, still needed to run its obituary, but I hoped that would be the end of any media interest in the case.

Avery came through the door with a lanky plainclothes detective wearing the badge of an ATF Agent. Avery managed to fit his large frame on a varnished wood stool and introduced Ned Davis as we were approached by one of the new daytime waitresses. I told her to tell Tony there would be three of us eating lunch. Chef Tony tries his new dishes out on Avery, less because of any culinary insight than his willingness to eat anything put in front of him. Today it was going to be a passion fruit salsa over some sort of grilled fish set on a bed of rice with Caribbean seasonings.

Agent Ned Jackson described the dead ends the ATF encountered when they followed up on Tyshika's tip about Biggie's storage locker full of guns. The locker was not only empty of guns, it had been rented to a different tenant three months earlier. The company ownership changed hands in that same time period, but the new owners retained the previous owners' records. There was no indication that the locker Tyshika sent them to could be linked to Biggie. The ATF's interviews with Biggie's musicians verified her story that they gave their weapons to Biggie, which made the Feds all the more anxious to find them.

It was going to be difficult to track down the person renting the locker when Biggie was allegedly using it as a weapons cache. The young woman who rented the locker either wore a bad wig or colored their hair with a temporary dye job when she had her picture taken for what proved to be a fake ID of very good quality. The license plate on the Yukon Denali she drove turned out to belong to a family sedan sold for scrap a few days earlier.

I brought Chief Avery up to speed on my revitalized investigation. I explained the pit bull could only have been switched when it was loaded into its carrier. The carrier was covered in gift wrap to conceal the ruse, with its latch in the open position and held in place by the paper. The person, or persons, who wrapped the carrier and loaded it into the Land Rover absolutely knew what was going to happen. I told Avery that I had Cisco's admission to dyeing the dog and wrapping the kennel. I could arrest him as an accessory on the strength of that, but we both knew he would swear everything he did was on someone else's orders. Only three other people involved with the dog that day were still alive. They were Bumper, Tyshika, and Jerry. I only believed the last two in this trio to be unlikely perpetrators. I also knew myself well enough to know Bumper was only a suspect because I didn't like the guy for reasons even I didn't know.

I told Avery about the possible link between the Alpha Dog Kennels and an illegal dogfight in Slidell. Avery said I could get a search warrant for Jerry's business based on what I was presenting, but neither of us really expected to turn anything up by pulling the place apart.

Tyshika may have wanted Biggie dead because she was confident his will would provide for her. I doubted she could analyze her situation that well, and Avery wondered why she would have assumed she was the main beneficiary even if she knew there was a will. They weren't married.

Bumper's reputation was not going to benefit from losing a high profile client. We kicked around the idea that

Bumper may have had a gripe with Biggie, or thought killing him would better his position with either Tyshika or the studio's next owner. He alone claimed to any advance knowledge of the details of the will.

I mentioned Amanda and the adoption in passing, and the blackmail not at all. Even if there was blackmail involved, I had a hard time imagining Amanda would hire someone like Cisco to kill Biggie to eliminate whatever threat he posed to Parker's adoption. She certainly had the financial resources to hire someone more experienced to have done so, just as she had more than enough money to pay a blackmailer indefinitely. I wanted to believe she was more likely to have continued paying for silence than to be the one who permanently silenced Biggie.

Avery suggested I do some research on Bumper Jackson's background while he and our guest enjoyed a bruschetta appetizer. I remembered Bumper said he had played football at the University of Oklahoma until he suffered a career-ending knee injury. It struck all three of us that it was more than a little odd that someone with any amount of education wound up as the mindless muscle for someone as uneducated and crude as Biggie Charles Lynley.

I moved to the bar once Avery set to work on the plate of fish Tony personally brought to the table. I dialed 411 to get the phone number to the university's switchboard in Norman. I patiently worked my way up the phone tree from the receptionist to the Director of Alumni Relations.

"This is Hank Farrell." The Director had an inflection as flat as the prairie stretching outside his office window.

"Good morning, Mister Farrell. My name is Detective Holland and I am the lead investigator on a homicide case in New Orleans. I was hoping you might give me some information on one of your graduates."

"Oh, my. I will certainly do my best."

"I need to know what you can tell me about Bumper Jackson. I understand he played football for your university a few years back."

"He sure did. Is he alright? I actually played on the football team with him."

"Oh, he's just great." I felt like I had struck oil. I might get a lot more from Farrell than could be found on Bumper's transcript. What I needed to know about Jackson had nothing to do with his GPA. "He busted up a knee, right?"

"Yes. You could hear it in the stands." I could almost see Farrell wince as he recalled the injury. "He had the knee replaced, but the injury ended his football career. He gave up his scholarship for his last year here."

"So how did he finish his degree? Did his family have money?" I was just making conversation now. The Bumper Jackson I was dealing with said he had not had surgery.

"No, he was able to get an ROTC scholarship after his knee healed enough to pass their physical."

"The ROTC?" The guy I met did not look like he spent any time in the ROTC. The military teaches you a way to carry yourself and stand that stays with you a long time after you have any use for the training. I am still unable to slouch.

"Sure thing," Farrell said with obvious pride in his former teammate. "He joined the Army and has been sending us great letters from Afghanistan since he deployed there for his third tour of duty."

"Bumper Jackson is serving in the Army, and he is overseas?"

"Yes, sir. He's commands an Apache helicopter wing in Afghanistan."

"I guess I am thinking of the wrong guy. The guy I am talking about is about six foot ten, weighs maybe two sixty or eighty, with a shaved head. He may have had hair when you knew him."

"That sure isn't Bumper Jackson." Farrell sounded very certain of his recollections. Even if he wasn't, I knew that Bumper would never fit in an Apache helicopter.

I had no immediate follow-up question and the conversation lagged. I was left to wonder who would know enough about Jackson to try to impersonate him, especially anyone who might know he wouldn't be showing up here unexpectedly. "But, you know what? That does sort of sound like his younger brother."

"Brother?"

"Yeah, Eric Jackson. He was here on an academic scholarship. Eric earned an accounting degree and went to work for our Highway Patrol. He ran into some trouble and I heard he had transferred to the police department in New

Orleans a few years ago. That's if I remember right."

"He joined NOPD?"

"I don't remember the circumstances, but I'm sure that's right. I think it was about 2003 or 2004."

I knew I could find him easily enough now that I had this much information. It also confirmed my suspicions about Bumper after our last meeting.

"I can look into that from my end." I thanked Farrell for his time and recollections and was still grinning when I returned to my seat across from Chief Avery.

"Solved the case have you?"

"Actually I just may have kicked over a hornet's nest."

"Nothing new there," Avery grumbled as he forked another bite of fish into his mouth.

"The bodyguard was apparently an NOPD officer just before Hurricane Katrina. Does the name Eric Jackson ring a bell?"

"Not off hand, but it's easy enough to check out." I could tell he wouldn't be very happy to find out Eric Jackson was a rogue cop. "What else did you find out?"

"The alumni office says that the real Bumper Jackson is an Apache chopper pilot in Afghanistan, but Eric Jackson was an accounting major who was booted out of the Oklahoma State Patrol before he joined NOPD."

"Hopefully he is someone else's problem these days. Maybe he's working undercover for someone that has neglected to inform my office. I guess I'll have to make some calls though, huh?" Avery sighed, but the sigh was for my benefit. Avery's week would be made if he were able to blow the cover off a Federal undercover operation he had not been informed about in advance, because *not* blowing the guy's cover would give him a very large IOU from whoever was running that undercover operation. "Do I have to tell you to stay away from the guy until I get back to you?"

"You just did." I was starting to miss the simplicity of looking for Avery's bail jumpers and warrant eluders.

21

AVERY CAME BY THE BISTRO during Thursday afternoon's Happy Hour with the news that a search warrant for Alpha Dog Kennels was waiting for me in St. Tammany Parish. He said I needed to call the detectives at the St. Tammany Sheriff's Department Monday morning after ten o'clock to arrange a day and time to serve the warrant.

I repeated my misgivings about serving the warrant. I believed that showing up with a convoy of officers to comb through every inch of the kennel while it was open would be devastating to the business. Very few scenarios I could dream up required Jerome Washington being involved in any plot to kill Biggie with a ringer dog. He owned the place, but the physical handling of the kennel's canines was done by his employees. Chief Avery shrugged his shoulders, finished his beer, and told me to give him a call when I decided what I wanted to do.

My solution to the dilemma of potentially damaging Jerry Washington's business by turning his operation upside down without knowing what I was even looking for was to call him about the search warrant. I explained I was required to execute it during business hours. That was all it took for him to agree to escort me on a tour of the facility after closing time that very evening.

I ran a risk of valuable evidence being destroyed in the meantime. I'd already considered the likelihood that there was no evidence left to destroy. The best piece of evidence would be the real Taz, but I didn't think for a second that Biggie's pit bull was still at the kennel. That dog would be long gone if whoever made the switch had any sense at all. Beyond that, I was not really sure just what I could hope to find. Dye packets and rolls of wrapping paper would not be any evidence, as it was uncontested that the animal was dyed blue and the carrier was already gift wrapped when it was loaded into the back of Biggie's Land Rover.

Jerry Washington was alone in the lobby when I arrived just after ten o-clock that evening. He thanked me profusely for giving him a chance to cooperate rather than descending on him with a search warrant and a pack of local news reporters. Nobody cared that Biggie was dead, well almost nobody, but everybody loves a juicy murder story. This one could easily become a tabloid's dream come true.

"Let's take a look at the kennels, alright?"

Jerry agreed and led the way across the patio where we had our last meeting. A set of stone steps led to a basic cement sidewalk running through the middle of a U-shape created by three cinder-block buildings. Two air-conditioned kennel buildings flanked the sidewalk. Their green-painted exteriors were broken at intervals by dog runs. The twenty-foot by four-foot exercise pens extending perpendicularly from each building marked the territory of each dog. The dog doors to the runs were closed for the night. The trainers' building at the far end of the walkway formed the center of the squared off U-shape.

I intended to focus my search on the trainers. It was the obvious place to look for anything to make the trip out here worthwhile. The trainers' building was painted green like the other buildings, but this one had a mural of ivy growing over the surface. The windows were not designed to be opened and the door was a heavy metal one. This seemed to be an unusually high level of security for a business and building unlikely to be burglarized. Then again, the only things people leave unprotected are things they do not value, and people lock up even their backyard tool sheds.

The building's interior featured a large open space for handling dogs. This was flanked by the trainers' individual offices. The shared lavatory was on the far wall between the offices and behind the dog handling area. The office doors were locked, but Jerry carried keys to both offices. Each office had a heavy metal desk, a mesh-backed office chair, and a wooden chair set in front of the desk. The floors throughout the building were tinted and polished concrete. Carpeting would have been a bad idea. Each office had a two drawer filing cabinet, both of which were locked. Each office also had an older desktop computer and a basic inkjet printer.

I made note of the personal differences in the offices. One was well decorated with photographs of what looked like a happy family, with dad and mom and three grade-school-aged children. The office was meticulous and the bookshelf held a dozen well-used reference books on animal training and veterinary medicine.

The second office was the one I assumed was used by Tyshika's cousin. It was practically a stereotype of what the office of someone who knows gangstas ought to look like. The pictures on the walls were of Cisco with famous clients and their dogs. I was not surprised to find there were two pictures of Biggie Charles in the collection. I would not have thought them to be much in the way of a recommendation to anyone looking at the gallery. There were also metal die cast models of Maserati and Ferrari coupes being used as paperweights, perhaps betraying a desire to reach the level of income and prestige his clients possessed. This was a man who loved what money can buy, but could probably be bought just by stroking his ego.

"I am going to guess that this is Cisco's office." We had spoken barely ten words between us since I had arrived. I had a job to do and the kennel owner was obviously deeply concerned that my doing my job was going to cost him his business.

"You're racial profiling." I looked up to see Jerry had finally managed to smile.

I leafed through the puddles of papers and folders on the desktop and tried to access the computer, but didn't have the patience to try to guess his password. Jerry knew the password and booted the computer, but I had no immediate idea what I might look for that would shed light on the case I was investigating. I was beginning think I was as stupid as I suspected Cisco thought I was, but I still did not think of him as the sort to have made a to-do list to kill Biggie and leave it on his computer. I was certain that it would prove to be fairly simple to have someone look at all of the files if I decided to impound it.

I spotted brightly colored pieces of paper in the trash

basket as I leaned over to look in the drawers. The pieces of paper proved to be a postcard card-sized party invitation torn into quarters. The front side was a multi-colored design built around the Greek letter Omega over the dark red silhouette of a Rottweiler. The invitation was printed on the back of the card. The design allowed for the time and GPS coordinates of the event to be hand-written into designated spaces before mailing it. I remembered the tattoo on the Rottweilers from the raided dogfight. I felt a joyful shiver run down my spine when it occurred to me what I held in my hand. Cisco must have thought anyone who came across this would not make a connection to dogfighting, and I might not have either had I not already crossed paths with one of his tattooed dogs.

The name of the intended recipient may have been removed from the guest list after the card was made up. The name was heavily inked over before Cisco tossed the card aside, which demonstrated consciousness of the criminality of his actions. The location, date, and time were simply scratched out. I knew the gals in the crime lab would have no trouble retrieving the name on the card if need be.

"Recognize this?" I assembled the scraps of paper face-up on the desk. Jerry rose from the chair where he had been watching me rummage through Cisco's things. I have searched this way in the past and feel like I am playing a game of 'Hotter/Colder' as I move about a suspect's space.

"No. What do you think it is?"

"Well, it looks like an invitation to a dogfight." I turned the pieces over and reassembled them.

"That son-of-a-bitch."

This reaction was not a performance for my benefit. Jerry was convincingly upset and I could see veins bulging in his neck. He really needed something to break, but there was nothing he could destroy without betraying our visit.

"This is a good thing."

"For you. Not so much for me." He continued to grow more aggravated over Cisco's betrayal and the legal position Cisco placed him in with me. His good reputation in a community unfamiliar with rumors of his own past was also now in danger.

"I can use this to catch Cisco organizing a dogfight. That

is a major felony and catching him in the act will give me a lot to bargain with when I ask him to explain his role in Biggie's murder."

"So, he had a part in that, too," Jerry must have agreed to lead me around only because he hoped I would come up empty and decide I was on a wild goose chase.

"At the very least he switched the dogs and wrapped the cage. Let's just assume he was also the guy who didn't latch the cage so the dog could get free."

"I don't think he even knew Biggie before his cousin bought the dog."

"Tyshika certainly knew Biggie well enough to wish him dead," I had to remind him. "Even so, I don't think she was the one who put Cisco up to this."

"Then who did?" I stopped Jerry from touching the invitation. I certainly didn't want his prints on it if they were not already there. I believed his innocence only so far.

"I'll ask Cisco that very question after I arrest him at his dog fight." I transferred the paper scraps into an evidence bag and labeled it with a Sharpie. "You can't let Cisco know I have this, or that I was even here tonight."

"I think I just got sick, anyway. I'd better stay home for a few days or I might kill the guy."

I was sure that catching Cisco in the act of sponsoring the dogfight would make the dog trainer a lot more agreeable about discussing a plea deal on any other charges I might throw at him in exchange for a better explanation of the details of Biggies murder. Cisco didn't strike me as the sort who would take anyone's rap but his own.

I also believed that being ahead of the curve on the dog fight would allow for a much more successful raid and the possibility of making solid arrests of the fight's organizers rather than only its slowest running spectators. It would be good for those responsible for such animal cruelty to have to fight for their own lives for a change.

22

IT WAS APPROACHING MIDNIGHT but Avery somehow knew I was calling to make a report about what I found at the kennel.

"Whatca got?" he half-mumbled as he awoke to my call.

"How would you like to bust a dogfight? I think I have a solid lead that the kennel's dog trainer is organizing fights and has one scheduled for this weekend."

"That's not really part of your case, is it? Don't tell me you've now set out to save every dog in Louisiana."

"I'll bet I can get a lot more out of Cisco if he's facing felony dogfighting charges rather than just my suspicion of his involvement in Biggie's murder."

"Alright, what do you need from me?"

"Who should I call with the tip?"

"That would be Candice Martin with the LA/SPCA."

The relief in his voice was almost comical. He's tired of reminding the NOPD detectives that I am a useful part of the department when he provides me with resources or personnel. At least this time the person I needed did not work for NOPD. He gave me a telephone number in Baton Rouge and hung up.

Candice Martin was ecstatic with my call the next morning and insisted on driving to meet me for lunch in New Orleans. She was reluctant to discuss any details over the phone, but she agreed to have a burger at Port of Call on Esplanade when I offered to pay. The place is famous for its huge burgers and equally large baked potatoes. I arrived early to be sure our name was high on the lunchtime waiting list. I was still standing beside the place's vaguely Tiki-styled bar when Candice came through the door.

She was in her late twenties, about five foot six and was

obviously on some sort of exercise regimen. She had dark hair pulled into a ponytail. She also wore a simple gold wedding band with no diamond that might get knocked loose in her line of work. She must have spoken with Avery because she seemed to know exactly who to look for when she arrived.

"How long on the table?" She shook my hand and ordered a beer from the bartender. I was about to answer when the hostess stepped up and led us to a corner table in the far dining room, next to a large bay window looking out on the Marigny neighborhood.

"Chief Avery said you might be a bit of a wild card but that you could be trusted. Are you sure about the lead on the dogfight?"

"I have an actual invitation. I know the exact date, time, and place. I believe it's being organized by the same crew as the one you raided a couple of days ago. I figure this fight must be to make up for that one."

She did not concur. She seemed to doubt what I was saying was even true. "Are you sure of the source? We get lots of false leads meant to distract us."

"Positive," I said as the waitress came and took our orders, hers for a regular burger and mine for a bacon cheeseburger. We both ordered fresh beers as well.

"Tell me what you have," she said as soon as the waitress was out of earshot. The nearest table was too engrossed in their own conversation to listen to anything we were discussing.

"There is a dogfight scheduled this Friday night just west of Houma."

I showed her a photocopy of the reconstructed invitation and this seemed to convince her that my information was worth pursuing. I also handed her an aerial photograph I pulled off of Google Earth that morning using the coordinates on the back of the invitation. She folded both pieces of paper and placed them into her shirt pocket.

"Avery says to just ask if there anything you need from NOPD on this."

"There's not. I try to hold information like this to a core group. I have a tactical team and a special squad I can call up from the State Patrol. We work together all the time."

"You've had leaks."

Blood sports like cockfighting and dogfighting have remained popular in the Deep South despite being targeted by new laws with stiff penalties. Recent legislation against cockfighting in Louisiana placed a ban only on bringing fighting birds across the state line to compete. This makes it harder to stage fights for high stakes, but not any harder to have a cockfight. Dog fighting has become a Federal offense in my own lifetime, but public sentiment only recently began favoring prosecution of participants as well as organizers. The conviction of an NFL quarterback on dogfighting charges increased public awareness of the sport, and that fresh attention increased its unpopularity.

All of this attention has made dogfighting aficionados even more insular. Organizers go to elaborate means to conceal their activities because some of the most devoted fight fans are police officers at local and state levels and even judges who might find themselves presiding over cases involving other participants.

"Your information will give us the chance to put our people in place before they even set up. We usually have to raid the site from the outside, but they always have escape routes set up and we only round up the stragglers. Our biggest offenders are good at constantly rotating sites."

"Are you familiar with this place?"

"There are a number of sites in that area. I will cross-reference what you gave me with the ones we know about. I doubt it will be a new one."

"Somehow that is not at all comforting."

The waitress returned with our lunch and we chewed our first bites of the juicy grilled burgers and piled butter and sour cream into the steaming Idaho potatoes in a reverent silence. Our conversation shifted from work to the traditional Louisiana table conversation about other meals. Louisianans like to sit at lunch and discuss what and where we had breakfast and where and what we will have for supper. I invited Candice to drop by the bistro for dinner on me the next time she and her husband were in town, and she was delighted to accept.

"Why are you still working as a cop if you own such a great restaurant?"

"My ownership stake consists of my name being on the liquor license in exchange for the use of an apartment upstairs, but that does make for handy room service."

We were through with lunch and I reached for the ticket, but Candice snagged it first. "It's the least I can do for what you have brought us."

"We'd have eaten at Galatoire's had I known you were going to be so grateful."

23

CANDICE ALLOWED ME TO JOIN her raiding party because I needed to be sure Cisco was caught in the act and arrested by me on the spot. I offered to handle over-watch, which would mean hiding in a tree and relaying information about the fight to the raiding party. It might also involve doubling as a sniper if Candice's officers met armed resistance. It had been years since I handled such duties, but I keep the tools of the trade and looked forward to getting to relive what I still think of as my glory days.

I store a number of hunting and semi-automatic weapons in a heavy safe in my apartment, but the most lethal weapons in my personal arsenal are stored at The Security Center. The Center is actually the former Federal Reserve building located in the Central Business District. It is privately owned and offers the security and anonymity of a good Swiss bank. Tony and I are more interested in the heavy security for what we store there than we are in being able to do so anonymously. The massive safe which once stored the government's gold is now lined with numbered safety deposit boxes, but our personal safes are in a locked room on an upper floor. What we keep secret cannot be accommodated within their largest safety deposit boxes.

I try not to think what Tony might have locked away, but my personal locker at the Center contains a dozen long rifles, primarily licensed Class 3 automatic and suppressed weapons, and a variety of handguns. I have lost my appetite for the barely constrained violence my former choice of professions required, but I do still love the feel of a firearm in my hand and work hard at maintaining my formidable marksmanship. I have carried a firearm for half my life.

The rifle I selected for this occasion was a .45 caliber

clip-fed automatic rifle in a bullpup design manufactured by Kriss. There was a suppressor for it but I wanted the confusion firing it from high above the dogfight could cause. Candice agreed with my plan to destroy the engine blocks of any vehicles present in order to make flight difficult for the dog owners and their guests. I packed the rifle into a hard case and loaded ammo and everything else I thought might be useful into a rucksack and headed back to the bistro for a bite to eat before hurrying to meet Candice's team at the McDonald's in Raceland.

Candice's hand-picked team was already assembled by the time I arrived. Her plan was to use the knowledge of the precise location of the dogfight to our advantage and to have the raid team situated well ahead of the arrival of anyone hired to scout the site in advance of the dogfight. Candice brought a dozen LA/SPCA officers and six State Troopers to the assembly point. I'd worked with two of the State Police troopers in 2006 when NOPD had to supplement its ranks with any officers it could borrow or beg for help. It was this manpower shortage that provided the cover for my own presence in New Orleans. I was the last full-time State Police detective assigned to the city on 'temporary' duty. I would retire on that same status if everything worked right.

The weather forecast was for a very warm afternoon, but with clear skies for the rest of the day and night. The bugs and mosquitoes seemed to be fairly light, and I hoped the Deep Woods OFF would keep them at bay. Everyone was aware that the dangerous predators in the swamp the dry ground the site of this dog fight rose from ranged from alligators and cotton-mouth snakes to wild boars and bears.

The site we were staking out was an illegal garbage dump, with a single dirt track leading off of State Highway 182 flanking Bayou Black and running south and west of Houma. It was just over a set of railroad tracks which doubled as a surge levee during hurricane season.

We squeezed into as few vehicles as possible and staggered our arrival at the location over the next two hours to avoid raising suspicions of anyone living near the site. The officers used branches to sweep over their tire tracks after they drove along the marsh side of the rail embankment and found a place to pull into the foliage. They camouflaged their vehicles with netting and bits of loose brush before joining the agents and troopers who would be the blocking force at the highway for the last briefing. I climbed a half-dozen trees to mount remote-controlled video cameras in order to have solid evidence of what happened that evening. Candice's team of officers and state troopers were divided into four teams, two on either side of the road as it came over the levee and into the clearing where we assumed the dogfight would be set up. The teams would move closer after the sun set in order to position themselves between any lookouts and the dogfight. The squad members were each equipped with a high powered spotlight and a semi-automatic carbine equipped with laser sights. You have to be especially stupid to pull a weapon on a trained police officer holding a laser dot on your chest with a gun holding enough ammunition to cut you in two, but some people are just that stupid.

Candice and the lieutenant commanding the other State Patrol officers parked his unmarked sedan behind an abandoned gas station half a mile away. They had a line of sight to the turnoff leading over the railroad tracks and used a spotting scope to record the license numbers of every vehicle heading over the embankment in case someone managed to squirt past the units that would block the road once we sprang our trap. Candice would contact the local authorities only moments ahead of the raid in case a local deputy tried to tip Cisco off about her trap.

I was in contact with Candice by phone from my perch in a cypress tree at the water's edge of the clearing below. I wore a sniper's Gilly suit decorated with Spanish moss and cradled my carbine on my lap. I placed a flash suppressor, instead of a sound suppressor, on the barrel. I wanted the sound of the gunshots to add to the level of confusion we wanted to create, but I didn't want to risk becoming an easy target by giving away my own exposed location.

A late model Chevy pickup truck stopped atop the levee just after four o'clock and two middle-aged men in jeans and T-shirts looked around for a few minutes. They looked both ways down the railroad tracks and then headed off to wherever they came from.

I had arranged for a separate surveillance team of

troopers from the headquarters unit in Metairie to watch Cisco's house and received a text message that dogs were being loaded into a pickup truck shortly after seven o'clock. They followed Cisco at a greater than usual distance as his truck made its way south on the Causeway, merged onto I-10 and then turned south and west towards Houma on I-310 and US 90. They broke off pursuit in Paradis, when the truck turned onto a narrow two-lane road towards Houma instead of staying on the faster four-lane. This would add a minimum of a half hour to Cisco's driving time to our location over using the main roads, but Cisco likely chose that route to expose anyone tailing him. The troopers were well out of their district and turned around to go back to their normal patrol duties after alerting me to Cisco's maneuver. I had the advantage of already being in position at the suspect's assumed final destination, so letting the surveillance team head for home was not likely to be a regrettable decision.

Cisco parked almost directly beneath my position just before eight o'clock and the last vehicle arrived at the location an hour or so later. There were twenty cars and trucks, each with two or three occupants. The transports lined up alongside Cisco while the patrons parked anywhere they could find a piece of dry ground. The transports parked facing forward so their headlights could illuminate the dogfights. Six of the handlers erected a sturdy wire enclosure for the fighting ring. I ran the video cameras for a few minutes to have evidence against those directly involved in setting up the dogfight. Cisco and one of his passengers mounted a pair of massive loudspeakers atop his truck and the annoying thumping bass of hip-hop music filled my ears. I looked forward to putting a bullet through the engine block of Cisco's truck with my first shot, in the hope it would stop the horrible noise beneath me.

The aggression level of the caged fighting dogs ramped up once the music began. I suddenly recalled the disc the lab techs pulled from the CD player in Biggie Charles' Land Rover. It occurred to me the CD may have set Taz in motion since it was probably a dog Cisco chose from the snarling canines arrayed directly below me. Two of the dogs, a Rottweiler from Omega Dog and a Doberman Pincher held by a tall white guy in jeans and a Hornets T-shirt were set in the arena and I hastily began turning on the video cameras. The music stopped in mid-song and a new piece of music began, which immediately drove the dogs upon one another. The dogs around the arena strained harder at their chains as well. The lyrics were lost in the noise of the lousy guitar playing, but there was a compelling beat to the song. The Rottweiler took barely five minutes to dispatch the taller, but lighter, opponent. The losing dog owner stepped into the cage to retrieve the carcass of his dog and tossed it into the dark bayou. I could hear, but luckily not see, the sound of an alligator dragging the evidence away.

One dogfight was all we needed for a case and all I had the stomach for. I had a fuller understanding of what Biggie's last moments must have been like. He would not have gotten a shot off if he held a pistol in his hand in the instant it took Taz to leap from his cage. I called Candice and waited for the four flashes of light from each group in the woods to mark their position, before pressing the bull-pup carbine to my shoulder.

The first round of metal jacketed ammunition tore through the radiator of Cisco's Ford pickup and into its engine block, but it took two rounds to its battery to kill the music. I placed rounds into the remaining transport vehicles in the next ten seconds, a pace slow enough to immobilize them while causing the desired amount of confusion. Darkness filled the site as the lights went out on each truck I disabled. The loud report of my weapon was soon drowned out by the angry and confused voices below. The spacing between my shots kept anyone below me from getting a clear picture of where I was. I created a level of pandemonium which disrupted whatever normal routine Cisco and the other dog handlers used to escape.

The agents in the tree line turned on their floodlights and blinded the gathering while the marked units parked down the levee roared forward to block the exit road as the spectators began to realize that what was happening wasn't part of the evening's entertainment. The attendees had to make a choice: surrender or make a break for it through the swamp in the dark. Dark was where the alligators, like the one that had chomped the evidence, lay in wait and there were plenty out there. I could see reflections from their pupils when someone's light flashed in that direction.

Handguns were tossed into the water and bushes as hands began to raise skyward. A weapon in the possession of any of the dog handlers added years to any sentence and a change from State to Federal jurisdiction. I roped down from my nest and shrugged off my bulky camouflage. I slung the rifle over my left shoulder and pulled my handgun from its shoulder holster to join the officers in rounding up the suspects. My focus was on finding Cisco.

An SPCA officer found him hiding in a large puddle of radiator fluid under his truck. He was marched to me wearing mud smeared jeans and a polo shirt embroidered with the Omega Dog emblem, as though owning the death franchise were something to be proud of. He was not wearing what I thought of as his trademark hat and glasses, but they may have been affectations for Alpha Dog Kennel's middle-class clientele. He still wore a Tag Hauer watch that looked massive on his thin left wrist. The pat-down turned up only an empty holster for what had probably been a medium sized semi-automatic pistol, and five grand in cash.

"How's it going Cisco?" The dog trainer was leaned over his truck's shot-up engine hood as he was handcuffed. He looked at me across the hood of the truck.

"What the hell are you doing here?"

I pulled my badge out from under my sweaty black T-shirt and dropped it on my chest. "I needed to be sure you were taken alive. I'm your new best friend."

"Ain't no cop gonna be a friend to me."

"I already have been. I could have shot you myself."

I grabbed his shoulders to spin him around and look him in the face. "You have the entire weekend to decide whether you're going to rot in Angola for dog fighting or for Biggie's murder before we speak again."

"Murder? What the hell are you talking about, man?"

"Biggie Charles. Surely you know that it was the dog you switched out for Taz that killed him."

I did not know if it was his idea to use a dog to kill the music mogul. I did know he had to be the one to switch the dogs, and the look on his face right then told me I struck a nerve. Cisco obviously grasped that any charges he faced for his part in this event were nothing compared to a very high-profile murder charge. Biggie Charles dead from a dog attack was justice to anyone who knew him, but being the one to murder Biggie Charles with a dog was going to be front page news. All of Biggie's pals in Angola Prison would have a special welcome ready upon Cisco's arrival.

I did not give Cisco a chance to speak to me about anything right then. I wanted him to spend the rest of the weekend wondering what I did or did not know. I tucked one of my State Patrol business cards into his hip pocket, handed him off to a uniformed officer and walked away to assist the LA/SPCA and other state officers in getting the dogs into the nearest cage. Flashing red lights coming over the levee announced the arrival of Candice Martin and the local authorities.

Candice had a huge grin on her face and gave me a friendly hug for giving her a tip that paid off so handsomely. This had to be a lot better result than she was used to. One of her agents approached us with one of the video cameras and she gave me a thumbs-up as they played back the digital recording. The agent also handed me an evidence bag containing the CD from Cisco's truck I asked him to collect.

I hitched a ride back to the staging area with one of the State Troopers not assigned to transport the prisoners or dogs. He was one of the patrolmen I worked with in New Orleans and we exchanged a few stories and thoughts on the city's troubled recovery and FEMA's red-tape hurdles. The trooper dropped me off at the rally point and I set the bag with my Gilly suit on the front floorboards of my car, next to my messenger bag. I set my rifle in its case and locked it in my convertible's trunk, next to the overnight bag from which I pulled a towel and a clean shirt.

I wiped the sweat and grime from my torso before I put on the clean shirt. I sat with my car's air conditioning on its highest setting a moment before I reached for the duplicate of the CD from the Land Rover. I reluctantly placed it into my vehicle's player. It took barely a minute of the first song for me to start skipping forward in search of the fight song I heard this evening. It was the sixth song on the disc, but then I had to time how long the CD played before reaching this track. I had less trouble sitting in a tree for six hours than I did listening to twenty-five minutes and forty seconds of the disc, but now I had a possible trigger for the attack, and a time frame to work in.

My new theory was that Biggie played the CD and become concerned about the noises the dog in the cage began to make once Cisco's dogfighting song began. Biggie might have assumed his time working with Taz would let him calm the dog down. Perhaps he opened the wrapped cage door and only realized the switch at the last minute. The rips to the paper covering the cage meant it was more likely his only clue something was wrong was a strange blue blur going for his throat. I allowed myself the smug satisfaction of knowing Cisco would sit wide-awake in his cell and worry about prison for the next couple of days.

I made two calls before going to bed. The first was to wake Avery up from a sound sleep to tell him I would be arranging to have the search warrant executed to impound Cisco's computer and address book on Monday. The second call was to Candice. She agreed to arrange for a canine officer to meet me at the boathouse at nine o'clock the next morning with his bulky padded suit in tow. I was hoping enough of the pieces were now in place to stage a repeat of the dog attack on a better-prepared subject.

I needed the dog we were still calling Taz to attack someone to further narrowing my list of suspects, in case Cisco unwisely chose not to hand me the person who paid for his part in murdering Charles Lynley. I felt confident Tyshika or Bumper would be in custody by noon on Monday, but I needed to remain open to further unforeseen possibilities. I had become a magnet for such things.

24

I WANTED TO HAVE A FEW MINUTES ALONE with Roger and Taz before the canine officer arrived the next morning. I put the top down on my XLR and headed east. I took the Chef Menteur exit off of I-10 just after eight o'clock. This was the longest route to my mother's house. It led through the neighborhoods and commercial strips which were among the last to rebound from Katrina. The homes along here were mostly occupied by poorer Hispanic and Vietnamese immigrants who arrived in town well after I was born and were some of the least insured in the city. The clusters of houses were almost all built on slab foundations and stewed in the fetid and brackish floodwater for weeks. The chickens and hogs they had kept behind their homes had either broken free or drowned in the flooding. I had heard stories of police officers hunting the feral hogs for food after the storm. The businesses which formerly occupied the buildings along the Chef Menteur corridor operated on thin profit margins or tried to skirt the environmental laws before the storm came. Some of the old businesses had returned, but it looked like most of the reclaimed storefronts were occupied by entirely new tenants, most of whom were likely in situations similar to their predecessors.

Traffic was sparse so it took me only a moment to spot the annoying Navigator in my rear view mirror. I sighed and continued driving east until I passed the NASA facility at Michoud where the divided roadway merges into the two lanes of old Federal Highway 90 linking New Orleans to the sandy beaches and casinos in Mississippi. My unwelcome tail found it harder and harder to find other vehicles to hide behind as the traffic thinned out, and the driver was too unaware of the route we were taking to realize how few other roads intersected the highway before they reached the Mississippi state line. I could have left him in a cloud of dust as my XLR was literally a rocket compared to the top-heavy Lincoln SUV, but I needed to stop their tailing me for good.

The highway had been lined with clusters of clapboard weekend camps for decades before the storm, all of which had been repaired from damage in other hurricanes over the years. They were the sort of weathered shacks with cute names like "The Hideout." Hurricane Katrina used a wall of water to bulldoze the communities. The depth and force of its storm surge lodged refrigerators in leafless tree branches twenty feet above the debris field which marked where the camps once sat. Like so many other neighborhoods in the storm's multi-state path, the storm surge didn't just take away the buildings; it destroyed an entire way of life.

The powerful waves ripped out the power lines, which the utility companies expected the landowners to pay to replace if they rebuilt their camps. This added thousands of dollars to the cost of re-building properties most of the owners had never even insured. There was a cluster of new camps being built just east of my mother's place. The camps were all being constructed atop unusually high pilings and incorporated every construction lesson the builders learned from the devastation. What my mother's new neighbors thought of her prideful decision to rebuild a house on its original at-grade slab foundation was anyone's guess. Most of the homeowners either knew or had worked with my father, so their opinions of her were formed long before they became neighbors.

It was paramount to me that Arnold and his gun-toting cohorts not know the address of my mother's house, or even of its existence. I decided it was time to not just stop them from following me today, but to discourage any interest in their doing so in the future.

I swerved into the parking lot of an empty commercial property quickly enough that my pursuers couldn't make the turn. The parking lot was only fifty yards deep, with a deep canal at the far end. The Kriss carbine from the night before was still in the trunk, so I retrieved it before the young driver in the Navigator turned around and come charging towards me across the crushed oyster shell lot.

I stood on the far side of my car, leaning my left hand above the front windshield as the foursome exited their vehicle with their weapons drawn. They may or may not have thought to wonder what I held in my unseen right hand when they lined up in front of their SUV. I made no shift in my apparently passive stance. They had me out-numbered but clearly lacked a plan of attack now that we were facing one another. Arnold and his brother held handguns, but their companions in the back seat came out of the Navigator holding AK-47s. I recognized the back seat passengers as the blustery pair I encountered when I interviewed Biggie's grandmother. I cursed them all under my breath because, frankly, I was in no mood to be shot by any more angry young men with AK-47s.

"Well, come on, let's do this. I have a busy schedule today." The only thing keeping them alive was that killing just one of them meant being put on desk duty and having to fill out more paperwork and sit through more interviews than it was worth. Killing all four was not out of the question because the paperwork wasn't much thicker.

They all stepped forward at the same time holding their weapons beside their bodies rather than pointed at me. I decided to kill them using a steady left to right arm movement. Normally I shoot the first assailant to move because they have a plan or some experience to draw upon.

"I distinctly remember telling you to stop following me, Arnold. Yet here you are. And I see you brought some friends."

"This here is my brother and these guys is in his band," Arnold didn't realize identifying everyone made it easier to round them up later if need be. "What you found out 'bout Biggie? We ain't seen nothing in the paper 'bout nothing."

"Then you should have assumed I haven't solved the case. I'm not the star of some TV cop show. This is going to take a bit longer than an hour to solve, kiddo."

"Don't call me kiddo. My name's Shooter!"

"Nah, today your name is Stupid and the rest of you should call me Detective Holland." My right arm started to come up on its own. Playtime was over.

"I ain't stupid." I honestly thought Arnold was going to

cry.

"I hate to say so but you are." I was pushing him.

"Who are you calling stupid? There's four of us and just one of you, and we're the ones with the guns." The boy standing behind Arnold shouted at me. My right hand come up and I set the bright beam of emerald green light from my weapon's laser sight in the center of his chest as I steadied the Kriss against my shoulder. The steadiness of the laser light was as unnerving as the twitch in my trigger finger. It was abundantly clear that I was far more prepared for this showdown than they expected.

"Not true. Who wants to try me first?"

"Whoa, whoa," Arnold's big brother said and tossed his gun to the ground. Arnold hesitated, and dropped his, but only when the green dot moved to his own forehead. The other two dropped the rifles when Arnold surrendered his weapon.

"Toss me the car keys." Arnold's brother tossed his keys, but they fell well short of my car. We both stared at them for a moment. It wasn't a trick. The kid was just nervous. "Okay, get back in your vehicle."

I waited until they were in the Navigator before I reached for the key ring. I kept the laser sight aimed at the driver's window as I moved about. I was afraid one of them might have a second gun and think they could fire faster than I could react. I tossed their firearms into the canal behind me before I got back into my vehicle and started the engine.

I pulled alongside the Navigator and laughed when Arnold's brother had to open his door and twist in his seat to get into the open enough to hear me because his power windows didn't work without the keys I waved at him.

"I'm going to drop these on the shoulder three miles up the road. When you find them, drive back to town and leave me the hell alone. You'll need pallbearers the next time any of you pull a gun on me. Are we clear?" He just nodded and closed his car door.

I drove barely a mile before I pulled over and set the keys in the middle of the pavement. I wanted to believe that the boys would do as instructed and I would never have to deal with any of them again, but I watched the rear view mirror all the way to my mother's house.

25

MY MOTHER WAS STANDING was standing beside Roger as he exercised Taz near the old boat slip. The two of them stood so close they were nearly touching as I approached, but Roger stepped to his left after I announced my presence. They seemed to have been in the middle of a conversation that had my mother smiling, which was something I found to be quite uncharacteristic.

"Good morning, Mother. Roger."

"What brings you out of your beloved city?" My mother managed to welcome me and still fit in a bit of reproach about how seldom I make the drive.

"I can't just stop by and say hi?" She gave me a disbelieving look and Roger didn't try to hide his smirk.

"Do you have some new idea you want to try out?" Roger wondered.

"Yes. There's a canine officer coming in a while."

"I'll let you boys play with your doggie. Roger, you can bring Taz to the house for brunch when you're through, if you wish."

"Thanks, Mrs. Holland."

"I told you to call me Camille." I was fairly certain that he was already calling her Camille. My mother was trying to make some point that I didn't want to pick up on.

I looked at Roger but he said nothing, though he did shrug his shoulders and grinned. I hugged my mother as she passed and then I shook hands with my increasingly expensive dog sitter.

"My friends don't even get to call her that. So I guess you two are getting along." I mentally blocked any images of the two of them alone together.

"You might say we have reached a certain détente. She

professes to hate Taz, but mostly she apologizes because she thinks you and your sister abandoned me here. Don't rush your investigation for my sake. I don't mind being paid to live like this," Roger grinned.

"I think my mother needs the company. Her friends don't come out here much and, however little she thought she had in common with her old neighbors, her new ones likely think she is an idiot for rebuilding this house."

"That's true." Roger laughed as though he knew more about the situation than I did. We crossed the wide slate-tiled patio between the house and the breakwater as I recounted the previous night's dogfight. He thought the use of some sort of sonic or aural cue might be the best solution to our mystery.

Roger and I reached the boathouse just as a white SUV with the State Patrol emblem turned off the highway and came towards us. The trooper introduced himself as Kevin Barnes. He had a sergeant's stripes but looked like he was still in his early to mid-twenties, tall and stocky, with short blonde hair. Barnes was an instructor with the State Patrol's K-9 Unit, which probably made him an ideal animal handler for Candice when the need arose.

"So you know what we're up to then?" I figured Candice would have explained why he was expected to drive so far on a Sunday morning.

"No, not really." He shrugged and took another sip of his filling-station cappuccino.

I did not want the reason I asked for his help to be a total surprise. "We want to see if we can duplicate an animal attack. You've heard about the pit bull attack on Biggie Charles, the rap music guy, right? We have been trying to figure out what set the dog off and have come up with a couple of theories to try out."

"That's the dog that killed Lynley? What is it you want me to do with it?" His eyes locked onto Taz.

"To stand in for Biggie. You brought the big suit, right?"

"Yeah. I don't know if it will be enough." Kevin seemed just a bit afraid for his personal safety doing what Roger and I were asking. "Maybe we should muzzle Taz. I don't think the muzzle would be much of a deterrent if one of your right ideas pans out."

"Well, suit up and let's get started," I said and followed Roger towards Kevin's vehicle while he struggled into the bulky canine training suit. My mother was on her patio, watching with interest from what she considered to be a safe distance.

Roger and Kevin loaded Taz into the large dog kennel while I set up video cameras to record whatever transpired. I focused one through the front windshield and the second one through the lowered passenger window on the driver's side, opposite of where the trooper would sit.

Taz had no objection to being placed in the cage or wearing a muzzle. If anything, it seemed to make him more alert to what was happening around him. The trooper's Chevy Suburban stood in for the Land Rover and the pair had no difficulty loading the kennel into the spacious rear of the vehicle. None of us claimed to be good with wrapping paper so Roger satisfied the requirement for covering the front of the cage by using a pair of blankets. I wondered aloud if there might be an element of claustrophobia involved, but the rear of the kennel being left open ruined any chance of getting an answer to that question.

I next tried sprinkling some of Biggie's cologne on my hand and held it near the front of the cage. Taz sniffed at it and we waited for another moment or two for his reaction. Roger said Taz registered only mild interest before moving away from the rather strong scent. The odor would have been familiar to the real Taz, but this dog had never seen Biggie Charles until the moment he stormed from the cage and attacked the fat man.

Kevin approached the vehicle wearing what looked like a squishy sumo wrestler Halloween costume, but it was specifically designed to withstand animal bites. Kevin took the additional measure of donning a lightweight ballistic vest and chain-mail gloves, the sort normally associated with use in shark cages or shucking oysters. I would have worn nothing less if I were in his position.

Lowering the Suburban's third-row seat allowed almost two feet between the front of the cage and the passenger seat Kevin wedged himself into. Seeing Kevin crammed into the space gave me a clue of how little room Biggie Charles had to defend himself in the Land Rover.

"Here we go with the Big Bang Theory," I said as I loaded the CD recovered from Biggie's CD player into Roger's portable boom box. Roger suggested using a portable CD player rather the vehicle's player because doing so would make it easier, not to mention safer, to control the music than having to reach inside the vehicle with an angry dog in the mix. We heard the dog begin to whine anxiously the moment the music that played the night it attacked Biggie began to come from the speakers, but Taz's level of agitation didn't begin to approach what I witnessed among the dogs the night before.

"I still have my doubts," Kevin decided when it became apparent that music might hold the key to the attack on Biggie Charles. Kevin managed to turn sideways in his seat and reached back with his left hand to try to open the animal carrier.

"I can't reach the latch."

Roger and I approached the vehicle and witnessed his struggles. It was very obvious to me that there was no way Biggie could have turned around in his seat and done anything with the dog or its kennel the night the dog killed him. He definitely could not have reached his pistol.

The dog burst through the blankets covering the kennel in a blur and made a bee-line for Kevin the minute the fight song began to play.

It did not, however begin to attack the trooper as we anticipated. The dog began pounding its muzzled jaws against Kevin's chest and headgear but it whined rather than growled as it did so. The trooper began petting the pitiful creature as a reflex to its distress. I turned off the music and Roger and I looked at one another and shrugged. This established that the song itself was enough to agitate the dog into bolting from its cage. The lack of a substantial violent reaction did not entirely disprove our theory. The ridiculous suit, or some other cue, may have been enough to confuse the dog about its target. A visible physical and emotional change washed over the fevered animal before it stretched out on the seat next to Kevin.

I was the first to speak. "That was a bit disappointing."

Kevin stepped out and pulled apart the heavy suit. He used a towel to wipe off the sweat built up in the suit. "It seemed to me that the dog was begging me to shut the music off. I didn't feel it was intent on attacking me."

Roger held his own counsel for a long moment before speaking. "Why don't we try the other CD as well? You know that it caused a distinct response last night."

I did not expect an entirely different reaction since the songs sounded identical to my ears but I agreed that it was best not to leave any stone unturned. Roger inserted the CD confiscated Cisco's from truck into his boom box while I reloaded Taz into the cage and Kevin donned the suit.

The second CD brought a wholly unexpected reaction, even though it was the exact one we were hoping to recreate all along. Taz heard something in the second version that sent him hurtling upon the surprised Trooper like a cannonball with teeth. Turning the music off initially had only a minimal effect, but the dog did become manageable after a few moments of silence and firm restraint by Kevin.

Roger and I looked at one another as the K-9 officer pulled himself out of the vehicle and began peeling off the layers of protection. I silently watched Roger reach out to pet the pit pull's still heaving haunches before he moved his hands slowly forward and tightened his grip on its leash before removing the muzzle. The dog seemed to grin after it stretched its jaws in a large yawn. It stretched out on the warm driveway and rested its head on its forepaws.

Roger left me with the dog while he walked around the vehicle to turn off the video cameras and collect the digital recordings while I dialed Avery's number. Roger and Kevin pulled the carrier from the vehicle and loaded the pit bull back inside.

I called Chief Avery with the news. "Hey, guess what. We were able to duplicate the attack just now. The dog attacked when it heard one of the songs on the CD I took out of Cisco's truck last night."

"What about the one from Biggie's car?"

"Taz reacted to it, but not as violently," I admitted.

"Well, congratulations. Now you have a genuine clue in your murder investigation. How does it feel to have been proven right?"

"Not as good as I imagined."

Avery didn't ask for an explanation. He just told me he

wanted to speak with me before I interrogated Cisco. He agreed to drop by the bistro for breakfast in the morning to pick up the video discs Roger handed me.

I looked at my watch and saw I had plenty of time to get home before the Saints tried to add the Miami Dolphins to their undefeated season. New Orleans had no idea how to handle being home to a winning football team, but every fan hoped the winning streak wouldn't end by losing to the Miami Dolphins.

I decided to visit with my mother while she and Roger ate the delicious looking meal my mother's sixty-year-old Vietnamese housekeeper prepared. The woman's son did the heavy yard work and mowing. My mother told me yet again how ecstatic she was to find help willing to work for what she paid servants before the storm. I was relieved she decided to repeat this only after the housekeeper was out of earshot.

"Have you made any progress on your father's disappearance this week?" my mother demanded as I sat at the table opposite of Roger.

"I have been working on the murder investigation." The explanation did nothing to remove the look of extreme disapproval on my mother's face. "What was I supposed to do when Tulip insisted I keep them from shooting the dog?"

"Well...." she trailed off. She is no better at resisting my sister's entreaties than I am.

"You've been in touch with the Great and Powerful Oz, haven't you?" I could not bring myself to say the name of the internet medium who'd been charging my mother for twice-weekly readings during the past four years.

"Yes," she said a bit defiantly. "I told him about your case and he has advice for you."

"Oh, joy."

"Let me see if I remember this right. He said to tell you that, quote short men aim too high yet tall men still live in their shadows unquote. Does any of that make sense?"

"Of course not. I cannot believe you spend money on this drivel," I mocked her yet again for giving a moment's consideration to anything she was being told by someone whose junk e-mail she answered in a moment of profound sorrow and weakness.

"Well, he still says that we are close to the answer to our question. I assume he means closer to learning what became of your father."

My mother began having a recurring dream of my father waving to her from the parapet of the pre-Civil War fort on the opposite bank of the inlet after she took up permanent residence here. Her internet psychic managed to convince her she was actually hearing from her vanished husband and not simply losing her mind. She remodeled this masonry shell of a disaster-waiting-to-happen-again because the unseen shaman told her that she was safest where she felt closest to my father.

"We? As in you and who else?"

"I know, I think it's a bit strange myself, but I assume he means you."

"You would," I muttered, but I knew she heard me. I didn't have the time to try to debate semantics just then. It didn't matter. She was already storming off with her usual injured pride and dignity whenever I scoffed at her online wizard who only spoke in fortune cookie riddles.

"Why are you and Avery worried about what happened to that horrible man anyway?" She spun around and demanded to know.

"Avery's certainly not very worried. He'd let me drop the case any time. Making the dog a material witness was the only idea I had for keeping it alive when Tulip begged me not to let anyone shoot it."

My mother gave me one of her wry grins. "I'm happy to see you're developing a sentimental side. That was something else my psychic said to me, but I think it applies to you more than it does me. You have to have a heart to learn how to love."

Expressing affection is not something that runs in my family. Living under my parent's roof taught me far more about living with roommates than what it takes to have a loving relationship. As for being sentimental, I love being home but I've lived away from here far longer than I have lived in the city of my birth. New Orleans and I have both changed quite dramatically since I departed as a teenager, and August of 2005 turned too much of what I once knew and loved about New Orleans into what people began to describe as things that "ain't dere no more."

"So how's the case coming?" My mother softened a bit. "It looked like you had some luck getting the dog to attack that poor man from the State Police. You two should be ashamed of yourselves for dragging him into this."

My mother had proven to be a reliable sounding board with other situations I have handled for Avery. I know a lot about investigating, but not much about police work and almost fifty years of marriage to a detective left her with a mind full of ideas I am able to draw upon when I have none.

"It has begun to get a little messy. So far I have one person in custody I know I could convict. The list of other suspects is mercifully short. Biggie treated his long-term girlfriend like crap and left her nothing in his will. There is an undercover informant who posed as Biggie's bodyguard. There is the kennel owner, but I doubt he had any involvement or motive. There is also a woman who adopted Biggie's child years ago. All I know for certain is that the trainer was involved. He knew which dog was in that kennel when he helped load it up for delivery."

"That's quite a cast of characters," Roger agreed.

"Well, the suspects aren't my problem. The dead guy and his girlfriend put their kid up for adoption a few years ago, but Biggie left his business to the son he gave up."

"How is that a problem?" my mother asked.

"I've been spending time with the boy's adoptive mother. Do you remember the actress Amanda Rhodes?"

Roger studied my face for a moment and then burst into laughter.

"Oh, right." I shrugged. "Like you wouldn't be doing the same thing if you were in my shoes."

"Really?" My mother cut short our male bonding. "You certainly should not compromise yourself with anyone connected to the case until this matter is through the court system. You need to start watching that blind spot in your pants a lot closer. Your father had that problem."

I was not about to abandon the budding romance with Amanda Rhodes because of questions about my ethical or professionalism, or family traditions I knew nothing about. The work I do for NOPD is to stay sane, not to pay my bills, and Avery is free to fire me any day he thinks I have strayed too far across the line.

If nothing else, for once my mother's psychic said something useful about my own life. I was finally opening myself up to another person for the first time in decades. I found that what I feared would make me vulnerable as an individual made me stronger as a partner. I probably should have told my mother all of this as well, but I couldn't bear the thought of suggesting her psychic wasn't just spouting nonsense.

26

MY FIRST APPOINTMENT MONDAY morning was with Cisco Barnes, who was being held without bail before his preliminary hearing that afternoon. He had been informed there was a delay in charging him while the decision was made on whether to file state or Federal animal cruelty charges. This was actually just a ruse to make him nervous, and to give his attorney a reason to encourage him to cooperate with whoever drew the straw to prosecute him. There was already a long list of people eager to make plea bargains by offering testimony against him. I was going to be able to interview him before he was formally charged by the state's prosecutor. Avery told me to meet someone named Katie Reilly from the State Attorney's Office and to have her sit in on Cisco's questioning.

Avery was responsible for the story about the possibility of Federal prosecution, and for requiring me to conduct the interview in the company of the prosecutor. His favorite interrogation technique was to include someone from the prosecutor's office who could imply they might be the one to decide whether a suspect spent years in a prison or might be offered a plea bargain. Our hope was that Cisco used his weekend in custody to consider what limited options he faced. He used part of that time to hire a good defense attorney, someone who would defend him even if he lied to them. He hired Dan Logan.

Chief Avery informed me Katie Reilly had worked for the district attorney before moving up to the State Attorney's office, but he failed to mention I already knew her. She was a couple of years younger than myself and babysat my sister when we were all kids. I failed to connect her married name with the beat cop I heard she had married shortly before I returned to New Orleans. Being married, and to an NOPD patrolman at that, was what kept me from ever trying to reconnect with her.

Her looks had matured but not really changed over the years. Her thick auburn hair still reached below her shoulders. This morning it was folded into a long braid that looked like an Indian war bonnet. I was glad to be on the good side of the fierceness her green eyes still held. She was nearly my height, but her height was no problem when she locked eyes with me to explain her ground rules for the interview. I was to make no threats or promises and would restrict myself to an exchange of facts in an effort to extract more information.

She did not press me on the specifics of the working relationship I have with NOPD's Chief of Detectives. Katie had dealt with Logan in the past and held him in no higher esteem than I did. Still, I did not make a good impression with Katie when Logan and I began to engage one another in banter when we met outside of the interrogation room.

"Should I look surprised?" I sighed at the thought of having to deal with him.

"If it makes you feel any better." He was studiously avoiding even looking at the comely prosecutor. "Tell me what you're looking for, maybe my client can help."

"Justice. So that's not likely."

Katie leaned against the opposite wall while Logan and I continued to posture a bit.

"You didn't think you'd get to him before he lawyered-up did you?"

"No, I just hoped he'd get a better one." With that said I reached for the doorknob. Logan laughed and waved Katie into the room ahead of himself. He sat next to his client, who was handcuffed to the metal table. I turned towards Katie and she just shrugged and sat back. She understood that Avery only wanted her there to intimidate Cisco. This was something the two of them apparently did fairly often.

"This is the most important day of your life. You get to choose between pleading guilty to any charges from the dogfight and being charged with the first-degree murder of Charles Lynley." I addressed Cisco directly. I wanted him to lose track of everyone else in the room except me. I ignored the very sharp kick I received from the prosecutor to remind me who actually gets to determine such things.

"Murder?" Cisco was still trying to act uninvolved in Biggie's death despite being the only person I knew had played a part. Logan appeared to be genuinely surprised at the suggestion his client played any role in his better client's murder. I could see the gears begin spinning behind Logan's impassive stare, but his client wasn't a clever enough criminal to pull off acting confused. Cisco may have planned to use the knowledge he had of the murder as a bargaining tool on the dog fight charges. He would lose that leverage if he was formally charged with murder himself.

"Murder in the first degree. Death penalty murder." I ignored Logan and kept staring into Cisco's eyes. That description was true, but my next gambit was all bluff. "You didn't really think your involvement in the murder of Biggie Charles was going to stay a secret, did you? And every piece of evidence I have only points to you."

"I need to talk to my client!" Logan was on his feet and shouting. "Alone."

"Fair enough, but the likelihood of a deal gets smaller each time we leave this room," Katie said and stood up. The prosecutor played her part magnificently and we headed for the door.

"No. Wait. You sit down," Cisco yelled, and gave Logan the universally understood 'shut-up' glare. "I am not going down for murdering that piece of crap. Not alone."

"So, tell me what you know and I'll tell you what that's worth." I avoided using the 'we' or 'us' words so he would focus on me and not start playing to the prosecutor. "Just know that whatever lies you tell will be an anchor sinking you deeper instead of being your only lifeline."

"I know you got me on the dog charges, but the Biggie thing was not my idea. I was asked about switching dogs as a surprise. I was told to swap the breeder dog for the dog I sent to Biggie."

"Partial truths aren't going to save you. You don't get to be honest about everyone else and lie about yourself, Cisco. I need names, not pronouns."

I could see where he was headed with this, and I didn't want to waste anyone's time with the version of this story he began practicing over the weekend.

"What do you mean?"

"It doesn't matter whether you were specifically told that the intention was to kill Biggie. I could see where you would agree to swap out the dogs as a joke, but you knew what was going to happen the minute you switched dogs and gift-wrapped one of your own fighting dogs."

"Why do you think it was a fighting dog?"

"You did a lousy job erasing the tattoo. You know, the one that will match the ones in your other fighting dogs that only attack when they hear the fight song you play at your matches. Did you think I wouldn't do my homework?" He stared at me for a very short moment and then looked at his cuffed wrists. "So, get it out and get it straight."

"Okay. Okay."

He doubted that I knew everything, but was sure I knew enough to catch more of his lies. I needed him to believe any leniency he could expect from the woman next to me would be determined by how satisfied he made me with his next version of how the murder was planned and executed.

"Can we make a deal first?" Logan interrupted. Katie stared him down.

Cisco took that as his cue to begin. "I used to be at parties at Biggie's a lot because of my cousin. This girl I met there told me Bumper was blackmailing her boss lady, but she never said what for. She told me Bumper was trying to make it look like Biggie was doing it, but that she was paying the money right to Bumper and Biggie never mentioned it. I believed the girl because Bumper treated everyone around him like crap and it sounded like something he would do. She also said Bumper was hitting on her anytime she went by the studio to see Biggie. Anyway, she wanted to buy a dog that would keep Bumper away. She said she wanted it to hurt him enough so he'd lose his job, but I don't think she would have minded if it killed him, neither."

"And the name of this girl you keep talking about?" I had a name in mind.

"Tanya. Tanya Lansing." I couldn't hide my relief that he had not named Amanda or Georgia. I was buoyed by the prospect of Bumper having blackmailed multiple victims. He was likely to have been as sloppy in any other attempts as he was at blackmailing Amanda. I was also tempted to dismiss the whole blackmail story as something he had been fed, if only because his lawyer was intimately familiar with Amanda's situation.

One thing began to bother me. I never considered that anyone but Biggie was the intended target of the dog's vicious attack. He pressed on, not sure how much, if any, of this explanation I was buying. "So, Tanya started to work on Bumper about having Biggie to get a dog. Tyshika told me they was looking for one and I had her bring them to the kennel. I suggested Biggie buy the real Taz and train with him. I had one of the groomers put that dye on one of the dogs I was training for the fights and we put him in the cage. The dog was supposed to kill Bumper, not Biggie. Biggie used to drive his-self and Bumper would sit in the back seat when Tyshika was in the car with them. I figured the dog would break through the paper and attack Bumper on the way across the Causeway."

"How much did you sell the real Taz for?" I wanted to know for my own sake. It was not a useful piece of information in his prosecution.

"I've still got him," Cisco admitted. He seemed surprised I hadn't figured this out, but I had not yet heard back about the search of Cisco's house Avery told me he would be conducting that morning. I would have to be sure to ask Roger to comb through the impounded dogs. "I was gonna keep the dog and breed him."

"Walk me through that Friday afternoon. Who helped you wrap the cage?"

"Nobody helped me with that. The groomers dyed the dog I gave them and I wrapped the cage in my office and they helped me load it in the SUV when I was done."

"And Jerry didn't bother to check to be sure it was the right dog?"

"Why would he?" This was a fair question. Jerry should be able to trust his trainers.

"Tyshika didn't want to see what she bought?"

"Nah," he laughed. "She didn't want to get her dress dirty looking at no dogs. One of the dogs had pissed in the lobby and I thought she was going to puke. I told her I had made it blue because someone left a message to do that.

Biggie loved them blue dog paintings so it made sense to give him a live one for his birthday. Tyshika laughed about it but didn't ask to see what I did."

"Why did you really give the dog a dye job?" I was not convinced the trainer really knew about Biggie's interest in Rodrique's artwork.

"I thought sure the cops would shoot the dog when it attacked Bumper," he admitted. "If they did then nobody would have probably washed the dog off and found out it was a different dog. Only one who would have recognized it anyway was Biggie."

This was exactly what I thought after I learned about the switch myself. It was a perfect plan until my kid sister ruined it. I wonder what would have happened when Biggie let that pit bull loose in his white-on-white world in that lakefront condo. Tyshika probably would have killed Biggie for doing so. I gave all of this a moment's before deciding I didn't trust his version of things. I doubt Logan wanted his client to lie to me, but someone else may have had fewer concerns. I believed Cisco would lie to me if someone he was afraid of told him to do so. Someone like Bumper, who may have had connections at Central Lockup, could have gotten to Cisco by now. Maybe Bumper believed I wouldn't suspect him of the crime if I thought he was the intended victim. He would be underestimating how much I hated him and wanted to see him in handcuffs and his smugness crushed. It was also possible Cisco would shield someone else if he knew he couldn't escape going to prison for his own role.

"I don't believe your story, but I'll check it out. I still like your cousin for this," I told him. "The money Tyshika will get from suing the kennel could easily pay you off for helping her kill Biggie."

"Sure my cousin could get some money suing Jerry, but does she strike you as the kind of person that will split a nickel two ways?" Cisco proved to be a lot wiser than I gave him credit for being. "And I swear that whatever reason you have to think I am lying is wrong. I will admit to my part, but I won't take the all the blame for killing Biggie."

"So that's your story and you're sticking to it?" This had hardly played out the way I thought it would. Everyone in the room agreed that Tyshika was likely innocent but no saint. Cisco had just confessed to killing Biggie, though apparently by accident, on the orders of someone named Tanya Lansing. This Tanya Lansing might have been a made-up name, but at least for now the conspirator that I was looking for was not named Amanda Rhodes.

"I don't have anything else to tell you," Cisco declared and sat back in his chair.

"I only have one more thing. What's up with the fight song you played at the fight? Why did all those dogs get so excited?"

"Dog whistles, man. We recorded six of those whistles only the dogs can hear and put that up under the song. It drives them nuts." He sounded rather proud of this idea.

"It sure does." I had to agree. The genius of this was debatable, but the effect was immediate and certain. I had seen the efficiency twice so far. "Here's another one you know the answer to. It's been bugging me since I watched those two dogs fight. When a dog attacks, will it focus on one spot or will it look for any spot it can bite?"

"Once. They always go for the throat first and will keep at it until they get there."

"Why would the dog have chewed on Biggie in two places then?"

"Maybe he was holding it down. The dog would have gone straight for the throat, but I guess it would bite him anywhere he couldn't defend. It's how they're trained."

I thanked him for his help and advised him to learn to go without showers, as pretty boys like him didn't do well in the showers at Angola. It was just a mean thing to say.

Katie wasted no time pinning my ears back once we closed the door behind us.

"I'm not sure what I can do with any of that. You do know you didn't read him his rights."

"Yep."

"Do you think Logan didn't notice?" We both knew the answer to that question. "Why the hell didn't you read him his rights?"

"So he'd talk. You have him solid on the dog charges. He will plead to whatever you want on that just to beat the murder rap. I don't think anyone cares if he ever does a day for his work on the Biggie's murder. The kennel Cisco works for is going to take a pretty big hit just from the dogfighting story. Being even remotely involved with a dog murdering its owner would put them out of business. Cisco is not the big fish I want to catch, and now you can get him to testify against anyone else in the dogfighting case without having to go into court admitting you made any deals."

"Tulip said I'd want to slap you if we ever worked together."

"Well, my sister certainly didn't fill me in on you, Mrs. Reilly."

"Reilly was my married name, but I'm divorced. My father doesn't have very nice things to say about you these days, either. He says you called him some pretty men things when you phoned him to say you were looking for your father."

"Yeah, I was a little rough when I called him," I admitted. I had all but accused him of trying to cover up whatever happened. I brought the subject back to our immediate situation. "Did Avery happen to tell you who we are looking at for orchestrating the murder?"

"No."

"Despite what Cisco is trying to sell us, I may hand you a crooked Fed on a silver platter. I can probably get the blackmail charge to stick, but I am a lot more interested in nailing him on the murder charge."

"Keep me posted." Katie sighed deeply before she opened the door to the interrogation room and then turned to reach out and touch my arm as I began to turn away. "It was nice seeing you again, Cooter."

"Interesting anyway," I chuckled and left her to deal with Cisco and Logan alone.

27

IT WOULD BE A FEW DAYS before I could ask Amanda or Georgia if they knew anyone named Tanya Lansing. Amanda took Georgia and Parker to Mobile for a USO fundraiser on the USS Alabama. Amanda told me she avoids trading on her background as a debutante, but that she is always ready to play the part of the Southern belle that made it big in Hollywood if it serves a good purpose. She also confided to me that she had no intention of ever touring with the USO in Afghanistan or Iraq. Her reluctance had less to do with the time away from Parker than the fear of people shooting at her. I bit my tongue to keep from telling her what little difference I feel there is between those foreign streets and the ones I patrol in New Orleans.

I decided to use the time to work on getting Bumper Jackson to implicate himself. I broke my promise to Avery to stay away from the man until Avery was able to confirm Bumper's true identity and role. I didn't care who he really was, only whether or not I could deliver a prosecutable case for blackmail or homicide against the guy. Something about Bumper was beginning to really annoy me. I had to constantly remind myself that he might be innocent and that it was entirely possible I simply hated him.

I returned to BC Studios the next afternoon and found Bumper and a mixing engineer laying percussion tracks under what passed for a song. Bumper paused the recorder and whispered something to the engineer before the man left the room. I took a seat in the engineer's empty chair.

"What can I do for you, Detective?" Bumper spoke the last word with the touch of derision he tried to inject whenever possible.

"I suppose you confessing to blackmail and murder is

out of the question." I stretched my feet out ahead of me to block his exit. Bumper wasn't going anywhere anyway.

"Yeah, that's probably not going to happen," Bumper chortled, but he didn't say he had no idea what I was talking about. He also didn't immediately plead innocence. He was going to make me do all the talking, perhaps hoping that I would show my hand before he played his own cards.

"Everyone seems to be sending me your way about Biggie's murder these days." I tried lying because I still had nothing solid to use against him. "One story is you had to get Biggie out of the way to make the moves on Tyshika. I doubt she'd have you, but maybe you just wanted to take over the record label and studio. I even have the CD with the track that makes the dog attack. Those are the theories, but I like the evidence. And just the other day someone was telling me about a ten grand a month scam you have going to keep quiet about the adoption of Biggie's kid. I'm also planning to tie you to Biggie's gun locker out in Harahan."

I hoped to feed him enough tidbits of what I had to spark some debate so I could steer him into a position where he would defend himself against any accusation he thought I might actually have enough to get an indictment. That slip-up would tell me where to focus my efforts to find the evidence to actually do so.

"I doubt a jury is going to convict me of lying about giving bad advice on pets and I have no idea whatever blackmail you are talking about." Bumper threw up both hands in mock defense. "The CD I gave Biggie was just a collection of songs some of his bands were working on. I don't know a thing about any hidden messages. Do you have the CD with you?"

"Funny you should ask," I gloated and took the CD recovered from Biggie's CD player from its evidence bag. Bumper did not seem unnerved by the word EVIDENCE printed on the bag.

Bumper loaded the CD into a player next to the huge mixing board and cued up the track that caused the pit bull to simply lunge at the trooper the day before. The song was even more annoying now that I was having to listen to it through professional loudspeakers. Bumper started to grin as he manipulated the mixing board spread out before him.

"What's so funny?"

"There's nothing here that should have made the dog go after Biggie. Watch the bar graph over there."

Bumper pointed to a set of lights and began removing frequencies one at a time. Each time he made an adjustment I could hear a difference in the music. He removed the last tonal abomination and the graph was black before us. I had no idea what this meant but assumed my theory had just sprung a leak when I saw his triumphant grin.

"Try this one." I offered him the CD from the dogfight. He repeated the process, but this time the board remained lit up with frequencies we were unable to hear.

"Those are some ultra-high frequencies," Bumper pointed to the graph and moved more things about on the board. "I'd guess it's a dog whistle."

"Why do you think it's a dog whistle?" I understood he could isolate the tone, but to be able to immediately identify the source of the tone made him seem a little too smart about such things.

"Because I was here when Cisco added some to a CD. I'm guessing that this is probably that same CD. I thought he was doing it as some sort of practical joke. So, you thought I had added a dog whistle to the CD I gave Biggie? That would have been pretty dumb of me. Sooner or later someone would have thought to run a test like this."

"So you're saying you knew about Cisco's dog fighting operation?" I shifted gears. The idea that the two of them sat here and made the alteration without Cisco giving the real reason for doing so seemed far-fetched at best.

"I knew, but knowing isn't a crime. As for the dog that killed Biggie, getting a dog at all was Biggie's idea. I'm sure it was Tyshika that paid the trainer to switch the dogs so she could sue the kennel for wrongful death. She may have thought she'd inherit the business. Cisco did tell me how easy it would be to switch the dogs and kill someone if I were ever interested in doing so, but I told him to get lost. My job was to protect the big man, so I would hardly plan to kill him."

"You wouldn't be the first bodyguard to kill his master. You've also had plenty of time to make up an alibi." I had to admit that his story could be enough to give a jury in

Orleans Parish reasonable doubt. Arguing that protecting his undercover status rather than exposing crimes the subject of his investigation was not directly involved in would probably work in his favor with a lot of juries. Being a cop might work against me in a New Orleans courtroom. Juries of the average New Orleans' peers have shown far less willingness to automatically believe a police officer's testimony to be totally honest since the storm.

Bumper handed me my CDs and stood up abruptly. He motioned for me to follow him out of the recording studio. I looked around the room as we walked out, and my eyes fell on a series of framed pictures in the hallway. Most of them were of the bands under contract to Biggie, and most of these had Biggie or the engineers posed with them. A few of them were taken in the nightclub. The ones which drew my attention featured Biggie with a very young boy on his lap. There was a strong paternal look on Biggie's face as he looked towards Parker. Bumper followed my gaze and started to laugh.

"Oh, man, you hadn't figured that out yet?" I managed to figure out he was an undercover cop, but I was entirely unprepared for these pictures. I thought that finding a way to corroborate Cisco's story about Georgia bringing the boy to see Biggie was going to be harder than this. "The kid is Biggie's."

"I know about the adoption, but I didn't realize Biggie had any contact with his son after the adoption. These look fairly new." I pulled a picture off the wall to study it closer.

"They sure are. That one was taken a week before Biggie died. Biggie bribed the kid's nanny behind that actress, Amanda something or another's, back. She'd bring him by once a week or so." The way Bumper said this was likely to try to put some distance between himself and Amanda. At least he didn't indicate he was aware of my budding romance with Amanda. He also may have been keeping any knowledge of that to himself to use later. Bumper led me to his office while I tried to keep the conversation going.

"Why would the nanny do that?"

"Biggie told her he regretted the deal he made. He told her how he met Amanda's husband and found out the actress chick couldn't have any babies. He told me he sold them his kid in exchange for the money to get started here."

"He actually said that he sold them the kid?"

"Well, no, the way he described it sounded more like they made some sort of a trade, but her husband did give Biggie money to get started right after the adoption went through. Then Biggie kept hitting the guy up for money whenever the studio fell short of cash. Biggie told the couple he would go public about the adoption if his credit was cut off. The husband kept paying, but he also took a piece of the action and that really pissed off Biggie. He told me more than once that he planned to have the nanny bring the kid to him if the husband ever tried to take his studio away."

We made it to his office and he closed the door behind us, just as Bumper finished with these disclosures. I had my doubts that I could get him to repeat any of them under oath. Bumper silently motioned for me to have a seat, but I remained standing while he went to a filing cabinet behind the desk and began thumbing through a file drawer.

"Is that what you went undercover to investigate, whether Biggie was extorting money?" I brought the subject back to what I believed was his real purpose in getting close to Biggie, and to who I thought he was.

"That's not my job. I'm the bodyguard and you're the investigator, remember?" Bumper said and turned around with a slim file in his hand. He waved the file and motioned for me to follow him once again. I assumed, correctly, that we were headed back to the false privacy of the VIP lounge.

"So what's this?" The folder he handed me once we were seated consisted of fifteen single-spaced pages of firearm descriptions and serial numbers. I estimated the total number of rifles and pistols listed at just over five hundred.

"That's an inventory of every weapon anyone under contract to Biggie turned in. Biggie planned to cash all of them in during one of the city's buy-back publicity stunts. Biggie thought he could get some positive press if it looked like he getting guns off the street, but he'd profit as well."

"Where are the guns now?"

"The hell if I know," Bumper actually sounded like he was telling the truth. "Biggie told me to hire someone to rent the locker so it couldn't be linked back to either of us until he turned the guns over. I went out there a few months ago and the locker was empty. Biggie said to just let it go. He couldn't make a big stink about losing guns when he wasn't even supposed to be around them, and you can't do much with that list without the actual guns or the person I hired to rent the locker. If anybody asks I will deny ever having seen that list. So, do whatever you want with it."

"Who did you hire to rent the locker?"

"You really think I'd tell you that? The guns are long gone and even with the serial numbers you can't link them to either of us unless I testify, and what are the odds of that?"

Bumper sounded as though he was laughing as he opened the refrigerator and removed Heinekens for each of us. He opened them behind the bar and handed me one of the frigid green bottles before he reclaimed his seat on the sofa. I was sitting on the coffee table facing him. I wanted to be sure I was well inside his comfort zone.

"Losing the guns must have been a kick in the balls to whoever you're really working for. A firearm case that big against Biggie would have been a real feather in their cap."

"You keep making it sound like I am some kind of undercover cop or something." Bumper forced a chuckle. "I'm just a guy trying to make a living and I didn't give a damn about any of it, really. The guns were a bad idea all along. My only concern was who Biggie would get into any other business with. The club was a magnet for criminals and people who liked hanging out with them. I kept an eye open for anyone who might try to muscle in on Biggie, or who Biggie might try to take advantage of. The mess with Biggie's son was one that couple created for themselves. I don't think the movie actress even knew what was going on between Biggie and her husband. On the other hand, it would make her a suspect for murdering Biggie if he was blackmailing her for something, wouldn't it?"

Bumper phrased his response to not actually betray whether or not he was ever there to do anything but to protect his employer. He was clearly intent on encouraging me to focus my investigation on any suspect besides himself. It was beginning to look like good advice. I definitely needed to speak about Biggie with Georgia.

"It could be made to look that way, I'm sure." I needed

to chart a new direction. "I just find it interesting that every time we have these little chats you find something for me to investigate someone else about." I waved the file as an example. "It's like you were just a spectator and never got your own hands dirty in anything."

"Okay, it's just you and me sitting here having a beer. Maybe you should tell me what you think you know." Bumper stretched his arms across the back of the leather sofa and relaxed. I am sure he thought he had a good handle on things right then. Biggie was dead, so there'd be no prosecution for his possession of the guns because Bumper wasn't going to face prosecution without testifying to his own involvement. Even then, he could trade the name of the person who rented the locker for his own freedom. He was trying hard to make me think of Amanda as a suspect because of Biggie's blackmail threat. He should have been more worried that he was next in line if she'd killed Biggie.

"Here's what I know. I know it takes a particular sort of person to be a good undercover agent. They have to be able to spend all day pretending to be someone they would ordinarily hate. I know an agent could very easily find it is far more fun living life without rules than living a life full of them. Someone living undercover might go off the rails and then tell himself he can walk away from any mess he makes by claiming he needed to maintain his cover. That might work for doing a little blow or losing a truckload of guns, but I doubt it will explain away a murder or blackmail."

"You think a lot don't you?" Bumper slapped his hands on his legs. I was paying a lot of attention to his hands, and it occurred to me just then how very little I trusted the man. Avery was still trying to confirm whether or not he was an undercover Federal agent, and if so which agency's. My concern was whether or not Bumper pulled a gun on me. I sensed that he was waiting for me to draw first. "Why in the hell are you so convinced that I'm working undercover?"

"The Bumper Jackson who played football at Oklahoma is currently deployed as a helicopter pilot in Afghanistan. He is there, and yet you are here. That Bumper also had his knee surgically repaired, and his brother is a crooked cop."

Bumper mumbled something and leaned back. His fingers began to twitch like he was making a decision.

"I'm going to make a suggestion. Don't come back here unless you plan to make an arrest. Because, while I may be your favorite suspect, I am also a can of worms you do not want to open." Bumper stood up, gave me a patronizing pat on the head and left me alone in the room without another word. I heard the heavy metal door to the offices open and slam shut a moment later. Elvis, or whoever this guy proved to be, had truly left the building.

28

CHIEF AVERY MET with Bumper's supervising Agent at the FBI for supper at Bon Ton Cafe a few hours after I tucked my tail between my legs and left BC Productions to regroup and calm down.

Bon Ton Cafe on Magazine Street has the distinction of being New Orleans' original Cajun restaurant. The Cafe is the last building on its side of a long block. Half of the remainder of the block was paved to create a parking for the Federal Building directly across Poydras Street. The food was as much of an attraction as the location when Avery invited Bumper's supervising agent to dinner, at Avery's expense, after receiving an especially angry call from SAC Conroy about my latest visit to the studio.

Avery had the sense that the Special Agent in Charge intended to make the call for a while, but he wasn't prepared to do so when he was going to have to apologize to Avery for keeping NOPD out of the loop. Protocol dictated that he should have notified NOPD before he put Bumper beside Biggie. Agent James Gabb was Bumper's supervising agent and he contacted Avery moments after Conroy hung up, in a transparent good-cop/bad-cop ploy. Gabb agreed to sit down with my boss at a location of Avery's choosing. Buying the FBI Agent dinner at one of his own favorite restaurants at NOPD's expense was Avery's self-serving way of choosing a neutral location and getting a free meal for doing his job.

Avery immediately thought of Napoleon when Gabb introduced himself. He was shorter than average and rail thin, with slick brown hair and unusually dark eyes. His face had a naturally smug expression that Avery took an immediate dislike towards. Gabb had the handshake and long foot stride of an ambitious man well on his way to where he wanted to be. The agent's suit coat flared open to expose his badge and sidearm.

"Thanks for meeting with me," Avery said as they took their seats at a corner table.

"Well, it's always hard to turn down a free meal. We probably should have done this some time ago."

"Probably so." Avery chose not to use this as an opening to berate the agent in public.

"Well, then, let's take a look at the menu."

Avery knew what he wanted and Gabb needed only a couple of moments before he set down his own menu. Their waitress gathered up the menus from the starched white tablecloth and took their drink and food orders. Gabb waited until she was out of earshot before he spoke again.

"The Bureau definitely should have informed your department that we had an informant working close to Biggie Charles. There was some concern about security because he used to be a patrolman with NOPD."

"We're already aware of that situation."

Gabb was obviously surprised to find Avery so well informed, but Avery only showed his practiced expression of almost paternal disapproval for how SAC Conroy and Gabb handled their agency's UC operation. The waitress returned with Avery's glass of merlot and Gabb's iced tea. Both men ordered bowls of turtle soup to start their meal and it arrived a moment later with a basket of warm bread. Gabb waited until the back waiter was gone to start talking again.

"It was an operation to see what flies might be attracted to a rap music studio. It has been a dry hole, but we've invested nearly two years on the operation. We were building a case for some gun charges when Biggie died. How did you figure it out, not to slight NOPD's abilities?"

"No offense taken. I've got a special investigator on the case and he figured it out when he did background on your guy's cover story. The real Bumper Jackson is in the Army, and in Afghanistan. We believe his brother, Eric, is using his brother's name and college background as his cover. Eric was a patrolman with NOPD until he resigned a few weeks after Hurricane Katrina. He was immediately hired by one of the private security firms working here at the time, but then a year or so ago you made a personal recommendation that he become a confidential informant. I find that especially curious."

"Sloppy work on our part about the cover. What do you find curious?"

"How the two of you even know one another." Avery was trying to make this seem like a casual conversation and not the formal questioning he really wanted to put Gabb through.

"I met Eric while we were doing joint operations here after the storm and he seemed a bit more ambitious than the average rookie cop so, yeah, when I bumped into him again a couple of years later I approached him about working for the FBI as our eyes and ears inside of Biggie's operation."

"We're not interested in compromising anyone's cover. I came here to reassure you that we don't intend to blow up your investigation while we conduct ours."

"Well, obviously not exposing our guy would be very helpful. I don't want to have to make a stink out of your detective, either. I was surprised to learn he is actually a detective from the State Police. In fact, he is their only member of that rank permanently assigned to NOPD. I'm told you personally assign his cases. Are you running some sort of rogue operation of your own?"

Avery sensed the quid pro quo of each side keeping its mouth shut as house salads replaced the soup bowls. He also sensed that the FBI's background investigation ran far deeper than a simple call to the State Patrol.

"Not at all. I was his father's partner years ago, so of course, I naturally welcomed Cooter when he came to us after Katrina. Surely you remember how short-handed NOPD was right after the storm. He helped track down some suspects we lost track of while waiting for the courts to re-open. Lately, I have used him to handle oddball cases, such as determining whether Biggie's pit bull killed him on its own or was trained to do so. Nobody else seems to care about the answer than Detective Holland, and I let him pursue it more as a training exercise than anything else."

"So NOPD doesn't really consider Biggie's murder to be important?"

"The dog killed Biggie no matter what Cooter finds." Avery downplayed my investigation all that he could, but they both understood there was a huge difference in the dog being a murderer or being a murder weapon. "Cooter started this only because his sister didn't want to see the dog get shot. We never know how these cases will develop, but so far it's led to a blind alley on some guns Biggie had supposedly stockpiled. On a positive note, it also led to that dogfighting raid last weekend. I assume the dead end he hit was the same as the case your man was putting together?"

"I'm sure finding our UC and the dogfighting arrests were feathers in your cap." Gabb's glib response did not include answering Avery's question about any investigation into the missing guns.

Avery just gave a self-deprecating shrug rather than allow the meal to become an exchange of veiled insults, backhanded compliments, and obstruction. Unfortunately, those seemed to be the reasons Gabb agreed to the meeting.

"You are aware that your detective is considered something of damaged goods by the State Patrol, aren't you?" Avery had anticipated this sort of personal attack.

"How so?" Avery doubted Gabb had found anything substantial in his background check before it would have run into roadblocks Avery personally helped to set in place.

"Our UC asked me to check on Detective Holland after their first meeting. He wondered how an NOPD detective could afford to drive a brand new Cadillac as a work vehicle. Your detective's nickname is Cadillac, of all things. Bumper gave me a beer bottle with Detective Holland's fingerprints so I could run a basic background check in our own system. I was referred to the State Patrol by NOPD's Human Resources department and was surprised, to say the least, that Detective Holland graduated the LASP academy at the rank of detective. I imagine his mother being part of the Deveraux family played a part in that. I also found out there is a Homeland Security block on the last fifteen years of his life before he attended the academy. I understand he had trouble passing the Patrol's psychological exam, which I assume has something to do with all those missing years. He was assigned to your care the day he graduated and the State Patrol doesn't seem to have a lot of interest in getting him back. One of our anti-terrorism agents spent a year in Iraq and recognized your guy's name. He said Holland did classified work there until he was wounded in some sort of ambush and was slipped out of the country before he could be questioned about diverted recovery funds. The agent offered to make some calls, but then our SAC received a call and we were instructed to drop any investigation into your guy unless he could be charged with a criminal act. We have never been waved away from a basic background check." Agent Gabb detailed these problems with his investigation of my background with very obvious displeasure. The call from FBI Headquarters must not have been a very sociable one. "So, I am asking you, who is Detective Holland and is Cooter even his real name?"

"It really is Cooter Holland, and your version of a basic background check sounds a lot like a serious vetting. I know Cooter was wounded in Iraq, but your own agent probably knows more about what Cooter was doing there than I do." Avery held up a hand before his guest could raise further points. "Cooter came home after the storm, like you said, but he planned to do nothing other than investigate his father's disappearance. His family asked me to make an arrangement where he could trade having access to the police department's resources to do his investigation in exchange for helping NOPD by tracking down defendants we lost track of after Katrina. I was entirely aware that there were issues getting him cleared to join the State Patrol, but I was briefed on why that was and I still agreed to take him on as a detective. So far it has worked out fine."

"What does he think happened to his father?" Avery hoped this was a sign Gabb was trying to change the subject.

"Neither of us has any idea. I didn't even know Ralph was helping us at the time. He had retired but apparently showed up at the command post in Algiers when he couldn't get across the bridge. Ralph linked up with our SWAT guys and a mixed bag of Feds who were doing house to house searches and gathering up every hard case they found to get them out of town. Cooter found that his father went out on a night patrol with guys nobody remembers and ran into an ambush of his own. Everyone but Ralph was later accounted for. Most of the officers Cooter spoke with have apparently retired or left town. All of them claim to not be able to remember a thing that's been helpful." Avery summed up four years' worth of what I found in about a hundred words.

"Well, whoever Cooter is, he wasted no time sniffing out our informant. I'd say he's pretty good at what he does."

"You don't seem especially enamored of the Biggie Charles undercover operation yourself. Do you mind me asking what's going on there?"

Avery only came here to reassure the agent in charge of the FBI's operation that he was not going to expose their informant. They both knew he was lying when Avery said he harbored no hostility about the FBI leaving him in the dark for the last two years.

"I'm worried our informant may be involved in some criminal activity himself. He was personally responsible for handling all of the firearms that went missing. Our SAC was looking for a reason to close shop even before Biggie died and that incident nearly did the trick. I just hate to see so much work go for nothing."

"How did the operation against Biggie get started? What drew your interest?"

"Well," Gabb started speaking but then paused almost theatrically before continuing. Avery thought he might be trying to remember a scripted response. "My brother was Biggie's attorney at his murder trial, which has remained a family embarrassment ever since. I saw an opportunity to try to set things right and got a green light on the operation once I had an informant I could put in place."

"The agency approved your UC operation even though you have a potential family conflict of interest?" Avery was barely able to contain his skepticism.

Gabb objected to Avery's implication. "First of all, we have only been investigating Biggie's activities since he left Angola. Secondly, there is actually no family conflict. It was my brother who represented Biggie at trial and we have had no discussions about my investigation. The only thing that we both wanted was to see Biggie back in Angola for good. Just like everyone else."

Avery and Gabb found other things to discuss over their entrees, but both men were ready for the meal to be over by the time the waitress offered them dessert.

29

THE UNEASINESS AVERY FELT when he parted company with Agent Gabb increased during his short drive to Strada Ammazarre. I expected his visit because he promised to drop by if there were things we needed to discuss.

"Apparently dinner did not go well." I had a cold beer waiting for him when he came through the door.

"You could say that." Avery took a swig of his beer. "The FBI dug into your background. I'm not sure what all they found, but someone in Washington told the local office to shut down Gabb's background check on you. This is what you told me we needed to avoid, remember?"

Avery's frown was one I've seen rarely in the past. I saw a flicker in Tony's eyes before he looked away from us. The chef normally heads to the kitchen when Avery and I talk shop, but he remained rooted to his seat.

"I do. But, it's not like we don't have their agent in a worse corner than they can paint me into." I could tell Avery was not comfortable with the idea of engaging in tit for tat with the FBI. "And you just said they were ordered to drop the investigation, right?"

"Let's hope they really have. You promised me to tell me anything I wanted to know about your past. I've never taken you up on that, but now I think I should. I don't want to get blindsided by something they found and are saving up."

I glanced at Tony before I agreed to keep my promise. "This is a conversation we should have upstairs."

"You cannot imagine how little I wanted that to be your answer."

Avery followed Tony and me to the elevator. Avery did not question why Tony was part of our discussions, but the chef's presence only compounded Chief Avery's anxiety. I opened the heavy metal door to my apartment. This was Avery's first visit to my place since a cursory walk-through while the entire building's interior was under construction. He complimented the finished decorating in the front rooms and kitchen, but held his comments on my office, with its well-stocked gun cabinet and a pair of large chalkboards flanking the desk. The post-it notes and writing on one of these were a timeline of events between August 29, 2004 and the night my father disappeared.

I poured bourbon for Tony and myself and took a cold beer from the fridge for Avery. My boss avoids hard liquor rather than giving up alcohol entirely. He is a mean drunk but no alcoholic, at least not by local standards.

Avery settled onto the heavy Stickley sofa's leather cushions and put his feet up on the coffee table. Tony took a seat in a low backed leather chair, identical to the one I sat in, and waited to see what I divulged to Chief Avery. Tony and I had rehearsed this presentation dozens of times.

"I need some idea of the depth of the hole I am in if the SAC learned anything before Gabb had to stop vetting you." Avery glanced in my direction, but wouldn't make eye contact. Mike Conroy ran the local FBI office like his own fiefdom and was always looking for an advantage to use against NOPD.

"Even if my telling you deepens that hole?" I offered him a chance to stop. Avery gave this only a moment's consideration.

"Yeah."

I sighed and took a drink from my tumbler. "Tell me what you already know."

"Your dad was proud of you when you made the Green Berets, but worried as hell when you went to Somalia and things went bad. He told me you jumped to some super-secret outfit in the Army when you came back and then all he ever seemed to know came from postcards you sent from overseas that said nothing other than you were okay. He knew you went into Afghanistan right after 9/11, and everyone thought you were probably safer when you took that State Department job, at least until you were reported dead and they couldn't produce your body."

"Well, everything you know up until the Green Berets is

about right. I did transfer to what you know as Delta Force and was kept busy even before 9/11. I blew out my knee in a helicopter accident, but I came out of physical rehab and found contract work with our intelligence agencies. I took an assignment with a State Department cover in Baghdad, but wasn't actually working for them, right after Hussein high-tailed it out of town."

"What sort of contract work?" Avery asked.

"The sort of work the media speculates about but that nobody directly involved talks about. It's the kind of work my employers needed to keep plausible deniability about in case something went wrong," I said and let Avery decide where to take the conversation. I wasn't going to give him specific details and was sure he didn't want them anyway.

"So, what, you were sending guys to Guantanamo?" Avery said to get the conversation moving again.

"No. The guys in Guantanamo were taken alive. My job was to stop the missions the guys in Gitmo already had in motion. My job required a particular mindset."

"What sort of job and mindset are we talking about?"

"My job didn't involve taking prisoners." I could see the blood drain from Avery's face. "I had to change the way I do a lot of things when I came to work for you."

"Sweet Jesus," Avery muttered and finished his beer. Tony was pouring fresh rounds for the two of us and Avery abruptly switched to Scotch. I waited while Avery took a long sip from his tumbler. His hand was trembling and I knew he needed the shortest version of things possible. "What was your mission when you were injured?"

"What do you know about the money our government sent to Iraq after the war?"

"Not much. Didn't we release some money impounded after they invaded Kuwait?"

"That and the money from the UN-sanctioned Food-For-Oil program came to a little over twelve billion dollars. It was delivered by the pallet load to the Iraqi Provisional Authority in freshly-minted American currency. It arrived on the same size planes we use to ship tanks overseas."

"Twelve billion dollars in cash?" Avery repeated the number to himself a few times.

"The Americans running the Provisional Government

made the cash the responsibility of the Iraqis they were about to put in charge of running their own country. The country had no economy to speak of and there were no functional banks. Everything about the rebuilding process was being paid in cash. The accounting system was a joke."

"What does any of this have to do with what you were doing?"

"Like I said, my work in Iraq involved tracking down individuals behind the attacks on our troops. The mission changed when we found out we were financing the attacks on our own troops. We started to follow the money to the bad guys."

"And how do you fit into this?" Avery turned and asked Tony.

"I helped him." This was the largest understatement ever uttered.

"So you were some sort of spy like Cooter?"

"Not really. We wanted to kill some of the same men." Avery frowned at the thought his favorite chef was anything but what he believed him to be. "My father was an Iraqi intelligence officer using diplomatic cover at our consulate in Rome. He fell in love with my mother, who is from Sicily, and was sent back to Baghdad after they secretly married. Saddam had my father killed when I was ten years old. My mother and I were kicked out of Iraq and we returned to Sicily. I was a chef in Palermo when Saddam's secret police told me to work for them or they would kill my mother. I went back to Iraq to hunt down the men who killed my father after your army captured Saddam. The man your President sent to run Iraq fired the army and ordered everyone who worked for Mukhabarat rounded up, as you say. I was arrested and treated like a criminal, but Cooter hired me to help him find the men who were financing and directing the Iraqis attacking your soldiers."

I began explaining my own role before Avery could ask Tony questions I knew he wouldn't answer. "The men we were looking for wanted to keep the country stirred up. They killed Sunnis and Shia to make it look like there was a civil war and they killed anyone who helped the Americans. They needed lots of confusion so they could rob the country just like they had when Saddam ran the country."

"So they killed their own people just to steal the money we sent them?" Repeating our statements showed Avery's struggles with his new understanding of Tony and myself.

"Tony recruited a team of former Mukhabarat agents to track the money and lead us to anyone paying people to kill Coalition troops. It is wiser to stop a snake by chopping off its head than by stepping on its tail."

"One of these men shot my father. He was a colonel in the Republican Guard and was working side by side with the Coalition troops he was targeting. We found his family stole thirty million dollars from Saddam, and more from the money your country gave back. This man's brother was going to be part of the new Iraqi government."

"I reported this to my case officer and things went crazy," I picked up the thread again. "My report was sent to the State Department in Washington, which probably shared it with the White House. We were allowed to freeze the accounts but were told to leave the colonel alone. We did that. The colonel threw a tantrum until the Iraqi Governing Council protested the account freeze to the Provisional Government. There was also an increase in attacks on our troops, so my team drove out and picked up the colonel for questioning. We were ambushed on our way back to Baghdad."

"And what happened to the colonel?"

"He disappeared, along with the money in the bank accounts we had frozen."

"So I guess you rescued Cooter in the ambush?" Avery turned towards Tony.

"Yes." Tony continued while he poured more Scotch into Avery's glass. "I drove Cooter to a hospital in the city rather than to your own military's and moved him to safety when the Iraqis started hunting us."

Avery now turned back to me. "You were pretty badly injured."

"Every plan has its flaws."

"Why did the Iraqis want to question you after the ambush? And why are your records sealed?" Avery knew, by now, that this conversation involved far more classified information than he should know. Tony and I were doing our best to avoid giving him the names, dates, or precise locations involved.

"The Interim Government saw the colonel even being investigated as an insult to his family. They were livid about my detaining him, especially after he vanished with the family's fortune. I'm sure his family was more upset their money was gone than that he was missing. The Iraqis tried to convince the State Department my team abducted the colonel to force him to drain the accounts before we killed him. Tony and I were declared persona non grata by the State Department, Department of Defense, and CIA. They threw us under the bus to maintain their fragile relationship with the Iraqis they were committed to putting in charge of the country when the Provisional Government pulled out. They also couldn't let it get out that the new politicians our government helped get elected to the new council were as corrupt as the men our army fought a war to get rid of." I said and hid my face behind my tumbler of bourbon.

"That sounds like something out of a bad movie."

"It was a bad movie. I was dressed as an Iraqi police officer and was admitted to the civilian hospital under that identity. The State Department declared me dead because a jacket with my name in the liner was found on a body after the ambush scene was secured. They knew it wasn't me, but there was a fear I was abducted by the same people who grabbed the colonel. Declaring me dead removed my value to kidnappers and temporarily solved their publicity and security nightmares."

Tony told Avery the rest of the story. "I knew people who could protect us in Italy so I chartered a plane to fly us out of Iraq. The Iraqis lost interest when they could not question us and believed we could not embarrass them."

"So where did the story that Tulip told me about how you were injured come from?"

"I was in a coma for nearly two months because of the swelling in my head. I woke up to discover the State Department told my family I died in a botched carjacking somewhere in Africa. Tony began using the Italian cover identity the Iraqi's gave him to do their dirty work. Tulip showed up at the hospital and Tony told her he was a friend I'd made on one of my vacations. She believed him because I spent all of my vacation time in Europe. My last visit to New

Orleans was Tulip's graduation from Tulane in 2000."

"I assume Tony's background is why you try to keep the two of them apart." Avery has daughters of his own. I nodded. Tony tried to ignore us.

"Did I miss the part where you said how you came up the money to open the restaurant?" It was a roundabout way of asking if we had the missing money.

"The attacks against your troops dropped off after the colonel disappeared. Your State Department had a bounty for information about the attacks on Americans. They paid me well for the help I gave to Cooter, and they gave me permission to come to America with him," Tony gave Avery the story the State Department would verify if asked.

"The State Department accepted the Italian identity I was using when they issued my visa and identity card because they would rather explain an Italian chef getting a visa than admit they let a killer for the Iraqis move here." I explained. This was less verifiable, but it was entirely true.

"How likely is any of this to become public if the FBI keeps pressing?" Avery finally returned to the concern that brought him here.

"None at all. Homeland Security will never open my files to anyone. They barely want to admit the intelligence agencies ever knew me. There's every reason to believe that the investigation has hit its stone wall. The question now is whether you can keep our secret."

"Who do I know that would want to hear this? What I am going to do is to go home and finish getting drunk. Then I can wake up thinking of tonight as a bad dream."

Avery sighed and stood up before adjusting his tie and jacket. He didn't say goodbye or look at either of us before he stepped into the empty elevator.

"I hope your friend can keep his promise." Tony said and looked me in the eye. I understood the veiled threat that came with my partner's concern, but chose to shrug rather than choose between him and Avery for who lived or died.

Avery brought fresh bad news with him when he came for breakfast the next day. He greeted the chef as though the previous evening never happened and displayed no signs that anything had changed in his relationship with Tony, but the three of us knew everything was changed forever. Chef Tony and Miss J, the cantankerous Black woman who taught Tony how to cook for the locals, served us plates of scrambled eggs nested atop smoked pork shoulder and baked cheese grits topped with a Tabasco-infused hollandaise sauce. Tony contributed a basket of fresh beignets and buttermilk biscuits, most of which came to rest at the bottom of Avery's pit of a stomach.

"The FBI isn't dropping the background check on you. Their SAC personally requested your file from the State Patrol this morning, including your fingerprint records. They are looking for anything they can use to discredit you if you blow their UC operation. It's not like there aren't things to find, as I found out last night."

"I thought Gabb said they were told to stand down."

"Yes, but Mike Conroy isn't a great listener."

Avery was not immediately reassured by my grin. "I can do more than embarrass them. I can make a provable case that the FBI's informant withheld information about felonies he was directly involved in and can make a circumstantial case that he was involved in Biggie's murder."

"That should give them something else to worry about than you two. Someday these guys will learn not to play in my backyard without permission."

"Do you mind if I have a little chat with Agent Gabb?"

"Of course I do, but I checked and he will be at Brother Martin tonight since his nephew is playing ball against John Curtis. The family supposedly goes to Brocato's for ice cream right after the game." This was Avery's way of suggesting I not storm the FBI offices.

"I'll let you know how it goes."

"I'll just stare at the horizon and wait for the fireworks."

AVERY'S INFORMATION WAS ACCURATE, but the only description I had for Agent Jim Gabb was Avery's saying that he was "a short man with a big swagger and a face you just want to punch." The posture of a career FBI Agent gave him away as well. He was also paying as much attention to what was going on around him as he was to the lackluster performance of his nephew at wide receiver. I tactfully decided my opening statement shouldn't be that someone was going to be paying full price to send the kid to college.

I arrived in time for the second half and immediately decided the bleachers were a bad place for a meeting that was certain to get heated. I took a chance on the veracity of Avery's information about the family's ritual. I have always been amazed at how many people's personal details my boss keeps stored away.

"Your nephew's got good speed." I used the lie to break the ice as the family passed me in the gravel parking lot next to the ice cream parlor. The proud father smiled as he turned to the sound of my voice but Gabb froze when he recognized me.

"Why are you here?" Agent Gabb glanced around to be sure I was alone. My being alone unnerved him even more. He placed himself between his family and me. "You need to leave here right now and come see me in my office Monday morning."

"You don't want me in your office."

Gabb moved towards me. "The truth is, I have no idea who you even are. I ran a background check on you and my boss received a call saying that there is a Homeland Security block on your files and to drop the matter. All we found out is that you graduated from a military prep-school, have a degree in economics from LSU, and were a repeatedly decorated Green Beret. Then there is a big gap before you joined the State Patrol. That probably means you went to work for the CIA or some other intelligence outfit. As it turns out, we have agents in our office who worked in Iraq and remember your name. They told me that you were at the center of a pretty intense diplomatic incident in Iraq, in which you were wounded and an important Iraqi went missing. I can't find out anything else about that, but now here you are, a State Trooper in business with a foreign national the State Department will only tell us is here legally. So, yeah, I have been trying to figure out what to make of you. I don't suppose you'd care to elaborate?"

"Let me put it to you this way. Do you like sausage, yes or no?"

"Yes." Gabb played along because he expected me to get back to the topic.

"Would you care to see it made?"

Gabb understood my point and shook his head.

"Well, that was the sort of black-ops work I was doing in those years you can't find."

"How did you even wind up in New Orleans?" the Agent misunderstood my presence in this parking lot if he thought I wanted a long polite conversation. "I doubt your father's disappearance was enough of a reason. You hadn't lived here for years so I don't believe homesickness brought you back."

"You have no idea what it really means to miss New Orleans. And what I came to discuss with you would not be good to have on anyone's official record."

Agent Gabb's stance shifted to one he thought offered more protection. I was mildly amused by his efforts because I'd already figured out three ways I could kill him. He waved his brother's family ahead. His sister-in-law's face showed her own terror as she shooed the children ahead of her.

"What would that be?"

"Let's start with your informant calling himself Bumper Jackson."

"You can understand when I say that is a classified operation."

"Well, your guy is going way off the rails. I can link him to a blackmail scheme and intend to prove he helped with

Biggie's murder. I'll bet he drags you down with him."

There were other people coming and going in the gravel parking lot, but it wasn't very many people and none of them paid us any mind.

"Do you really think you have enough for an indictment? It's going to be your word against the FBI's. And you might have a lot of explaining of your own to do if we're pressed."

"I don't care what you think you know about me, but I won't stop until I have enough to put a needle in your informant's arm and force an early retirement for you and your boss."

Agent Gabb stared me in the eye for a moment, but he was the one who blinked.

"Damn you."

"That answers that. You already know your operation is a fiasco. All is not lost, though. Your digging probably gave you some idea about how discreet my investigations tend to be."

"Your arrangement with Chief Avery does sound unique." The FBI Agent forced a weak grin. "What are you suggesting?"

"Someone's going to have to arrest Bumper, but it doesn't have to be me." I didn't want the agent to imagine there was any resolution that did not involve Bumper's arrest. "The idea of running an undercover operation is not too bad either, especially here. Your problem now is that the subject of the investigation is dead. Biggie left the business to his son, but the boy's adoptive mother wants nothing to do with it. The FBI could buy the label from her, using new agents, and own the place. I can see to it that Biggie's death is closed as the animal attack everyone thinks it is. Arresting your informant ends the blackmail and creates a job opening for any undercover agent you put in his place."

"I'm not sure they make a rug big enough to sweep all of this under."

"The last I knew, I am the only detective looking into the possibility of this being a murder and not an accident. That is unless you want to start your own investigation."

"We'll pass, thank you. So you cover up the crimes, then what?"

"Cover up is a strong word. Think of it as reaching a

conclusion in line with the public perception of justice."

"I'm gonna write that one down!" Gabb finally felt comfortable enough to laugh at something.

"Anyway, give Bumper a plea bargain on whatever charges you want. It would be best if they didn't bring publicity to Amanda Rhodes and her son."

"So, the FBI gives a plea bargain to my informant, buys the studio from the boy's mother, puts in new agents, and we act like nothing happened? That's your plan?"

We faced each other in silence for a couple of minutes while he rolled the proposition around in his head. I already knew Avery was going to accept anything plausible that I came up with, and it would ruin the surprise if I admitted to Agent Gabb that I wasn't going to rest until he was sitting in a cell beside Bumper. He had to be aware of most, if not all, of what his man was doing. What I wanted him to take from this conversation was my promise to close his operation down. I would give Agent Gabb one last opportunity to get himself on the right side of things before that day came.

"And you can prove everything you have on my informant, right?"

"Absolutely."

"I know my boss would definitely have more confidence in your case if you could get Bumper to confess to everything you believe he did. We'll all feel crappier about the situation, but better about the strength of your case." I understood his point, but I think the real point he was trying to make was that he wasn't going to let himself be implicated by me in anything his own informant wouldn't say he had done. I doubt he thought for a second that Bumper would possibly roll over on him, which meant he had something else on Bumper than whatever was going on at the studio. That added another layer to my investigation. The agent and I had very little else to discuss, but I realized there was another matter we could talk about.

"There is a price tag, of course."

"There always seems to be." This part of our chat was what made him the most nervous.

"Drop the investigation into my background. Who has the file you started on my partner and me?"

"The formal inquiry never got off the ground. I looked

over your State Patrol and Army records and made a couple of unofficial phone calls." Gabb was anxious to downplay the background check now that he saw the size of the hornet's nest he was kicking.

"So nobody will miss your notes when you give them to me." I didn't want him to misinterpret this as a suggestion.

"Oh, these are the sort of notes people in my position find very valuable." Gabb chose to start showing a little backbone.

"They are also the sort of thing people in my position shouldn't have to worry about. You can never really anticipate how I might react if I feel cornered."

"And just how might you react if you and your partner were investigated formally?"

"Probably violently." I took one short step forward and it was enough to make him break his stance and retreat.

"Are you threatening me?" The anxious agent's gun hand was beginning to bend upwards towards his sidearm. I kept my own hands in very plain sight. I had already made up my mind about how I would incapacitate him if he went for his weapon without using my own.

"No more than I feel threatened. Your own Bureau told your office to ignore my background, so just follow orders and remember I have far more experience making sausage than you do."

Agent Gabb's brother shouted from the corner of the ice cream shop and Gabb turned cautiously to let him know he was coming. He turned back and caught me sizing up his brother. The agent started to say something more but realized the smartest thing to do right then was to shut up.

31

TULIP AND I MEET for supper at the bistro on the second Wednesday of each month, and then we alternate having supper with our mother the following Friday. This allows us to plan a few safe talking points and an escape strategy for the sibling tasked with handling a month's worth of our mother's anxieties and opinions. This month, though, our topic of discussion was the blackmail case I pulled her into. She informed me Tyshika had abandoned her threatened lawsuit.

Tony sat down to eat with us at the Chef's Table in the bistro's kitchen. It was barely after five in the afternoon and the dinner rush was still hours away. We devoured a plate of fresh anti-pasta and then Tony brought Tulip's favorite dish, braised scallops and shrimp in a sauce tasting of little more than citrus and barely melted butter. One of the new servers prepared zabaglione table-side so Tony and I could see if she was ready to do so for our paying guests. Tony opened another bottle of wine as we pushed back from the meal and began to discuss my investigation.

The first thing Tony picked up on, which I had not, was how Bumper steered me into the VIP lounge any time we spoke. This made sense the first time because neither of us wanted our conversation overheard in the crowded outer office. Closing the office door would not have diminished the staff's interest in that discussion. He had to maintain his anti-cop appearance, after all. The last time we spoke, though, he still preferred the VIP lounge to the soundproof studio. The VIP lounge was likely equipped with either electronic counter-surveillance measures or wired for sound and video, maybe both. The latter scenario meant Bumper was able to share those meetings with Gabb. I saw no indication SAC Conroy watched any of the videos if this was the case. He would have let Chief Avery know every single thing I did which violated State Police policies.

"Do you think Bumper would pat you down if you confronted him with everything you know?" The question sprang from what Tony would do under the circumstances.

"I wouldn't talk unless I knew the cop wasn't wearing any sort of wire if I was in his shoes."

"Well neither of us would talk." Tulip gave us both a curious look when we laughed at Tony's comment.

"Won't he see you bug the place if there are cameras?" Tulip found something to contribute to the conversation. I could imagine Bumper and Agent Gabb having a good laugh at videotaping me planting video or voice recorders in a room they were already monitoring.

"Someone else needs to plant the bug before I get there." I had an epiphany. "I know who we could have used, but I think that is likely a dead end now."

"Arnold and his brother?" Tony was already a step ahead of me. I assumed the brother had an open invitation to the late night bacchanals at the studio whether they had released his album or not.

"Too bad we scared them off."

"Yeah." Tony opened the contacts in his phone and dialed a number. He stood up and started to walk away with the phone pressed to one ear. "Good thing I kept the kid's phone after we ambushed him that day. Leave it to me."

"Is this when I offer my professional advice about Amanda's situation?" Tulip had joined Amanda and me on our nightly rounds a couple of times and they seemed to get along, but Tulip's view of Amanda as being a tourist was always obvious. "Agent Gabb will implicate Amanda in something if you press Bumper too hard. You need to find a way to get Bumper to implicate Gabb when he confesses to the blackmail and murder. You still need to find out if Amanda or her nanny know Tanya Lansing, too."

"Well, then, let's pay them a visit." I sighed and stood up. I politely moved Tulip's chair away from the table and looked about for Tony, but he was not to be seen. I left word with his expediter that we left to see Amanda and I would check with him after the bistro closed.

There was another thing I had been meaning to ask Tulip about. Walking to Amanda's seemed like the best, if somewhat inappropriate, time to bring up Katie Reilly.

"The prosecutor on Cisco's case was a bit of a surprise," I said as casually as I could.

"It was time you two got reacquainted. She got a divorce last year and is ready to start dating again. Ray was a drip. He couldn't get promoted to detective at NOPD so he quit and started some sort of private security firm," Tulip said and gave me grin that let me know she hoped my interest was outside of work parameters.

"Would I be wrong if I were to accuse you of having Avery make sure she was assigned to the case?"

"Oh, no. You'd be absolutely right," Tulip admitted. "I think a local boy should be dating a local girl. You can keep dragging Amanda around town but she just is never going to understand things like Chalmations or the Skank Bank."

"All the same, I can worry about my own love life."

"Deal. You worry about yours and I'll worry about my own," Tulip said before we let the subject drop. It took me a few minutes to realize she had just out-negotiated me on a matter I considered to be non-negotiable.

32

GEORGIA GREETED US AT THE ELEVATOR in a pair of jeans and T-shirt. Georgia was surprised that I had arrived without Amanda having previously informed her that I was coming, and now she seemed conflicted on whether or not to allow me any further access. She was equally thrown off by my being accompanied by a female she didn't recognize.

"Georgia, this is my sister. Tulip this is Amanda's nanny, Georgia. I know it's an odd time to just show up, Georgia, but this is official business."

"Miss Amanda is in the television room." Georgia led the way rather than inquire about what was so important.

Amanda and Parker were seated on a sectional sofa and laughing at an animated movie. Amanda started to invite us to join them but our stances indicated this was not a social visit. Georgia took a seat on the opposite side of Parker so Amanda could excuse herself and come to us.

"Got a minute?" I asked after she stepped up and gave me a peck on the cheek and said hello to Tulip. She did not try to conceal the level of concern she was feeling.

"Would either of you like a beer, or something stronger maybe? Maybe just a big hug?"

"The hug, definitely, but in a minute. We need to discuss some new evidence in the case. There are some difficult questions I need to ask. You need to answer them honestly."

Amanda pointed us towards the pool and we took seats at the table. "You know I'll try."

"Here's the thing. There's a guy in police custody who is trying to make a deal on Biggie's murder. Do you know a woman named Tanya Lansing?"

"What could she possibly have to do with this?" Amanda not only wasn't denying knowing her, she was displaying nearly equal parts anger and disbelief that Tanya Lansing, whoever she was, had anything to do with Biggie.

"The man has little reason to make up anything he can't prove. He did not say you knew anything about the murder plot. What I need is to know everything I can about Tanya Lansing, good or bad. You obviously know the woman, and that is a bad enough place to start."

Amanda clutched my arm and pulled her legs under her before she began to speak in a very hesitant manner, choosing her words as if they were footsteps in a minefield.

"Georgia's real name is Tanya Lansing," Amanda said and watched my face drain a bit of its color. "We call her Georgia because that's where she used to go when she ran away from home. She's my cousin."

"So you've known her a lot longer than rehab," I said as calmly and flatly as I could. I felt myself begin to lean away from her as she told her story. I took a breath and calmed myself down, but found I needed to express my own anger and sense of betrayal that Amanda had chosen not to be honest with me from the beginning. Mostly I hated feeling that Cisco was so much more forthcoming and truthful than Amanda.

"My whole life," Amanda shrugged and looked at me for some sort of reassurance that simply wasn't there this time. "She turned up on my doorstep right out of high school. She was going to make it big like I did. Only she didn't. She wound up dating a member of one of the gangs out there that push drugs and guns. She came to me one day and said she was scared. She saw and heard things she shouldn't have and wanted to get away. So I hid her in rehab."

Tulip and I exchanged looks of disappointment about this disclosure, but said nothing before she continued.

"John was angry about my getting sucked into it and he pushed me down some stairs. I decided to check into the same place to get away from him, and they were happy to take my money. We were there when Hurricane Katrina hit New Orleans and I came up with a plan for us to both get away. I hired Georgia as my assistant and told John I was moving here to help with the city's recovery. John had no interest in leaving Los Angeles, but he was quick to help me get moved. We donated a lot of money and did some fundraisers in Los Angeles and here, and I think he met Dan Logan at one of them. They were peas in a pod. They were both looking for any way to make a buck out of the chaos following the storm. John would find a way to get a piece of any business deal he worked on. We kept our money and business separate because of the prenuptial agreement he made me sign, and my accountants and lawyers have been trying to sort it all out ever since he died. I guess it's a huge mess, but John made a lot of money I am only too happy to spend."

"And where did Biggie come into the picture?" I asked, less to keep her talking than to let her know I was listening to her story and not simply making judgments. I was also silently kicking myself for my own bad judgment.

"Logan was Biggie's attorney and knew he wanted to start his own record label and Logan knew John had music executives as clients in Los Angeles. Record labels involve a lot of pieces, and the labels in New Orleans at the time had flooded studios and most of their musicians were still evacuated. John saw an opportunity for Biggie to take the lead before they recovered. One day Biggie came to see John and brought Parker. He was two years old and my heart just melted. Georgia and I played with him and she said it was too bad he was going to grow up and be just like his daddy. I knew what she meant and I told John how worried I was. The next thing I knew John told me Biggie and his girlfriend had agreed to let us adopt Parker. I don't want to think there was an actual trade, but I'm sure that's what it looks like."

"Is that why didn't you announce the adoption? I would think you would have wanted the good publicity of having saved a Black child from a life of crime and poverty," Tulip asked, with sarcasm that Amanda did not seem to pick up on it as much as I did.

"I wanted to. John simply said to let the ink dry on the paperwork, and I took that to mean that there were some legal problems with the way he had handled it. What little I knew of Dan Logan just made me think so all the more. I didn't want to get into a custody battle with his parents. It would have been all over the papers."

Neither Tulip nor I said a word, and I consciously caught myself before I nodded affirmatively out of reflex. I could see the corners of my sister's mouth beginning to tighten and her fingers curling into tiny fists, but she held her silence. Her legal practice was built on fighting the sort of attorney John seems to have been, and Logan still is. Amanda wasn't improving her image with Tulip in the least when she said her primary concern about the custody fight was the possibility of bad publicity.

"John never liked that Parker got more of my attention than he did. We fought more. I should say he wanted to fight more, but Georgia kept facing him down and we were living apart by the time he died. A week before he died he came to New Orleans and we had dinner. John said he missed me, but he spent most of his time while he was here talking to Biggie about the way money was pouring through the studio accounts. The last night he was here we got into a shouting match and he tried to hit me. Georgia pushed him and John told me to fire Georgia or he would, but he couldn't and I refused. He stormed off and then a few days later he was dead. We never got to make up from the last fight."

"Do you think Georgia had anything to do with John's death?" Tulip spoke up. I was glad she was the one to ask the obvious, but awkward, question.

"I don't see how she could have been. She was here the whole time."

"Fine," I said and shifted the conversation to the next matter involving her cousin. "Tell us about the blackmail payments you have been making."

"Like I told you," Amanda began and reached out to take my hand. Hers was hot and sweaty but mine likely felt almost clammy to her. "Georgia came to me right after John died and said Biggie's bodyguard told her that Biggie would go to the press about the adoption unless I started paying him to keep quiet. He only wanted ten thousand dollars a month and that isn't a lot of money to me, and I know that sounds stupid, so I went along with it. I gave her an envelope full of cash at the first of every month and she gave it to the bodyguard to give to Biggie."

"And then Biggie died," I said as a way of marking the point at which my sister and I entered this circus.

"Right. Then she said the bodyguard said we had to pay him just like I paid Biggie. So I have been, but I don't trust him to keep quiet like I did Biggie."

"Any ideas, counselor?" I turned towards my sister. She had been unusually quiet, even for herself, throughout this entire conversation. I knew her well enough to know she sifted for anything she could use to her client's advantage.

"A couple of them actually," Tulip moved to sit beside Amanda. "I will go over some options with Amanda while you interview Georgia. She may hold the key to how to turn the tables on Bumper."

"I guess you'll need to take care of Parker while we do this." I held Amanda's hand as we walked through the house. She scooped her son up and returned to the deck.

I sat down on the sofa facing Georgia and turned off the television set. She shifted uncomfortably in her seat and waited for whatever was about to happen. She struck me as being one of those people who reacts quickly to the world around her, but does little to keep things from happening in the first place. She likely found her way out of her messes by following the path of least resistance. No doubt she sensed things were about to change again.

"You need to tell me everything, from the beginning." This was all I said to her. I did not want to give her the slightest clue of what I already knew. I was hoping she had never confided to Amanda the worst things she had done.

"About what?" She initially tried to stall, as I expected. I said nothing. "What did Amanda tell you?"

"What matters right now is what you tell me." Georgia seemed conflicted about what to tell me as I offered no clues to what I knew about anything. Right then I didn't really trust what I thought I knew. "Let me be clear. I did not come here planning to arrest you. I just need you to help me to connect some dots in my investigation."

She continued to stare at me as though she was weighing her options. "Whatever I have done was to protect Amanda and Parker."

"I understand that." I truly did.

"Amanda needs someone to be strong for her. She's always had lousy taste in men, and who to trust."

"So you're her self-appointed knight in shining armor?"

Georgia shook her head. "I just want to make sure she's okay. I took care of protecting her from John when he was still around. I have kept Bumper and Biggie from hurting her and Parker."

"Let's start over. Maybe begin with your relationship with Amanda."

"Our fathers are brothers, and both of them are mean drunks. I stole one of my daddy's junk cars and drove to Hollywood the night I graduated from school. Amanda had married John by then. They met at a party she was paid to be at, you know to look pretty. She moved in with him and he produced some of her movies, but it was all low budget stuff. She got herself a real agent and started getting good roles. John started beating on her when he lost control of her, but she wouldn't leave him. I got a job dancing in a joint on Sunset and took up with guys that weren't no better than my father. I wound up dating a guy in a biker gang that was selling dope and guns and I got scared of what would happen if I tried to break up with him. Amanda checked both of us into a rehab place that let us hide out while I got clean. We decided to come out here and start over."

"And what about your relationship with Bumper?"

"I met him at Biggie's nightclub right after it got opened. John asked me to check it out because Biggie kept asking him for more and more money and John wanted to know where the money was going. Bumper recognized me and reminded Biggie I was Parker's nanny. Biggie called me a couple of weeks later and asked if I'd like to make some extra money. He reminded me that he was Parker's real dad and he told me he just wanted to see his son. He wanted to know if I would bring Parker to the studio every week or so. He said he'd pay me five hundred bucks every time I did. I figured I could use the money and Amanda wouldn't have to know."

"This was part of your watching her back?" I said. Georgia scowled and I decided to hold my sarcasm in check. "When did Amanda find out about this?"

"She's never told me she knows anything. John was at the studio and saw a picture of me with Biggie and Parker and he called me from Los Angeles just before he got killed in that car-jacking. He said he was going to tell Amanda the next time he was here. I was going to tell her about Biggie myself after John's funeral and all, but Bumper told me

Biggie and him was going to blackmail her about the adoption. Did she tell you that?"

"Yes." This was not the response she expected. "She also said that she gave the money to you to pass on. How do we prove you weren't the one keeping the money?"

"Bumper would have hurt me bad if I didn't give him the money," she protested. I couldn't tell if she misunderstood my implication or if she thought I underestimated the huge bodyguard's strength and temper.

"What did Bumper do with the money?" I knew I was hoping for too much to think she may be able to put money in Gabb's hands. "Did Biggie ever mention the payoffs to you when you took Parker to see him, or was Bumper the only one telling you the money went to Biggie?"

"I don't know what Biggie knew about that money. He never brought it up and he just kept paying me to bring Parker by. So, you know, I did that. I'm really sorry about it, and I know Amanda will fire me for doing this when she finds out now."

"Probably. But I don't see why I need to be the one to tell her about it." Getting behind this woman's ingrained defenses was not unlike trying to pet a tiger with a steak in your other hand. "Tell me about the storage locker full of guns."

"Which storage locker?" Georgia immediately blurted. The choice of words suggested Biggie might have multiple arsenals stashed around the city.

"Are you the woman Bumper hired to rent a locker to store Biggie's guns in? You used a fake ID, and I assume you were driving a car he gave you, right?" I was fishing on a lot of this. Georgia nodded her head at these fresh accusations, but she was also carefully choosing her words.

"Bumper is the one who gave me the car to drive, and the ID I used. All he said was they needed a place to store something Biggie was collecting. I just did it as a favor for Biggie, not for Bumper."

"Where did he get the fake ID?'

"I don't know," she assured me. "He took my picture and the next day he gave me the driver's license. I had to give it back to him when I brought the car back."

"When did you find out what Biggie was storing?"

"Biggie told me a long time after I done this. He said he was collecting guns from the boys he signed to work for him and was going to turn them into the police when they did a buy-back thing. He just wanted to get some good publicity."

"And what became of the guns? They seem to have disappeared."

"I don't know." Her eyes closed when she told this lie.

The missing guns were becoming important for no useful reason I could see, except to know a fuller picture. The only two people who knew where they were stored were both denying any knowledge of their fate. Bumper was a proven liar. Even so, I still believed his denial more than I did Georgia's.

"Yes, you do. The guns are gone and there's not much I can do about them. I just have to know where they went."

Georgia stared at me for a long moment before she spoke. "I traded them to my ex-boyfriend in L. A."

"I thought the whole idea of moving here was to get away from him."

"It was, but he tracked me down. He'd call and threaten me about what would happen if I ever told anybody about what he did when we was together."

"I need to read you your rights before you go on, okay?" I said and hastily read them off to her. She listened to my recitation and took a deep breath before acknowledging she was in very deep trouble. "What did you get in exchange for the guns?'

"I told him John was trying to get me fired and he said he'd take care of that if I gave him the guns I told him Bumper had me hide for Biggie. I only told him about the guns so he would know I knew some people here that would make trouble for him if he came after me." This part of her story sounded like something she would do.

"What did you think he meant when he said he would take care of John? Is your old boyfriend a real persuasive talker?"

"I knew what he meant," Georgia said and tears began to flow. She understood she had confessed to doing a very bad thing to a detective who didn't like her very much.

Bumper had to realize that Georgia was responsible for the disappearance of Biggie's guns. Maybe he made the connection between the timing of the disappearance of the guns and John's death. He might be intending to use Georgia's role in hiding Biggie's guns and having John murdered to leverage Amanda into not pressing charges if his blackmail scheme was exposed. Bumper may have given me the list of guns as a way to let me know he had something on Amanda's nanny and could start a nasty tabloid feeding frenzy anytime he wanted.

That situation was bad, but the worst parts of it happened in a different jurisdiction. Now, though, it was time to confront her about what she knew of Cisco and Biggie's death. "I need to know what you know about the dog that killed Biggie."

"I didn't know it would be so messy. It wasn't what I wanted to happen at all," she sighed, close to tears. I was surprised enough that I just waited for her to start again. I made the dog statement only because of Cisco's contention that using a dog to scare Bumper was her idea. Georgia was full of bad news, and it was all going to come pouring out now because I had pulled the plug without realizing it.

"So you knew about the dog attack?" I sat back in my seat and braced myself for my theories about Bumper's being responsible to collapse. Georgia finally broke the silence that she had kept.

"I met Cisco at the club one night when he came in with Jerry. They were hanging with Tyshika. That's when I found out her cousin worked at the dog place. Anyway, Cisco and me hooked up. I went to his place and saw his dogs. I knew he was using them to fight. I told him about Bumper taking money from Amanda. I told Cisco I knew how we could kill Bumper with one of his dogs if we could get the dog close enough to him to kill him. I told Bumper it would make Biggie look badder if he had a big attack dog. He thought so, too, and started working on Biggie to get one. Biggie didn't want one because he was afraid of dogs, but Tyshika said her cousin was a dog trainer and could train one any way Biggie wanted. She had nothing to do with any of what Cisco and me had planned." Georgia seemed either unaware or unconcerned that her explanation for how Biggie decided to buy a dog was a confession to first-degree murder.

I understood why Cisco distanced himself from the plan

when I interrogated him. It occurred to me that, in a rare moment of clarity, he realized he was not in a healthy partnership after he got to know Georgia. I knew what she was telling me was as close to the truth as I was going to get from either of them. I also knew Georgia's version would change the instant the attorney Amanda would hire for her learned Cisco was trying to trade her in for a get-out-of-jail-free card.

"Tell me about the actual dog attack."

"Cisco said he had a way to make a dog go crazy. It was some crazy-assed dog whistle that only dogs can hear. All you had to do was blow it near the dog. Bumper cornered me at the studio a couple of weeks before Biggie got killed and said he knew all about my plan with Cisco. I swore we didn't plan to ever do nothing with the idea, but he said he was a cop and could arrest us just for thinking about it. He said he'd leave us alone if I helped him use the dog on Biggie instead of him. I didn't want to, but he had what Cisco and me talked about in that VIP room on some kind of tape. I agreed to help him, but I never told Cisco I changed the plan."

"Why not?"

"I was going to find some way to get the dog to kill Bumper and Biggie both. Then everybody would be rid of what they was doing. Bumper talked Biggie into having his birthday party at the Hard Rock Café and told me what day they would pick up that dog. I called Cisco and told him when to switch the dogs and then I blew on the whistle out on the balcony when Bumper went back to the car and gave me the signal. He was going to wave his hand just before he closed the door."

"And you never told Cisco that it was Bumper who was planning to use the dog to kill Biggie?"

"No. I thought he might chicken out if he knew there was that videotape. Bumper wanted Cisco to change the dogs before Tyshika picked up Biggie's dog. Cisco had a dog that would go nuts when it heard the whistle and he dyed it blue to hide the switch."

"It certainly did go nuts. You blew the dog whistle out on your balcony when Bumper wanted the dog to attack. Is that right?" I hated to ask the question because I truly did not want to hear another affirmative response. I also had a quick, random thought about how hard it is to find good help. A nanny willing to kill to protect you and your child is priceless.

She simply nodded. "He said to blow the whistle when he closed the door. I tried to get it to attack him, too, so I blew the whistle while he had the door open, but he got away."

"Why didn't you just call the cops about Amanda being blackmailed?"

"Bumper said he could make it look like I was doing the blackmail because I was the only one Amanda ever gave the money to. He showed me a badge and said he'd have me killed in jail if I ever said anything."

"Bumper told you he is a cop?" Arresting the arrogant son-of-a-bitch for impersonating a police officer was going to be nearly as satisfying as the murder charge.

"He told me he is an undercover cop. Is he lying?" I'm not sure why she thought I would know this much about Bumper's role in things. "Am I under arrest?"

"Let's say that you are just under house arrest for now," I made this up to maintain the appearance of knowing what the hell I was doing. Doing nothing would only confuse everybody. "Do not discuss any of this with anyone, especially Amanda or Bumper. I will see what I can work out in exchange for your testimony before I talk to you again. I am serious, Georgia, do not speak to anybody."

"Yes, sir." She had begun nervously rocking back and forth and now she began to cry.

I stood up and joined Amanda and Tulip on the deck. I said nothing of what Georgia and I had discussed, but my face must have betrayed the unpleasant nature of our conversation. My concern now was to distance Amanda not only from the press but from her homicidal cousin.

"What did you two come up with?" I asked my sister.

"Amanda asked Bumper to meet her at my office tomorrow morning," Tulip informed me. "I am going to draw up a contract between them which guarantees Bumper a job at the studio. I am inserting a clause that will make any future blackmail payoffs look like monthly bonuses."

"And how is that going to help anything?" I wondered.

"Because that clause will follow a million dollar golden parachute clause. The bonus clause will contain a legalese confession to taking blackmail payoffs prior to the agreement," Tulip explained and flashed the grin I always associate with her smelling blood in the water. "I am sure Bumper will focus on that million dollar payday and ignore the way the clause is worded, or the fact that signing it with anything but his real name means the contract cannot be enforced, but it still serves as a valid confession."

"I like your sister," Amanda was finally smiling. "I wish I could have hired her sooner and watched her cut John's balls off."

"I'll keep this in mind about both of you." I laughed. It hid the fact that I was already looking for flaws in their plan.

There were two immediate problems with Tulip's grand design. The first was that she needed ten thousand dollars in cash to pay a signing bonus tied to the clause implicating Bumper in the previous payoffs. This wasn't a problem because Tony kept more than that in the bistro's safe at any given moment. I would be up the rest of the night scanning the money to be able to trace the serial numbers of any cash Bumper spent.

The second issue was finding a place to hide Amanda, Georgia, and Parker until I arrested Bumper. I was on thin ice ethically just knowing Tulip's intended to harbor a capital-murder suspect, so I had to make a point of leaving while Tulip arranged for their disappearance. I didn't need to stick around to know that Tulip was almost certain to call our mother and ask if she could play hostess to a famous Hollywood actress for a few days. It would kill two birds with one big rock. The first was to hide Amanda and Georgia in case Agent Gabb figured out what she was up to and tried to pre-emptively arrest either of Tulip's new clients. The second, and very Tulip-like, reason was that doing so would distract our mother enough to spare Tulip from the monthly dinner she faced otherwise.

33

TULIP'S MEETING WITH BUMPER the next morning went more as she expected it to go than Bumper could have ever anticipated. The meeting took place in Tulip's office on Magazine Street. Her modest office is on the second floor of a two-story brick building near Jackson Avenue. Two other attorneys have offices on the lower floor and the three of them share a pair of paralegals and a legal secretary but are not formal partners. Tulip's office has a balcony, and that's where she stood to watch Bumper park his Lincoln Town Car. She noted he scanned the block before crossing the street and entering her building. He didn't spot me sitting in Tulip's Porsche Cayenne two blocks away, ready to pick him up if he headed downtown when he left. Tony positioned his Audi coupe at a Shell station on Jackson Avenue to follow Bumper if he left and headed towards the river or the lakefront.

Amanda's explanation to Bumper the night before was that she wanted to make their "arrangement" formal and secure for both parties. She claimed her accountants wanted her to pay the ten thousand dollars each month as a performance bonus rather than as a payoff for tax purposes and he was quick to agree to the arrangement.

Tulip waited until Bumper was on his way to her office and she was behind her desk to call me on her cell phone so I could listen to their conversation. She also turned on the digital voice recorder taped under her desk. I would have had to tell Avery too many things I wanted to hide to get a court's permission to monitor or record the meeting, but my sister could file a criminal complaint about the blackmail on Amanda's behalf and play the tape recording in court.

Tulip kept Amanda calm while they waited for Bumper

to step into the office. She encouraged Amanda to imagine she was playing another role in a movie. Bumper came in and took a seat without greeting either woman. Tulip did not offer him anything to drink out of spite for his manners.

Tulip had Amanda explain to Bumper that she wanted to create a long-term contract between them to be sure their "special arrangement" was secure once Logan filed Biggie's will and she was in a position to take control of the studio. Tulip confided that another part of Amanda's motivation was her concern that she would have to continue leading me on so I would be her protector and that having to live in New Orleans full time made it hard to earn a living. Amanda feared Bumper would expose the adoption if she left town and he thought she might stop paying him.

Bumper was quick to assure Amanda that her fears were justified. I lost track of what Tulip was saying for a moment while I pondered whether my sister was using this opportunity to put words in Amanda's mouth about our relationship. I knew Amanda was aware that I was listening to every word.

Tulip set the eight-page contract in front of Bumper and pointed out the clause guaranteeing him the generous golden parachute if he left the studio for any reason before Parker's eighteenth birthday and did not disclose his own knowledge of the adoption. This was the bright shiny thing she and Amanda were hoping he would focus on.

Tulip's tone and the dollar signs dancing in his head relaxed Bumper enough that he did not see the trap when Tulip casually asked him when Georgia began bringing him the payoffs. He told the women about John's death and the conversation he had with Biggie about the adoption which led to the payments in the first place. Biggie didn't need to blackmail Amanda to keep the studio afloat because John's accountants were willing to keep pumping money into the studio. Bumper's explanation was an admission that he was the only one blackmailing Amanda.

Tulip was being very careful not to act like blackmailing Amanda was a serious crime and risk making Bumper think twice about talking to them. Tulip was equally careful not to imply there was any assurance of either woman's confidentiality for what he told them. She gradually led him through the contract to reach the clause assuring him of a large annual salary plus the monthly bonus of ten thousand dollars. The bonus clause was phrased to make it clear he had been receiving this same amount of money for maintaining the confidentiality of the adoption before this contract was signed. He perked up at this for an instant, but Tulip waved off the concern and said it was just Amanda's accountants' way of accounting for the money that went towards the previous payments. She convinced Bumper it was always easier to justify continuing a payment than explaining why a new one was initiated when writing contracts.

Tulip eased a pen towards Bumper and asked him to sign it if he had no other questions and set the banded money for his payoff on her desk. Bumper glanced at the thick stack of bills and then at the contract. Amanda said she instructed Tulip to make the first monthly bonus payment once the contract was signed. Bumper immediately signed on the dotted line. Amanda signed the contract and Tulip passed the money to Bumper before he left the office with his own copy of the signed contract. I could almost hear Tulip's mental laughter at what she imagined Gabb's reaction would be when he read the payoff clause.

Bumper came out of the building, got into his car, and immediately dialed a number before he pulled away from the curb. Bumper turned his car around and turned right at Jackson Avenue and then turned to the right again. He headed towards downtown under the live oak canopy on Prytania Street. Tony fell in behind him and called me to give me Bumper's location. I intercepted the pair under the overpass on Camp Street, and fell in line behind Tony. We left a block between us while Tony kept an eye on the big man's rear view mirrors. Bumper seemed unconcerned with being followed. I was hopeful that he was headed to meet Agent Gabb, but worried that he may have done so before the meeting with Tulip. I was fairly certain that had not happened. Gabb would have sensed Tulip was a laying some sort of legal trap because of our family relationship and her reputation in civil litigation. That reputation was earned fighting insurance companies after the storm. All of them now beg for arbitration rather than face her in court.

I closed the distance on our quarry as our game of cat and mouse approached the Central Business District's dense traffic. Bumper turned left on Poydras, which has two lanes running in either direction between the river and the Superdome. Tony and I each took a position in one of the lanes behind Bumper to be able to follow him if he were to turn abruptly. When he did turn, it was a gentle right onto Baronne headed towards Canal Street. He pulled into a parking garage, which Tony followed him into, while I drove past and parked on the street. Tony lost his phone signal in the garage but called me back as he exited the garage on foot and said Bumper was walking towards Carondolet. I suspected I knew his destination. I was not only correct, but I was able to use my camera to record Bumper and Agent Gabb walking into The Security Center together.

I was impressed either of them thought to stash their ill-gotten gains there. Tony's money was probably headed to a safety deposit box in the massive vault. It would require knowing the precise number of the pair's box to get a search warrant in order to prove Bumper took the illicit payoff.

We positioned ourselves as unobtrusively as possible outside the building and waited until I could take their picture together. It was going to make my day, and Avery's year, if I could prove that somewhere inside the building was a lockbox containing at least one blackmail payoff with the full knowledge of an FBI agent.

CHIEF AVERY ARRANGED A MEETING with Katie Reilly and FBI Special-Agent-in-Charge Conroy at the bistro later that afternoon so I could present my evidence against Agent Gabb and Eric Jackson. I had absolutely no intention of sharing anything about what I knew of Georgia's involvement in the disappearance of Biggie's gun collection or the murder of at least two men.

I did tell Avery and Katie that my sister moved the women and the young boy to a safe location and listened contritely to Avery's dissertation about the legal problems caused by placing the pair in the care of my sister. Avery was also upset I used my own money to trick Bumper into leading me to his cash stash, but then admitted he would never have authorized police funds for the purpose. Katie was only upset that Tulip placed herself in physical danger by shielding the women and child. Conroy didn't believe any of this posed problems for his own agency and quietly enjoyed listening while the other two ripped into me.

Avery started the meeting by sharing everything we knew about Eric Jackson's time as a lawman. He was fired in Oklahoma for using excessive force and then resigned from NOPD rather than face charges of felony theft. Eric was caught with Rolex watches he stole from a jewelry store in Canal Place while he was on foot patrol following Katrina. Katie's opinion was that all any of the incidents showed was that Eric was a bad apple anywhere he went.

Conroy shared the results of an investigation into the personal bank accounts of both Bumper and Gabb by his agency's own forensic auditors, as well as both Amanda and Georgia, and he seemed rather smug that there was no indication either man was receiving any of the cash Amanda was withdrawing from her account each week. There was, luckily, also no evidence that Georgia was the one stashing the cash away, either. Conroy claimed there was no mention of any blackmail being committed by anyone at all in any of the reports Gabb filed, nor mention of an informant handling payments of any sort for Biggie. He declared he was convinced the blackmail story was a lie. He was certain that his agent was involved in nothing illegal, but then covered himself by stating Agent Gabb probably wouldn't have any knowledge of any illegal activities Bumper did on his own.

Conroy's grin collapsed when I showed him the contract, with the clause which served as Bumper's confession to blackmail highlighted. I followed this with the audio tapes from my sister's office and the one I made of my own conversation with Agent Gabb on Friday evening. I then showed everyone the videotape and photographs I took of Bumper and Agent Gabb outside of The Security Center. My male companions believed I had a good case. Katie insisted on playing the devil's advocate role and argued that the contract certainly indicated bad deeds in the past, and a willingness to be bought in the future, but she wasn't confident a grand jury would see what our trained eyes perceived. The audio tapes were inadmissible and the videotape was too inconclusive about what transpired. Georgia's testimony about Bumper blackmailing Amanda and Amanda's about making the payments still might not be enough to get a grand jury to issue an indictment.

The last piece of evidence I shared with the group was a PowerPoint presentation of the surveillance video from the parking lot at the Hard Rock Café. I had to use photographs because what I wanted to show them had eluded me the first two dozen times I watched the video. I began by playing the video at normal speed and then as slow as possible.

Bumper claimed he returned to the Land Rover and spoke only briefly with Biggie Charles before his boss sent him back inside with Tyshika. That is exactly what the video showed if that is all you knew to look for. The camera angle was such that the view into the back seat was partially blocked by the open door. There was a narrow gap between the vehicle and the door that gave a view which included both men and a corner of the kennel in the cargo area.

Bumper could be seen speaking with Biggie, who was unmistakably the guy sitting in the tight confines of the passenger compartment. Biggie appeared to be more surprised by the door opening than angry about Bumper opening it. Bumper's written statement made it sound as though Biggie waved him away in reaction to the intrusion. Bumper's body blocked the limited view as he leaned in to say something to Biggie before he slammed the door and walked away. The first spray of arterial blood crossed the vehicle windshield before Bumper was four steps from the vehicle. The image was digital, but still not of a great quality and taken from a distance of nearly thirty yards away. Even so, the surprise on Biggie's face and his blood were clear.

The presentation repeated the video frame by frame. It matched Bumper's story and what our eyes told us until Bumper abruptly moved away from Biggie and closed the door on the Land Rover. Reduced to individual images, we now saw Biggie was sitting bolt upright, with a look of intense pain on his face, just before Bumper slammed the door shut. It was an expression of someone in physical distress, not someone making an emotional outburst. He was definitely screaming something at Bumper as the bodyguard waved one hand above the door and slammed it shut. Bumper's right hand slipped very briefly into his pocket as he began walking back to the restaurant.

"What are we supposed to see?" Katie was the first to admit she missed what I did not see my first twenty times either. I handed each of them a set of photographs and led them through what I had finally seen again.

"Bumper was obviously with Biggie just moments before the dog took him apart. We know a dog whistle was used to make the dog attack. That may be what Bumper put in his pocket," I knew that was a lie. Georgia had already admitted to blowing the fatal dog whistle on her balcony. It was more likely that Bumper stabbed Biggie to make him bleed before the dog attacked him. The dog's teeth would have destroyed any sign of a small incision on Biggie's neck or crotch. "Bumper was the assassin. He just used the dog instead of a gun."

"Both of your people are dirty." Avery now weighed in

and I was not all that surprised when both Conroy and Katie agreed. The evidence was fairly damning, but it implicated only two bad apples under Conroy's command. He might be able to clean his shop without losing his job. Katie said she would have little trouble getting indictments in a city reeling from fresh accusations of police abuses in the wake of Hurricane Katrina. Everyone gathered at the table had no issue with offering Agent Gabb up to quiet the angry mobs.

"But, they're also innocent until proven guilty," Katie pointedly reminded us.

Avery threw his copies of the photos on the table and turned to me. "I guess that's where you come in. Nobody wants to open a criminal investigation based on what you have. The publicity of the investigation and a protracted trial are nothing this city needs right now. You need to bring us a case strong enough to force plea bargains."

"I can do that," I assured the skeptical trio. "With some help."

I CALLED ATF AGENT NED DAVIS to see if he still wanted to know what became of Biggie's locker full of guns. I offered to give him Bumper's list with the serial numbers of the missing weapons and a witness who could explain what became of them if he agreed not to charge her. Davis said he would take the offer to his boss and let me know. I had my answer within an hour.

SAC Conroy and Katie agreed to meet me for breakfast on Saturday morning before I staged my final interview with Bumper. Katie arrived ahead of the FBI agent and she briefed me on a list of subjects I needed to address with Bumper and the answers it would be best to hear from his own mouth. Confessions are always easier to sell to a grand jury than evidence. SAC Conroy arrived and drank coffee while Katie nibbled at a croissant. Conroy's wish list was shorter and sounded like nothing much more than damage control. Conroy needed for me to have Bumper clearly state that the FBI itself did not authorize anything illegal that Bumper and Gabb did during their undercover operation. Conroy also assured me that his surveillance and tactical teams were already in place, and the listening device I had arranged to plant in the VIP lounge was working.

I arrived at BC Studios just after nine o'clock. I was surprised by the number of cars in the parking lot. I also followed Logan's earlier example and parked well away from the door. The receptionist directed me to the soundstage when I asked to speak with Bumper.

It looked as though a party from the night before was just beginning to wind down in the vast area BC Studios used for its fake 'live' performances. Members of one of the bands still under contract to Biggie were on stage packing up their instruments. Attractive women milled about the room in their best club dresses and highest heels. Their hair, makeup, and fingernails were all a hot mess. The dress shirts on the male guests all seemed to be untucked and their ties were either loosened or jammed in a pocket. Everyone had the unfocused stare that comes from excessive imbibing and over-indulgence. Low tabletops in front of the sectional sofas alongside the dance floor were cluttered with empty imported beer and champagne bottles. Styrofoam boxes of partially eaten take-out food marked the spot wherever people took their last bite.

I found the newly appointed studio executive sprawled on one of the sectional sofas by the dance floor. There was a leggy blonde leaned against his shoulder, dead asleep. I took this as a sign that he wasn't expecting my visit.

"Can we talk privately?" I asked. I remained standing, which cued him to disengage from the blonde. Bumper led me upstairs to the VIP area. I positioned myself against the metal railing and let a body-builder sized guy from the studio's security detail use his bare hands to pat me down.

"This is a first," I commented when he snatched my own cell phone but left my handgun in its holster. He silently ran a security wand over me until he was satisfied I wasn't wearing a concealed wire or a miniature video camera. Bumper ordered him to place my cell phone in the beer fridge. The heavy metal icebox would cancel any signal.

"I'd say our relationship has changed since your last visit. I get the feeling you'd like to hang something on me."

"Well, thank you for noticing my hard work."

"I told you not to come back here unless you thought you could arrest me for something. You must think you found something." His demeanor made me worry whether someone at the FBI let my plan slip and that Bumper's overconfidence meant he was toying with me. Conroy might have felt he needed to choose between protecting his agent and getting on my bad side, and chosen badly.

Then again, there wasn't much about my investigation Bumper couldn't learn on his own. Cisco Barnes' involvement in a dogfighting ring became public knowledge when the *Times-Picayune* ran its long story on dogfighting right after his arrest. He may have worried Cisco would flip on him, but the trainer still believed killing Biggie was Georgia's idea. It was likely that Dan Logan was keeping Bumper informed about my involvement with Amanda Rhodes.

Arnold's brother walked by me in search of his wallet and cell phone. I wasn't counting on him seeing either of them again but helped him rummage about the dirty table tops while Bumper watched impatiently. I spotted an iPhone beside an empty Popeye's chicken box and waved it around for all to see and claim. The young man claimed it wasn't his, so I held onto it for the moment.

"I *am* here to arrest you." I took a moment to read him his Miranda rights, which he took as a joke or a bluff on my part when I made no move to handcuff him.

He responded with a bluff of his own. "It's too early to laugh this hard. Do you really think you've got a charge I can't beat?"

"You're not going to hide behind that whatever-I-did-was-to-maintain-my-cover crap are you?" Bumper's smug smile twitched just a bit. "You just don't get it. Impersonating a cop made me go after you all the harder. I know your real name is Eric and I know the details about your departures from the state police in Oklahoma and NOPD, you naughty boy. You're still wearing Rolex watches."

"Is there anything else you think you know about me?" Bumper asked as he subconsciously placed a hand over his watch. He wasn't smirking as much now that I had his full attention. Knowing about his fake claims of still being a police officer and my having access to his personnel files seemed to genuinely surprise him. I wondered if Gabb even told him about having dinner with Avery.

"Blackmail is ugly enough, but what chance do you think a twice fired cop turned informant will have in a New Orleans courtroom? People hate us these days. Did you not realize signing that contract with Amanda was just a way to get you to sign a confession?"

"How was that a confession?" He lost his grin entirely when he realized I knew about his agreement with Amanda.

"You don't remember meeting Amanda's attorney just yesterday morning? The contract was nothing more than a signed confession to your extorting payments in exchange for remaining silent about Amanda's adoption of Parker. Tulip made an audio recording of your conversation to turn over to me as evidence. I'll bet I can even tell you the serial number on any hundred dollar bills in your wallet."

"You're full of crap. That conversation is covered by attorney-client privilege."

"That only applies to my sister's clients, and you aren't one of them. Amanda is her client and Tulip is only obligated to protect Amanda's interests."

"You'll still have to prove it in court."

"Actually, I think you might plead to blackmail rather than murdering Biggie. A lot of people keep telling me how hard you pressed Biggie to get a dog, and then the dog killed him. That is some coincidence."

"I had nothing to do with that dog killing Biggie. Nothing! Just ask the trainer."

"I did. You almost had him scared enough to set up Amanda's nanny as being the mastermind. I think his story will change once you are sitting beside him in jail. I know you killed Biggie, but I still cannot figure out why. My guess is you decided to kill him to take over the studio. Did blackmail not pay enough?" I was doing my best bullfight picador imitation, but pricking Bumper wasn't working.

"Sure, I took the money from that actress, but then I passed all of it on to the fat man because that was my job. I gave Biggie's lawyer a will I made up with Biggie's name on it so she could get all of her money back. The amount of stuff you don't know is bigger than the little bit you think you have on me."

He certainly had me there.

"You do realize forgery is a crime, right?"

"I don't think she is going to contest it. Of course, I read that contract. Can you blame me for jumping at the chance to get paid legally for what Biggie did illegally?"

"The white hat you're trying to wear would fit better if you stopped blackmailing Amanda after Biggie died, but you went right on taking it and you put the money my sister gave you into a safety deposit box. I'll bet there are a lot of other envelopes in that box. I gave the FBI photographs of you and Agent Gabb taking the money my sister handed you to The

Security Center on Carondolet. Your handler coughed up the password to your account and the Special Agent in Charge is headed there right now with a search warrant. He seems very keen to wrap this up on a slow news day." This news finally jolted him a bit. "Maybe there are other skeletons to find in that box as well."

"Interesting choice of words. Go ahead and knock yourself out. The skeletons you're looking for aren't in there."

"I'd say that Biggie's skeleton will be enough. I've got pictures of you holding something shiny in your hand, and I can prove a shiny dog whistle is what set the dog off."

"It's quite a leap from shiny thing to dog whistle."

"I broke down the video from the parking lot. You two didn't argue like you told me. You blew that whistle and the dog was on him a second or two later."

"That's your version. I'm sure I can come up with a hundred stories for what's on that one camera's footage."

"Yeah, funny you mention that as well. It turns out that where you parked happened to be the single spot in the parking lot covered by only one camera. That must have taken some scouting to figure out."

I was not at all certain about how a defense strategy based on committing criminal acts to maintain Bumper's cover would play before a grand jury or in court. He was, at best or at worst, guilty of taking payments from a fool and killing a man everyone wanted dead. I was running out of things to throw at him. I had to admit he had done a pretty good job of batting even my best pitches away. I wasn't going to tell him everything I knew, but the damning accusations and evidence already rubbed in his face hadn't rattled his cage enough to even elicit a denial. He also didn't implicate Georgia as being the whistle blower, as it were. He might be saving that as a bargaining chip down the line, along with any number of other things. His ability to stonewall me was about to start giving him the upper hand. I continued poking at him because there were probably things he could reveal about Gabb if I got him to flip on the agent.

"Let's just sit here and wait for that FBI team you keep talking about." Bumper's tone was guarded, but most of his belligerence and hostility were gone.

I wanted to push Bumper's buttons a little more before I gave the signal for the arrest team to take him away. So far, I had let him know he was facing arrest for blackmail and possibly murder, lied to him about the proceeds from blackmailing Amanda being gone while also suggesting that his FBI handler was under internal investigation, and let him know his signature on Amanda's contract was a confession to a crime he wanted me to believe could be explained away as being part of his cover. None of this resulted in anything usable. It was time to get personal.

"Fine. We can talk about other things in the meantime. Maybe we could start with why you would do so many bad things using your brother's name. Is there some sort of family issue? Did big brother not love you enough?"

"You don't know a thing about me and my brother."

"You're right. All I know is that your name is Eric and you're going to prison for crimes you committed using your brother's name. That's going to come up at the family reunion, don't you think? I'm just disappointed that you seem okay that the statement Agent Gabb gave this morning will be the official record of what happened here."

Bumper's visceral reaction seemed to be more about Gabb giving the FBI a statement than about my knowing his handler's name. I had saved Gabb's name until I could use it against Bumper as a hammer instead of a nail in closing his coffin. This little bit of success encouraged me to bait him a bit more.

"Gabb's confession will probably only go to show how little imagination you two put into hiding your lies. How many other people knew what you and Agent Gabb have really been up to? Do you believe your partner gave the same story you'll give when you're questioned?" Maybe there was something to be gained from convincing him Gabb was less of a partner and more of a co-conspirator who might well make a deal that could dump everything on Bumper. "Close your eyes for just a second and imagine being a fly on the wall at Agent Gabb's interrogation. Is he throwing you under the bus or is he a stand-up guy taking equal responsibility for what the two of you did? I bet his statement is going to be way different than yours."

This was literally true. To the best of my knowledge,

Gabb had not even been questioned. Conroy told me over breakfast that he wasn't going to approach his agent until I had Bumper in handcuffs. He planned to send Gabb to Baton Rouge on an errand to separate the pair this morning.

The bodyguard was quiet for a long moment, his jaws visibly flexing and beads of sweat formed on his face as he began wondering what might have been said in the fictional interview. He abruptly stood up and went to lean on the railing with his back to me. This was a game of Liar's Poker, and I was running low on chips. Bumper said something I couldn't hear and pounded his clenched fists on the metal rail so hard I thought it might bend. He stormed back to the sofa and sat down. I chose to stay where I was.

"Look," Bumper said and gave me what was probably his scariest look. "I'll tell you everything I know, but I'm telling you all of this only so you'll know who you're dealing with."

"What I've been dealing with is a sucker and an overly ambitious FBI agent intent on framing Biggie to save his family honor. Your whole operation is headed for the toilet. The smartest thing you can do is testify against the guy. Start with how you two really met."

I casually set the stray cell phone I'd been holding in my hands on the coffee table between us as I moved my seat closer to Bumper. I also began paying a lot more attention to where and how he moved his hands. I assumed he still carried the pocket knife he used to stab Biggie. I made the accusation that he was the one who blew the dog whistle so that theory was in the mix for anyone else listening to our conversation.

"I graduated from the police academy about six months before Hurricane Katrina. I was stationed in Algiers when the storm came and didn't know my house was underwater for another week. NOPD's mission started out as doing rescues, but it became crowd control after people started breaking into places to get food and water." Bumper started to develop the blank stare of a man allowing himself to revisit memories he has spent a long time suppressing. I have a mental walk-in closet of dark memories all my own. "Gabb worked for a private security company FEMA hired to supplement NOPD. They were that same outfit that got in trouble for shooting a bunch of civilians in Iraq. They were teamed up with NOPD's SWAT guys to do house-to-house searches out in the East. Every cop in town had a list of lowlifes we hoped had evacuated. We checked all of their last known addresses and rounded up a lot of dangerous guys to ship out before they could make any trouble."

"Gabb wasn't an FBI agent?"

"Nah, but he used the contacts he made with FBI guys here during Katrina to get hired by the FBI after everything blew over." Conroy must have forgotten to mention that.

"So, how did you get from Katrina to here?"

"I got caught with some Rolex watches and NOPD let me resign rather than charge me with the theft. Jim put a word in for me with the private security company he worked for and I got a job patrolling empty government buildings. The pay and hours were a helluva lot better than doing the same thing for NOPD. I worked for them for a year or so and then went to work for a personal protection service in California. That was where I ran into him again."

I saw no reason to question anything he was saying so far, but I needed to get him to talk about the operation Gabb cooked up in New Orleans. "What happened then?"

"The FBI assigned Jim to Los Angeles when he got out of the Academy. He was already looking for a way to move up when I met him again. Jim's brother represented Biggie at his trial and told Jim that Biggie was out of prison and running a hip-hop music studio. That put Biggie in a great position to go back to dealing drugs or guns. Jim arranged for me to meet Biggie in L. A. so I could convince him to hire me as his bodyguard. When Biggie asked me to move back here, Gabb told the FBI he had an informant next to Biggie and wanted to run an operation to bring Biggie down. They gave him the green light in no time."

"Okay, but why did you start using your brother's name?"

"In case I ran into any cops who remembered me from when I worked here."

"So you thought being called Bumper instead of Eric was some sort of disguise?" I didn't even try not to laugh. "How was Biggie financing the operation?"

"We figured he was paying the bills by dealing drugs or guns but it turned out he was getting all of his money from

John Rhodes. I really think John believed he could make money investing in Biggie's studio. John introduced his wife to Biggie and she met Parker and then began pressuring her husband about finding a way to adopt the kid. She saw right through Biggie and knew he would destroy the boy's future. John didn't want any part of the kid, but he worked it out. It ended up creating problems in their marriage. I heard he started beating her until Georgia beat him up so bad one night that he moved back to Los Angeles. That was right before he got killed in that carjacking."

My reaction to all of this told him I already knew most of what he was telling me, and I suspected telling me all of this was an attempt to bait me into telling him what I had on him. He began again.

"Biggie was no businessman. He spent money like there was no tomorrow and kept hitting the lawyer up for more and more of it. John gave him money, but he took a piece of the company as well."

"How did that sit with Biggie?"

"Well the lawyer's dead, right? It was no secret Biggie wanted John out of the picture."

"You think Biggie was behind his death?"

"Sort of."

"What does that mean?"

"Biggie started paying Georgia to bring the kid around a few months after the adoption. They got to talking and she said she knew somebody that could take care of John."

Bumper took delight in how poorly I took the news that he was aware of Georgia's part in murdering John.

"You didn't think Georgia was some sort of Girl Scout, did you? Christ, she was screwing a member of one of L.A.'s biggest gangs. Those bikers are the go-to guys for guns for the Mexican cartels and street gangs and anybody wanting to get strapped up. Georgia got hooked on coke and had her cousin hide her in rehab because the Mexicans started saying they didn't trust her. She knew they'd kill her if the bikers didn't kill her first."

"So, you think Biggie had someone whack Amanda's husband?" I knew I was on the trail of something, but with so many people covertly monitoring our conversation, I needed to find a way to keep him from implicating anyone besides himself or Gabb in all that had happened.

"I don't know for a fact what happened. Besides, Jim was pissed that I blew the one thing we did have on Biggie. He was afraid his boss was going to close us down."

"What did you mess up?"

"Biggie used to make everyone promise to go straight when he signed them and made them give up their guns. That was a big problem because felons can't touch guns. Biggie told me to rent a storage locker where we could put them that wouldn't trace back to him."

"The locker out in Harahan."

"Right," Bumper blinked before he nodded. I don't think he gave me credit for knowing much about what happened with that locker full of guns, but I was sure he didn't know nearly as much as I did. That was a good thing. "So I did and we filled it all the way up with guns. Biggie planned to turn them in when NOPD had one of its big gun buy-backs. He thought he was going to drive up with this van full of guns and be some kind of hero. Jim planned to arrest him for gun possession before he dropped them off and pack his fat ass back to Angola. He was the one who told me to use Amanda's girl to rent that storage unit. He gave me an ID to have her use, and made me give it back to him when she was done so he'd have her fingerprints on it."

"Why was that so important?"

"Jim planned to use her history with her ex-boyfriend in California to link Biggie to their crimes because we had so little to work with here. He also figured he could force her to give any testimony he wanted rather than get Amanda Rhodes involved in all of this. She didn't even know what Biggie had in the locker."

"Apparently that didn't work out the way you wanted." I wasn't about to tell him how much Georgia did know.

"Hell, no," Bumper spat out. "I went out there one day and the guns were gone. Biggie said not to worry about them. It was certainly good for him that they were gone, but Jim almost strangled me when I told him what happened. The guns were the only thing he had Biggie dead to rights on. He had to start making up excuses to keep the FBI from shutting us down while he figured out another way to justify his operation."

"What did he come up with? The guns have been gone for quite a while, right?"

"How do you know that?" Bumper stopped his story long enough to admit his surprise that I knew this much. He was obviously saving details, like names and dates, he could use to negotiate a plea deal after I slapped the cuffs on him. The details were worthless if I already knew them.

"You told me not to come back unless I could make a case against you. I did my homework. So what did Gabb decide to do next?"

"He pressed me to get more involved in the operation, and Biggie was cool with that. I started handling more of the business side and less of the bodyguard stuff he didn't need anyway. I was supposed to find out where he was getting his money and what he was spending it on. All I found out was he was lousy with money and spent it on this place as fast as he could get it from John."

"What did Gabb have to say about that?"

"Gabb told me I had to figure out a way to get Biggie out of the picture. He figured that if he had an informant actually running the studio then the FBI would have to let him keep running the operation. He was sure he could make his career out of this."

"Sounds like he lost interest in putting Biggie back in jail."

"Maybe, but Jim didn't lose any interest in getting rid of him. He wanted him dead, but I didn't want to be the guy everyone came after when Biggie died."

"Sorry that hasn't worked out for you," I flashed him a smile. "So, you borrowed Cisco's idea about the dog. Who was going to suspect anyone if a dog killed him, right?"

"Yeah," Bumper readily admitted. "If they shot the dog when it was still blue nobody would have figured this out."

"You can thank my sister for that." I goaded him.

Bumper considered his options for a moment before he spoke again.

"You know none of this matters, right? It is just my word against yours if you try to use any of it. I'm not the guy you really need to worry about. Jim is going to get out on bail, and he won't go down easily. He will think nothing of making you disappear, just like he did your old man."

Bumper knew this was going to get my attention, and it did.

"You don't get to say something like that and not explain yourself."

"Like I said, Jim's skeletons aren't in any safety deposit box. Remember I said I met Jim when we were doing house searches after Hurricane Katrina? The governor issued an order to shoot to kill looters, but NOPD wanted none of that. The private security guys and some cops that came in from other places thought it was hunting season. Jim asked me if I might be up for what he called 'zombie patrol.' He wanted to check out the addresses of his brother's clients and their friends, but he needed an NOPD officer to accompany him. We decided they must have looted any supplies they had, so they were fair game if they resisted arrest. It sort of made sense, you know? We also knew we might catch more of them at night."

"Who approved this?" I was hoping it was SAC Conroy. And Gabb was right about using the cover of night. My interdiction team in Iraq scheduled most of its raids for the middle of the night.

"Nobody, as far as I ever knew. Like I said, the cops from New Orleans thought Governor Blank Stare had lost her damn mind." I could tell from the way he said this that Gabb's idea of going out at night was the first sign Gabb had something else in mind, but Bumper still went along with him anyway. It had been a while since I'd heard the derogatory name for then-Governor Blanco as well.

"Tell me how this relates to my father."

"We had a half dozen of the guys on his list flex-cuffed in the back of a pickup truck like bags of trash. Jim told me we were going to transport them to an evacuation center, but then he drove us out to a marsh and told me to pull them out of the truck. We lined them up on their knees with the truck headlights in their face. I thought he was just going to leave them there, but he opened up with an AK-47 he took from one of their houses. I had to help him toss the bodies into the water. Some weren't even dead yet. I was screaming at Jim that someone was going to find these guys, but he kept saying alligators would clean up the mess."

"So, you came back and reported him, right?"

As an urban legend, vigilante justice satisfies our desire for stability, but as an actual police action, it has no justification whatsoever. I doubt any cop or Federal agent in town during the city's darkest hours didn't at least consider committing such acts, but that is when things like oaths, training, and an admittedly fragile sense of humanity quieted those voices in their heads. I know all too well what happens when the forces of self-described good are empowered without rules or oversight. The result is not greater security, it's just better organized mayhem.

"That man is crazy. He swore he would kill me if I ever said anything. I believed him then, and I still do. Anyway, he got really nervous when we first saw each other in Los Angeles. He offered to make me the UC if I would go on keeping my mouth shut."

"So you traded this assignment for keeping your mouth shut about shooting drug dealers and petty criminals? You still haven't said how my father fit into this."

"Jim made me go with him two more times and we probably killed at least thirty guys. Your old man figured something was up because nobody else was going out on patrol after dark. Jim offered to let him ride along on the last trip we made. I have to give your dad credit. He tried to stop Jim once we had the bangers lined up. Jim turned on him with that AK and your daddy took off running. I have never seen a man that old run that fast. Jim let him get out in the water a ways and then sprayed a good dozen rounds after him. I heard his body splash in the water. We came back and said we were ambushed and got separated."

"Did you actually see my father's body?"

"It was pitch black. I saw him fall when the muzzle flashed and I heard him hit the water. I didn't hear any more noise after that. Gabb shot the others and we drove off."

"You said you were working with some of the SWAT cops, right?" These might have been the officers who resigned or retired before relocating after the storm that I interviewed over the phone. They included Katie's father.

"A half dozen of them went out with us the next afternoon. I think they knew something bad was going on, and a couple of them asked about how your dad disappeared. Jim talked to them and they never brought it up again. They kept their distance from us after that patrol. I was assigned to the First District a couple of days later. I didn't see Jim again until Los Angeles." Gabb's intimidation tactics were a good explanation for the memory lapses the men I spoke with developed about the night my father disappeared.

"And you two thought you'd never get found out?" I didn't let on to how well they stalled my investigation into my father's disappearance. "Exactly where did you do these shootings?"

"We took them out to some swamp out by Irish Bayou, near Highway 90. I went out there again a few months later and remember passing some old brick fort at the foot of a bridge on my way back to town. I can show you where the bodies are if you get me an immunity deal."

I almost threw up but was able to quell the urge. I was stumped on how to explain this to my mother. I knew it could not be in any fashion that made her damn psychic seem, well, psychic about how close she and I were to my father all along. Irish Bayou is practically within sight of my mother's house. She lives in the shadow of an old brick fort.

"But, you know the crazy part? We *are* going to get away with it. I'll deny everything I just said unless I get a really good immunity deal. I just thought you ought to know what happened to your old man. Jim will kill us both if you try to prove any of this once he gets out on bail."

"You've really thought this through, haven't you? It's like you needed to show everyone exactly how far you could push things and get away with them. But, you've really just been hiding behind your brother's name and your boss man's skirts this whole time."

"You're the one who thought he could take on an FBI agent." Bumper grinned at me and stood up. "What were *you* thinking?"

"What I am thinking right now is that you would probably make anything up to barter your way out of the extortion and murder charges I already have you on. I am certain the evidence is going to carry a lot more weight with the prosecutor than your version of things ever will."

"Well let's not forget your girlfriend and her assistant."

"You've already admitted that Gabb had you frame

Georgia for helping Biggie with the guns. You don't have any evidence tying her to either Biggie or John's murder, and you'll have an uphill fight trying to sell the idea that Amanda Rhodes was involved in anything except paying a blackmailer, and I can prove that blackmailer is you."

"That won't keep me from dragging their names into this if it will let me skate free. I'll bet that actress doesn't want anyone looking at her boy's adoption papers. I will not go down for killing a bunch of gang bangers, and I will not be the FBI's fall guy for what Jim Gabb did to pull off taking down Biggie."

"You could have kept a lot of this from getting any messier had you reported Gabb to his own agency."

"It wasn't anything the FBI was going to busy itself with and any time I argued with Jim about the case he reminded me of my involvement in that other thing."

"Nice euphemism." I couldn't believe this oaf had just summarized killing unarmed people, including my own father, as being "that other thing."

Bumper began to laugh. "You will never be able to use any of this. I'll deny everything I just told you and I had all of the microphones and cameras turned off up here last night, so you've got nothing. Nobody's come to arrest me but you, and you still haven't done so. Why don't you just get out of here and let me get back to what I was doing when you got here? And, for what's left of your family's sake, remember to stay away from Jim and me in the future."

"Well, I would, but I don't have to." I showed him the stray cell phone I had silently toyed with as he told me the lurid details he just swore he'd never repeat. "Did you know the FBI has the technology to make one of these into a bug?"

"Yeah, it's why I took yours away." He thought about it a moment while I continued waving the phone. I tossed the phone on the table and walked over to the railing.

The big man's expression changed once his brain fully processed my implication. He reached into his pocket and came out with a short-bladed flip-knife. Bumper charged me, leaning over at the waist and leading with the blade. I took two steps forward and shifted slightly to my left before I shoved my right foot into his supposedly weak knee as he barreled past me. He was knocked off balance and dropped the knife when his forearm caught the rail as he tumbled to the floor.

I instinctively pulled my handgun and aimed at the back of his head. I barely stopped myself before I fired two rounds of ten-millimeter hollow points at the base of his skull. I have killed other adversaries lying in his position, none of whom gave me such personal reasons to kill them. The red dot from my laser sight marked where the bullets would strike when vengeance was mine.

Bumper rolled over and looked up. It placed the red dot in the middle of his forehead. We both studied my trigger finger as I deliberated what to do next. I could say I didn't pull the trigger because I saw myself in his face just then. Tulip would point out that shooting men intent on harming civilians and our troops, but not actually engaged in doing so at the moment, was little different than rounding up known criminals and killing them before they carried out further crimes. I've had that debate with myself and found a way to live with myself in the narrow space between what the Geneva Convention allowed me to do and the way the codes of conduct require me to handle a criminal suspect in New Orleans. In the end I didn't pull the trigger simply because I wanted him to face a more public punishment than taking my own revenge would inflict upon him.

The sound of hurried footsteps behind me made us both exhale.

"Got a bit more than we were looking for." Avery pressed his hand across the slide of my pistol. I looked up, still fingering the trigger. SAC Conroy and three FBI agents busied themselves with arresting their informant while Avery's NOPD officers enjoyed the show. I engaged the safety and holstered my pistol. I handed the iPhone that Arnold's brother planted si I could "find" it to Conroy but neither of us felt like shaking one another's hands just then.

"Enough anyway. Do you believe him about the Katrina killings?" I asked Avery as I retrieved my own phone.

"There's a lot of things I believe that asshole is capable of, but being a good liar isn't one of them. You finally have the answer about Ralph, now you still need to settle up with the others involved in the dog case, alright?"

"Yeah, I know." I took a deep breath and looked Avery in

the eye. "And the other matters? Does Conroy believe he knows something about Amanda's assistant being involved in her husband and Biggie's deaths and the missing guns?"

Avery had probably been giving these matters a lot of thought in the few moments since he had heard about them. He had apparently already made up his mind to let me decide how we were going to handle this mess.

"I'll follow your lead. I think we can all sleep at night without trying to solve California's crimes for them. Letting Conroy clean his own house has dividends that you and I can both cash in down the road."

I sighed again and looked at his face. He did not hold my gaze. I stood up and followed him out of the building and into the bright mid-morning sun. My car was now blocked by the marked police cruisers and FBI vehicles of the officers and agents who waited for Conroy's signal to arrest his tainted agent's informant. It seemed like a good guess that Gabb was already in custody in Baton Rouge.

Reporters from the local television stations tipped off about the gathered police cars were busy setting up their live-shots despite having no idea of what was happening. I am certain nobody was willing to be the one to tell them this was about closing down an undercover operation run by a corrupt FBI agent. Conroy most likely was hoping he could use Bumper's cover identity as a means of getting him out of here without too much fanfare. The rubber-necking neighbors expected the studio to be shut down ages ago.

Conroy was about to learn a lesson about dealing with Bumper Jackson's criminal brother: Nothing works out as you either hope or plan. I'll admit I didn't consider every unforeseen consequence of using Arnold's brother to plant the cell phone in the VIP area for me to find. It was an easy answer to a complex problem and that part of the plan had worked perfectly. What I did not account for was how Arnold might interpret the phone being planted. The brothers were intent on finding Biggie's killer and I knew they already had a grudge against Biggie's successor. I should have considered their reaction to Bumper's arrest.

"Crap." It took me longer to say the word than it did for Shooter to live up to his name. I spotted the boy slip through the cordon and immediately began to run towards the car where Bumper sat in handcuffs. Arnold had distance in his favor and was clearly on a mission.

His hand came up with a heavy revolver and he fired three rounds into Bumper at almost point blank range. Two FBI agents guarding him realized what was about to happen about the same time I had, but they chose to shoot Arnold rather than disarm the boy. They dropped the young man in his tracks before he could fire a fourth time and then scanned the crowd for any further threats. Arnold's companions chose to blend into the fascinated and horrified crowd. Arnold's brother and I locked eyes for a moment before he led the other boys I'd dealt with away.

"What the hell was that?" Avery was shouting at me when I began to pay attention to my surroundings again. I tore my eyes away from the youngster lying sprawled face-up on the parking lot in a slowly expanding pool of blood.

"His brother planted the cell phone for us last night. I guess this one thought Bumper had something to do with Biggie's death."

"What do you suppose you gave him that idea?"

"I asked him why he was following me once and he said he wanted to kill the person that murdered Biggie. I told him to forget about revenge and let me handle Biggie's murder. I never told him I thought Bumper had anything to do with it." I belatedly filled him in.

Conroy joined his agents at the scene of the shooting. He looked in our direction. Avery just shook his head as if to say we had no idea what happened. It was going to make for interesting television, and I knew that the Special Agent in Charge was as practical of a politician as he was a lawman. He would spin Bumper's death to clear up as much of Gabb's mess as he could. Not having Bumper's testimony would complicate prosecuting Jim Gabb for the heinous crimes Bumper just accused him of committing, but the flip side of that for the FBI was that now there would never be an embarrassing trial on those charges either.

The death of the only cooperative witness in my father's death meant that I would have to recover my father's body, and evidence of the mass killings, without the assistance of either NOPD or the FBI. Neither organization had anything to gain by the negative publicity that would come with any such formal investigation.

I did not know if having a corpse and funeral would provide closure for my family as it was. I personally did not feel the burden of finding an answer to my father's disappearance was lifted from my shoulders by knowing the truth. My mother takes her comfort in being able to touch my face from time to time. Tulip just likes having her big brother home from the wars. My only peace of mind was going to be in letting them know that both of the men in their lives had died defending other people, and that I was a much different human being when I rejoined the living.

I WENT BACK INSIDE and washed my face in the club's bathroom and adjusted my expression into something passably civil before I faced my next challenge, which was finding a way out of the investigation's maze. A lot of lives could be ruined for very little good reason. Amanda and Parker had the most to lose and had done the least wrong. Georgia was just as ruthless as Biggie and Bumper, but only when it came to protecting her cousin and nephew. Nobody who knew Biggie, or John for that matter, were mourning the violent death of either of the controlling brutes. Bumper's death was unfortunate only because it eliminated his damning testimony against Gabb. Gabb was certainly on his way out the door at the FBI. Avery could use helping SAC Conroy make sure the rogue agent didn't spoil his career to Avery's advantage somewhere down the road.

Avery and I discussed the case and what I proposed to do about the many loose ends. I filled him in on my early morning conversation with Ned Davis and he accepted the deal I made with the ATF before repeating his admonition about my approaching other departments and agencies without his permission. He stayed on the topic of my taking him out of the loop by asking me about Arnold, and I told him almost everything I intentionally left out of my reports. The altercation in the French Market and the showdown on the way to my mother's house no longer mattered. Avery was seriously displeased I never mentioned Arnold and his brother but understood how I missed the potential for what happened that morning. The case had clearly worn him out, and listening to Bumper's confessions about the killing of my father and the corruption of FBI Agent Gabb was far more than he bargained for when he told me to look into a simple dog attack. We were both more than ready to find out if what I came up with would actually "match public perceptions of justice" as I suggested to Agent Gabb.

I followed my boss to my mother's house in my own car, which spared us any further discussions and let us each compose ourselves for what came next. Avery parked behind my mother's Mercedes-Benz sedan and I pulled in behind Tulip's Porsche Cayenne. I looked across the narrow strait of water at Fort Pike and imagined my father's ghost was waving at me from its parapet. I did not want this to be my thought every time I came to see my mother, or for her to live out her days in the shadow of the knowledge that her husband's remains were lying unclaimed in the wetlands nearby. Most of all, I did not want my mother to be able to use the relative accuracy of her damned psychic's fortune cookie advice as a means of defending their consultations.

We entered the living room unannounced. My mother and Roger were sitting on the sofa while she read a story to Parker. Amanda, Georgia, and Tulip were working on a jigsaw puzzle in the kitchen. Taz was chained up on a long cable run just beyond the patio. Roger took our arrival as his cue and asked Parker to help him tend to Taz.

Roger wanted to adopt the dog and argued that there was an operation that could keep it from hearing the high frequencies that triggered its attacks. I anticipated only perfunctory arguments before everyone else was happy to wash their hands of the dog. Roger and my mother helped Parker walk Taz along the breakwater and kept themselves well away from the house.

Amanda gave me a hug. I introduced her to Chief Avery while squeezing her hand reassuringly.

"You look like hell. What happened?" Amanda asked and kissed my cheek.

"I got Bumper's confession on tape. So the hard part's over." We held one another for a moment before she returned to where she had been sitting.

"What happens now?" Tulip was speaking now on behalf of her clients.

"Well, Amanda's name shouldn't be coming up at all." I assured her. Tulip glanced at Avery and he silently nodded his agreement with my assessment before he explained why.

"Biggie is dead. Everyone wants to believe a dog killed him, so we can just let them go on doing so. Cisco has plead guilty to all of the charges related to the dog fighting and agreed to testify against anyone we can tie to his fights from his computer records. Agent Gabb, who was supervising the undercover operation, will face some pretty stiff internal disciplinary action from the FBI. He'll be lucky if he's only fired. He has some things to negotiate with, but hopefully not enough to avoid prison."

"What will happen to Bumper?" Georgia needed to hear that the boogeyman was not going to get her after all.

"He's dead." Avery and I said in near unison.

The three women all turned to look at me as though I were responsible. Avery hastily fielded the explanation. "A young man shot him after he was taken into custody."

"Was it that boy who was following you?"

Avery frowned at me. "I really appreciate how your girlfriend knew about him before I did."

Tulip refocused the conversation. "How much trouble are my clients in?"

"What have they told you?"

"Amanda has explained the probability of legal issues with her adoption and about the payments to Biggie, and Georgia said she knew about the plot to kill Biggie with the dog. I knew things were probably pretty bad, but that Georgia was willing to kill Amanda's extortionist is a lot to wrap my head around."

I glanced at Avery, whose only input was a slight shrug, and then I looked at my sister. She started to open her mouth, but I motioned for her to stay quiet because it would have ruined what I came to say.

I would have handed the case back to Avery the day Biggie died if I had known what I would eventually uncover: The blackmail payments, Parker's questionable adoption that could possibly lead to Logan's disbarment and a feeding frenzy for the gossip magazines at Amanda's expense, the probability that Georgia orchestrated the murder of two unpleasant men, a slew of damaged FBI careers, and the discovery of how and why my father disappeared. I looked my sister in the eye and told her I meant to balance justice with preserving the lives of people caught up in events that had spun out of control.

"First off, Chief Avery will drive Georgia to the Federal building and turn her over to the ATF," I began. The women looked at me with varying degrees of confusion, Tulip most of all. I addressed Georgia directly and explained what she needed to do. "I have a list of firearms which Biggie said was stored in the storage locker you admitted to renting. They will put you into a witness protection program if you turn the list over to the ATF and agree to testify against the people you gave them to. That should make you safe from your ex-boyfriend and from the cartel."

"But then she can't have any contact with her family," Amanda immediately objected.

"My concern is for the physical safety of everyone at this table," I said and she quieted down and accepted the apparent necessity of protecting her cousin. It certainly wasn't Georgia's safety that inspired the deal I made with Agent Davis earlier in the day. This was the surest way I knew to put distance between Georgia and her famous cousin and Parker that didn't involve a trial or prison.

Amanda was shocked, but Georgia was absolutely stunned. Georgia was the only other person in the room aware of the full range of charges for which I could have put cuffs on her slender wrists. Avery was not pleased with this deal, but he was willing to bank yet another favor for saving the ATF's dead-end case. I told Georgia to make sure she limited her story to giving the guns to her ex-boyfriend without saying what she got in exchange. Hopefully, Georgia would wait until Amanda was in the clear before she slipped up and told the ATF the guns paid for John's murder. If that blew her deal and they decided to prosecute for the murder then that would happen way across the country from my jurisdiction and Avery wouldn't have to explain a thing to his own superiors.

"So who gets charged in Biggie's murder?" Tulip was left wondering.

"My final report will show what everyone already believes, which is that Biggie died because of a dog's attack. Cisco took payment for one pit bull but delivered a different one. Katie can add fraud charges to his other charges if she needs to in order to get a good sentence. Cisco will say he had no idea the dog he swapped out would attack Biggie that way and I don't think anyone cares that it did."

"So it wasn't even the dog he bought that attacked him?" Amanda wondered aloud. She looked at me as though I might answer the question. "Why would anyone have switched dogs?"

"I assume it was because he wanted to use one he knew would attack Biggie with the proper trigger. The real Taz was a dog the kennel used for breeding, and Cisco figured to use it for that himself." Amanda gave a quick glance out the window to where her son was walking close beside the murderous dog. The other two women glanced at Avery. He held his stony silence.

"Why would you do this?" Amanda took Georgia's hand, but her question was addressed to me. There was some visible disappointment on her face that I wanted to send Georgia into virtual oblivion. "If you are going to ignore Biggie being murdered, why can't you ignore that she did something bad with a few guns? I may never see my cousin again."

"Georgia played a part in a lot of other bad things she hasn't told you about. It's far more than helping Bumper blackmail you. What I have worked out for her is better than any plea deal she would get on any criminal charges."

Georgia looked at me before she answered. "He's right. Maybe I could use this as a real fresh start."

Amanda sighed and stood up. "Well, that's just great. Now, what am I supposed to do?"

Tulip came to my defense. "Cooter has been doing what he can to keep you and your son out of the papers. This might be a good time for everyone to come clean, don't you think?"

"You mean about the adoption?"

"Exactly. You should control the story. Don't keep letting it control you."

Amanda bit her lip but nodded. We sat quietly for a few minutes, each of us with plenty to talk about but little left to say. I finally stood up and Georgia started to rise as well, but I waved for her to sit back down.

"Avery will take you to the Federal Building when you're ready. He may need my help making sense out of all this later, but everything should work out well for everyone here."

Amanda took my hand and I followed her onto the patio. We kissed. I did not bring up the hurtful comments Tulip put in her mouth while trying to entice Bumper to sign the contract. I did not want to believe her affections were just a means of using me to keep Bumper and Gabb at bay, but I instinctively knew we were at the end of our time together anyway. Still, if things had to end, I wanted to believe we parted because being together would remind Amanda of all the bad things which had happened lately and not because her affections for me never even existed. I was likely kidding myself, but I liked that I no longer thought of myself as a collection of internal and external wounds no woman would ever love. I had even begun sleeping through the night and hadn't had a nightmare in almost a month.

"I know you're just doing what you think is best, but you're costing me a damn good nanny." Amanda sighed.

"The world is full of people who would love to take care of Parker. It would be best to find one with a better sense of the people they should get involved with."

Amanda shrugged sadly and pecked my cheek. "Is this when one of us says we'll always have Paris?"

"Or it could be where you say you are grateful for everything I have done and swear you have never been so in love." I had every intention of making a joke.

"I am grateful, even though you made a mess of things." I accepted her version of what I did to avert the impending disasters swirling around her before I arrived.

"Tell me something." I had her sit beside me on one of the lounge chairs. "Did you even start to love me, or was I just a wall you could put between yourself and Bumper?"

"I wanted to love you." Amanda pressed a finger to my lips before I could say anything. She could tell that what I just heard was not what she meant. "I just can't be with someone so comfortable with violence. I know it's a part of what you do for a living, but it's also become a part of you. I adopted Parker to get him away from people like that, and I can hardly bring you into his life just because you're one of the good guys. All that space in your heart that you want me to fill is already full of other things you need to work out."

"And what about your heart?" I did wonder how she was going to fill the vacuum she had been letting others control for so long.

"My heart is fine. I just need to stop filling up the rest of my life with distractions and excuses. I probably need to be a much better judge of people, too, don't you agree?"

"You'd lead a happier life," I admitted. We had a long last kiss.

Amanda went back inside and Tulip joined me on the seat a moment later. Avery watched us with sadness on his face, but he remained seated and went back to explaining the witness protection process to Georgia.

"Bill said there is something else I should know."

I took a deep breath and sat close enough to grab her if she fainted or decided she needed to throw things when I told her what Bumper revealed about our father's death.

"It seems the FBI has been sitting on some knowledge about our father's killing. He was shot by one of their agents to cover up the murder of some ex-cons he rounded up in the dead of night and executed right after Katrina." It wasn't the most accurate version of the story I could have told.

"Oh, my God." Tulip gasped but seemed to be holding herself together. "Have they arrested him?"

"The man who told me this story is the one who was killed today. The boy that shot him may have been the son of one of their other victims." That possibility only came to me as we were driving to the house and I remembered Arnold's story about his father's disappearance. "The agent he implicated is likely in FBI custody by now."

"I wish I could have been the one to shoot that son-of-a-bitch. *That* would be justice as far as I am concerned," my pacifist sister hissed as she wiped away one single tear.

Tulip looked at me and we both laughed at the sudden change in her position on capital punishment. "Christ, little sister, you're starting to sound like I do."

"I'm sure dad's made his peace wherever he is."

I did not tell her how close that actually was. She draped an arm across my slumped shoulders. "Are you going to stay around? I remember that you only agreed to come home to solve this."

"I think I might." I had only decided the matter at that

very moment. "I would already be gone had I wrapped this up right away. I like my job and it's nice to be rebuilding a city instead of blowing one up. It's also great to be part of the family again, our mother notwithstanding. Besides, I own half of a local restaurant thanks to you and Tony."

"Well it's nice having my big brother around again," she said and hugged me tightly. "Especially when you bring me so much business."

I held her until she was ready to tell our mother what I had just told her. I could have been the one to tell my mother, but the loss and its resolution was something the two of them shared far more than I ever would with either of them. I watched from the kitchen as the two women spoke on the patio and I averted my eyes as my mother walked directly to her bedroom without saying a word to me or Avery. I was sure I heard my mother crying a moment later but also knew to leave her to her grief until she was ready to talk to me again. I told Tulip the truth but, while I was born here, I grew up far away. Military school and college filled the time most people make life-long friendships and connections to places. The temporary nature of these places were followed by professional deployments. The brevity of time I spent in any one place eventually instilled a tendency to never become too attached to any one place or person. New Orleans, however, is a place that lives within you and not the other way around. The roots I pulled up decades earlier had dug themselves deeper than ever on my return. I couldn't leave again if I wanted to.

I SHARED BEIGNETS and coffee at Cafe du Monde with Katie Reilly two weeks later. It took that long to get up the courage to call her and invite her to breakfast before she headed to work. Avery joined us and confessed his envy of my practiced ability to keep the powdered sugar falling from the fried dough puffs off of my clothes. He showed me a small story buried inside the local section of the *Times-Picayune* about Jim Gabb dying in a fiery car crash a couple of days prior. It took a while to identify the body.

The story claimed the FBI had suspended him two days earlier, implying he may have committed suicide. Avery noticed the accident occurred on the highway which traverses Irish Bayou. He also told me Conroy told him Gabb's autopsy showed quite a few of the dead agent's injuries were inconsistent with those found in a car crash.

"I don't suppose you have anything I might tell the FBI about any of that."

"Good hunch."

"Well, Conroy wants you to have this." Avery passed a slim manila folder across the table. I didn't need to open it to know the SAC decided not to test my patience about surrendering the notes on the FBI's investigation into my background as his dead agent tried to do.

"I think you'll end up paying a fairly steep price for crossing Conroy," Katie joined the conversation. "He has informed the State Attorney General that the FBI plans to investigate the officer-involved shootings after Katrina."

I doubted the FBI's list would include my father's death.

"Is there anything besides the Danziger Bridge and Henry Glover shootings?" I wondered. Avery and Katie exchanged glances. They had been here in the horrible days immediately after the levees collapsed and took civil order with them. They knew better than I did what lay buried.

"I hate to think what else there may be," Avery admitted and shifted his gaze to his food. I didn't take this to be any reference to my father's murder, either.

I read an article in *Offbeat* magazine a week later about a couple of young out-of-town entrepreneurs purchasing Biggie's recording studio and their plans to move the operation to Atlanta in the months to come. The pair of thirty-something Black men made a pledge to build on the successful business model Biggie established. Biggie was fondly remembered for his promotion of local music and his efforts to get gangs off the street, and that his life was tragically cut short by the pit bull attack. The magazine's editor was also the one to finally put into print the bad joke that the music business is truly a "dog-eat-dog business." Logan shredded the will that Bumper forged so Biggie's grandmother, rather than the son he had put up for adoption, would become the sole beneficiary of his estate. Hopefully, she sold the studio to the FBI for enough to move out of the projects and back to Bogue Chitto.

I spotted a picture of Amanda and Parker on a *People* magazine cover in the check-out aisle at the Rouses Market on Royal Street. The article included a few photos, in which she was posed with the cute son of her new personal assistant. I had to look twice before I recognized the new assistant as Tyshika. Apparently Amanda had given up on trying to save the world and settled for reuniting one family. She also managed to trade one pit bull for another, but that was now a problem for her to solve on her own. Amanda also announced she would star in a television series being produced by her new boyfriend.

Avery and I did not discuss the topic of Biggie's murder case until he brought his family by for the Halloween party Tony and I threw for the bistro's regulars. Avery smiled a lot but said nothing about my chef and sister holding hands, or the displays of affection between me and the prettiest Assistant States' Attorney either of us knew.

The time since Biggie's murder allowed each of us to reflect on the day I accepted the arrangement hammered out between Avery and the Commander of the State Patrol. The commander actually argued against me being on anyone's police force, even with Avery's assurances that NOPD would take me off the Patrol's hands from day one.

I quoted Joseph Heller to Avery over lunch on my first day on the new job. It was a quote from Catch-22, which put forth that "justice is a knee in the gut from the floor." I had proven its truth when I put my knee into Bumper but vindicated Avery's trust in me when I didn't pull the trigger.

I could find no record of any of the men, other than my father, who may have been machine-gunned by Gabb ever having been investigated as missing persons by any law enforcement agency. The FBI had not seen fit to pursue the matter of my father's death any further or to provide NOPD with details from their interviews with the late Agent Gabb. I couldn't very well tell them what Gabb admitted to in his pain filled final hours, either. There was no massacre as far as anyone else on the planet knew, which meant it would be eventually forgotten by everyone but my family.

I'm not satisfied that I have all of the pieces to my father's disappearance, but that puzzle has been filed away and my family and I can move on with our lives. Even so, a part of me wants to believe that one of the men Gabb and Eric murdered was Arnold's father, and that it was Arnold who balanced the scale of justice for both of us.

OTHER BOOKS BY
H. MAX HILLER

Cadillac Holland Mysteries

Blowback
Can't Stop the Funk
Ghosts & Shadows

https://www.indiesunited.net/h-max-hiller

ABOUT THE AUTHOR

H. Max Hiller's first taste of New Orleans was as a cook on Bourbon Street at the age of seventeen. His resume now includes many of New Orleans' iconic dining and music destinations. These jobs have provided a lifetime of characters and anecdotes to add depth to the Detective Cooter 'Cadillac' Holland series. The author now divides his passions between writing at his home overlooking the Mississippi River and as a training chef aboard a boat traveling America's inland waterways, and is always living by the motto "be a New Orleanian wherever you are."